TINCTURE OF DEATH

Also by Ray Harrison:

Harvest of Death
A Season for Death
Counterfeit of Murder

RAY HARRISON

Tincture of Death

St. Martin's Press
New York

Library of Congress Cataloging-in-Publication Data

Harrison, Ray.
    Tincture of death / Ray Harrison.
            p.   cm.
    "A Thomas Dunne book."
    ISBN 0-312-03442-3
    I. Title.
PR6058.A69424T56   1989
823'.914—dc20   89-10356
                                                              CIP

First published in Great Britain by Quartet Books Limited.

First U.S. Edition

10 9 8 7 6 5 4 3 2 1

To Gareth and Sandra

1

Detective Sergeant Joseph Bragg pounded down Moorgate, the paving stones ringing beneath his boots. He twisted to avoid a stout woman walking her dog, and she turned to gaze at his coatless, collarless form trundling down the road. Still the running figure ahead of him was pulling away. He would never keep up with him, let alone catch him. He was losing his wind now, his heart thumping. Not surprising, either . . . he was forty-three, after all. He couldn't be expected to keep up with a twenty-seven-year-old . . . And all because Inspector Cotton had not got the brains to plan an operation properly . . . Even had he been fifteen years younger, Detective Constable Tofts could never have covered the back of that warehouse on his own. Now Cotton was blaming the escape of the screwsmen on Tofts; saying he was too slow and out of condition. And he had launched the detective division on a fitness crusade, to divert attention from his own ineptness . . . It was bloody stupid, sending everybody out on a three-mile run before starting work. It just buggered them up for the day . . . A sharp pain was growing in Bragg's ribs, and his lungs were gasping for the air. A cab-horse staled in the gutter as he passed, and he spat to clear the taint from his mouth. Damn this for a lark! . . . Constable Morton was lost in the distance now. He would be enjoying it, if no one else was. While they had looked thunderstruck, he had seemed pleased – said it would get him in trim for the cricket season. Stupid sod! . . . It was bringing the force into disrepute, as well – even if most of the route was out of the City. As Bragg laboured up to Finsbury Square, he could see a cluster of clerks on the corner, laughing and shouting derisively at the panting runners. What respect would they have for the police, after this? It was throwing away the only real advantage they had got – and for nothing. Cotton himself had soon dropped out. One run and he had looked fit for the knacker's yard. After that he'd been too busy! . . . The pavements were practically empty, now that he had got away from the business area. He felt a spot of rain on his forehead and looked up. A threatening black cloud was being driven towards the City on the blustery March wind. If he got caught in a rainstorm, he'd be having to go off home, to change his clothes. That would be the best part of the morning wasted . . . He glanced over his shoulder. There was no one in sight. He turned into an entry and, once out of view, walked painfully across the railway footbridge to Bishopsgate. Then he jogged slowly back to the headquarters building in Old Jewry. The desk-sergeant greeted him with a broad grin.

'You are looking younger every day, Joe! Mind you, I can't see you having the privilege much longer, after what happened this morning!'

'What was that?' asked Bragg, perching wearily on the corner of the desk.

'Haven't you heard? Detective Sergeant Spenlow is in a Metropolitan police nick! You know how clumsy he is. Well, he was just coming up to Worship Street, when he collided with a pedestrian. Knocked her down and scattered her belongings all over the pavement. She screamed blue murder, naturally. Spenlow said sorry, then ran on. She yelled "stop thief!", and there was a right hue and cry! By then he was knackered, of course; next thing you know, he's grabbed by the beat constable and arrested . . . No jacket, so no means of identification. At the moment he's in the cells at Nile Street, while Inspector Cotton tries to negotiate his release!'

'I hope they make him beg on his bloody knees,' Bragg said sourly. 'Anything happening, Bill?'

'Not apart from that.'

'Right.' Bragg walked stiffly up the stairs and went into his own room. He put on his jacket and tie, then flopped into his chair. He was just lighting a much-needed pipe, when Morton burst into the room, exuberant and full of vigour.

'Why, sir,' he exclaimed with a grin, 'I could have sworn that

I left you far behind me! It seems that I must have been mistaken!'

'What Inspector Cotton doesn't realise, lad, is that it's brains that gets results in this game, not brawn. Don't you forget that.'

'I will remember,' said Morton, donning his jacket. 'Did you have a good weekend?'

'As a matter of fact, I went down to Dorset,' Bragg said casually.

'Ah, yes. Is the partnership in your cousin's carriers business causing you concern? You seem to have to go down with some frequency.'

'No, lad. No. It's doing very nicely.'

'And the attractive Miss Hildred?'

'Well enough.'

Morton grinned. 'Then you will have returned like a giant refreshed.'

'Huh! Some hope . . . It's time we got on with what the public pays us for. Now, I want you to finish off the report on that breaking and entering. I am off to Davies and Royle, to go through the witness statements. I should be back by noon.'

There came a tap on the door and Sir William Sumner, the Commissioner, entered. 'Ah, Bragg, there you are,' he said diffidently. 'I don't suppose you have seen this morning's *Times*.'

'The *Standard* is more my mark, sir.'

'Then you will not have read about the sacking of the Chief Cashier of the Bank of England?'

'May? Good God! What did they do that for?'

'It is really because of the work you did on that counterfeiting case, Bragg. Once you had exposed the weaknesses in their system, they instituted a thorough review. It is said that the Bank has had to make a reserve of a quarter of a million pounds, to meet losses.'

'Good heavens!' Morton exclaimed.

'And May is the scapegoat, is he?' Bragg asked.

'Hardly that. He was the responsible official, under the Governor.'

'But the present Governor was Deputy-Governor at the time. He should swing, as well as May.'

'You seem in a rather jaundiced mood, today, Bragg,' Sir William said with a foxy smile.

'Me, sir? No. Never felt better.'

'Then, perhaps Inspector Cotton's regime is having some beneficial effect, after all!'

Bragg swivelled round with a snort and put down his pipe. 'So, you will be receiving a delegation from the Bank, expressing their gratitude for our work, will you sir?' he asked sardonically.

'I hardly think that is likely. We must be content with the knowledge that we have done our duty.'

'At least the Prince of Wales did make you a Knight Commander of the Bath,' Morton reminded him.

'True.' Sir William beamed with pleasure. 'Perhaps one can say that, nowadays, there is gratitude in princes, but not in officials. That is probably a good indication of where the real power lies. However, that was not the reason I dropped in.' He took a fold of paper from his pocket. 'I would like you to look into this report from last Saturday's *Echo*. According to them, the tea in one of the City's warehouses has been poisoned.'

Bragg took the cutting and glanced through it. 'I expect there is nothing to it, sir.'

'Nevertheless, it is a matter of public concern. I am bound to be asked what we are doing about it.'

'We have our hands full, at the moment,' Bragg said stolidly.

'But, damn it, Bragg, it's my own tea merchant!'

'I see, sir . . . The trouble is, this morning run shortens our day by an hour. We ought to be recruiting more officers, to compensate.'

'More officers!' Sir William exclaimed. 'The common council would never stand for it!'

'Then our service to the public is bound to suffer,' Bragg said placidly.

'You know that I cannot give you preferential treatment by exempting you from this training,' the Commissioner said petulantly.

'You could, of course, order us to do it in our own time,' said Bragg. 'That would not be a concession.'

'And would you do so?'

4

Bragg looked up. 'I expect so, sir.'

Sir William glared at him. 'Very well, Bragg. Then, let me know how you get on with Cassell Smith's. I suggest that you talk to Arthur Pixley. He is the managing partner.'

'Very good, sir.'

The Commissioner went out unhappily.

'I am not at all sure that I appreciate your guile on this occasion, sir,' Morton remarked. 'I suspect that, hereafter, I shall really have to do my training in my own time!'

'Not at all, lad. You can run down to Fenchurch Street and look in on Pixley. We can't have Sir William expiring over his breakfast blend, can we?'

Morton walked briskly down to the offices of Cassell Smith & Co., and was directed to their warehouse in Gould Square. The railway line to Fenchurch Street station had been carried across the square on a viaduct. Since then, almost all of the arches had been enclosed for commercial purposes. As a result, the square had virtually ceased to exist as an open space. It seemed that Cassell Smith's had taken almost all the premises. He went through a small door below an arch, and found himself in a vast, shadowy warehouse. A little daylight struggled through dusty windows, but the main illumination came from fishtail gas-jets. As his eyes became accustomed to the gloom, it seemed as if he was in the crypt of some great cathedral of commerce; the low, vaulted roof supported by the massive brick pillars of the viaduct. By the door was a small office, enclosed by glazed partitions. It was empty. Nearby, a man was stacking packets of tea, then parcelling them up in a large sheet of brown paper. He looked across at Morton, then went on with his work. In the middle of the warehouse, a section of the wall had been whitewashed to head height. By it there was a long, zinc-covered table on which tea was piled in greenish mounds. On each side of the table men were stationed, with brass scales and copper scoops, filling tea packets. These were whisked away by a couple of young girls to another table, where the tops were deftly folded over and secured by a label.

'Are you looking for someone?'

A slight man in a ginger check lounging suit was approaching him from the other end of the warehouse.

'I would like to speak to Mr Pixley,' said Morton.

The man smiled and held out his hand. 'That's me, Arthur Pixley, at your service.'

'I am a policeman. The Commissioner asked me to see you about this newspaper report.'

A frown settled on Pixley's brow. 'That's good of Sir William. I don't mind telling you that it has got us worried.'

'Is it possible that there could be any truth in the report?' asked Morton.

'I would be a fool if I gave a categoric no; but, for the life of me, I cannot see how – or why, for that matter.'

Morton glanced over at the men packeting the tea. 'Could it be that a disgruntled employee might have introduced some poisonous substance, at the packing stage?' he asked.

'We do not have disgruntled employees,' Pixley said brusquely. 'We pay good wages, and expect a good day's work. We never keep anybody who falls down on the job. Besides,' he added, 'no single packer could do it on his own, undetected; they would all have to be in on it. I just cannot credit that it could happen.'

'Perhaps you could explain what you do at these premises,' Morton suggested.

'Then, we must start at the beginning.' Pixley led him to the far end of the warehouse where large tea-chests were piled in pyramids. 'This is where the parcels of tea are stored, when they come from the docks.'

Morton read the label pasted on one of the chests. 'So the tea is consigned direct to you by the shipper?' he remarked.

'That's right. We have a big wholesale trade. Most of these chests will go out this week, to tea merchants up and down the country . . . which is why it is so worrying.'

'You mean that any poison could easily be spread throughout Britain?' Morton asked.

'I mean that if this report is taken up by the provincial newspapers it could kill our business stone dead!'

'I see . . . At all events, we have established that the label is attached to the chest by someone in India or China.'

'Not India,' Pixley interrupted. 'We do not touch Indian tea.'

'Why not?' Morton asked in surprise.

'Ours is a high-quality trade – the top of the market. Tea has only been grown in India for thirty years or so, and they have not really got the knack yet. It's cheap, I grant you, and it has got a third of the market now. But it is not for Cassell Smith & Co.'

'Are you saying that all these different teas are grown in China?' Morton asked, glancing around him.

'Bless you, yes! And more besides. We only take the pick of them.'

'The best of the best, eh?'

'That's right,' said Pixley emphatically. 'You see that small chest over there? Well, that is the most expensive tea in the world. Normally, you cannot buy it in western Europe, but we import a little for valued customers.'

'What is so special about it?' Morton asked with a smile.

'Well, for a start, it is the best tea that China produces. And there is not a lot of it, so it is mostly reserved for the wealthy Chinese. Then again, very little of it is exported, because it gets seasick.'

'Seasick?' exclaimed Morton incredulously.

'It is true! It cannot stand an ocean voyage, it loses all its virtue.'

'Then, why do you bother to import it?'

'This has been sent overland from China to Russia, where they prize it highly. I occasionally squeeze a little from one of my contacts in St Petersburg, and bring it by train to Calais.'

'Will it stand the Channel crossing?'

Pixley laughed. 'It is thirty years since I tasted it in China, so I cannot positively swear that it does!'

'You have been to China?'

'I went out as a young man, to learn the trade.'

'Then you must have a good idea of where poison might have been introduced into the tea.'

'Frankly, I do not see where or when. For a start, tea is grown on plantations. It is processed and packed there; and the chests are sent to the shipper sealed, as you see them now.'

'Could it happen during processing?'

'I suppose it could – though it is only a matter of heating and drying the leaves. But why should the producers poison their tea? What have they to gain? Anyway, the newspaper does not say that all China tea coming into the country is poisoned – just ours.'

'Could a competing firm have given the information to the *Echo*? If so, might they have procured the poisoning themselves?'

Pixley sighed. 'I have thought that over, as you can imagine. There are people who would profit, if we were put out of business – people like Jacksons or Moffats – but I could never believe that they would stoop to that. It is not a cut-throat trade. The market is growing; there is plenty of business in Indian teas, for those who want to expand.'

'Nevertheless, you have the reputation of supplying the highest in the land – including our Commissioner! Could it be that someone is trying to supplant you?'

'We have a good connection, I will admit. But we do not supply many personal blends, nowadays. It is just not commercial. If you can get a tea accepted widely, like Earl Grey's blend, then it is worthwhile. But not otherwise.'

'The Commissioner is highly favoured, then?' Morton remarked.

'Sir William is by way of being a connoisseur,' Pixley said. 'He has a fine palate, which I suppose he developed during his army service. We value his opinions and, in return, we indulge his whim.'

'What teas do you blend for him?' Morton asked with a grin.

'You don't expect me to give away our trade secrets, do you?'

'I am scarcely likely to become a competitor! But it is useful to be able to talk intelligently about the boss's personal interests.'

Pixley smiled. 'Well, don't you go saying I told you . . . His tea is a green gunpowder – a blend of Pin's-head and Imperial Moyune from Shanghai, with just a dash of Formosan.'

'I will be discreet!' Morton assured him. 'Now, can you tell me what is the earliest stage that anyone would be able to identify a chest of tea as being consigned to you?'

'In the shipper's godown.'

'Yet presumably the coolies would select the chests to fulfil your order, entirely at random.'

'I suppose so.'

'What happens then?'

'A label is stuck on the chest, or our name is stencilled on the side, and it goes straight to the ship.'

'Is it stored at the docks, for any length of time?'

'No. It takes up too much room.'

'You think it unlikely that a chest could be interfered with at that stage?'

'Damned near impossible, I'd say.'

'Presumably, it might happen during the voyage?'

'I doubt it. The ship's holds are kept closed – unless there is an emergency, like the cargo shifting . . . Even if you got into the hold, you would be lucky to locate parcels of tea consigned to any particular merchant.'

'It could, of course, be purely fortuitous that you are involved. Perhaps the perpetrators were just concerned to poison a chest or two of tea, and they happened to be ones consigned to you.'

'But why?' Pixley exclaimed in irritation.

'That, we may discover in time. For the moment, let us concentrate on how. If you were going to introduce poison into a sealed tea-chest, how would you set about it?'

'Well, you could not open one, without its being obvious. All the joints are covered by tin strapping. The only way I can think of, is if you squirted a liquid poison in, using a hypodermic syringe.'

'Have you followed up that idea?'

'I have. There is no way you could get a hypodermic needle through the wood, without breaking it. I reckon you would have to put a small nail through first. Last night I had the men examine every chest, with lanterns, but never a nail-hole did they find. Mind you, I cannot speak for the chests that have left here in the last few days.' Pixley began to walk back gloomily to his office. He paused and watched the girls sweeping tea dust from the now emptied table into a canvas bag. 'I let them take the dust back to the foundling hospital,' he said absently . . . 'You know, I reckon this is all a story.'

'A hoax, you mean?'

'Not a hoax – but if anyone wanted to ruin us, they would

only need to get some rag of a newspaper to print a report like that, and it would be as effective as if it were really true.'

'I suppose that is so.' Morton checked. 'Look! The chest that the men are bringing to the table! Surely that has been tampered with? The tin strapping on the top is all buckled!'

Pixley gave a grunt. 'That's the Customs,' he said. 'They have put their stamp on the side – see?'

'The Customs? Why are they concerned to open tea-chests?'

'They take samples, now and again, for testing.'

'Do they open the chests at the docks?'

'Yes, and close them again. Though they take the samples to their laboratory.'

'So a Customs officer has had access to this chest? That is worth pondering on.'

'Well, that's a job for you. I have to go and see my solicitor. I spoke to him briefly, last night. He said I should take samples from every chest and test them myself – then let the *Echo* know I was doing it. I shall follow his advice. But a rag like that would have no interest in printing what I had to say. It would only spoil their story.'

Catherine Marsden cleaned the nib of her pen and replaced it on the inkstand. It had been a good day. She had interviewed a prominent feminist who was to speak in the City later in the week. As a result she had written an article, which had received the grudging approval of the editor, Mr Tranter. But her real satisfaction lay in the feeling that the report was by no means as anodyne as he thought. She had, of course, toned down the vitriolic criticisms of men's attitudes to women, or the article would not have stood a chance of being published. But she felt that her own re-statement of the points was even more effective. To her mind, they now appeared as self-evident truths that no half-reasonable man could deny. On the question of enfranchising women, for instance, her presentation moved the argument away from whether, as being inevitable, to when. The men might dismiss it as another tiresome repetition of women's arguments, but Catherine hoped that their womenfolk would go to the meeting in droves.

She was tidying her desk when the office-boy poked his head round the door.

'A young lady to see you, miss,' he said chirpily.

'Who is it?'

'I dunno. She didn't say.'

'Then send her up.'

Catherine wondered if it could be her interviewee of the morning. But by no stretch of the imagination could she be called young. She took her mirror from her bag and checked her appearance. Then she heard a step on the landing, and a young woman came in.

'Louisa!' Catherine exclaimed, jumping up and enfolding her in a hug. 'I have not seen you since we left school! How are you? Goodness! how exciting!'

She held her at arm's length and scrutinised her. She still had her clear complexion and dark brown hair, but her face was thinner. It suited her. She no longer had that tabby-cat look of contentment, but she was certainly beautiful.

'Sit down, and tell me what you have been doing, these last three years. How did you find me?'

Louisa laughed uncertainly, then took the chair opposite Catherine.

'It was not difficult to find you,' she said. 'Everyone knows that you are a reporter on the *City Press*. You are held up to us lesser mortals as an example of what women can achieve.'

Was there a sour note in the bantering tone? Catherine wondered.

'What nonsense!' she said. 'Anyway, I would never have got the job, but for my father's influence.'

'Do you remember how we used to talk endlessly at Cheltenham?' Louisa asked with a smile. 'As I recall it, you were determined to be a High Court judge, one day!'

'Some people would say that I pronounce quite enough judgements, as it is! And what about you? You went to the Royal Academy school, didn't you?'

'Yes . . . I did.'

'How do you like it?'

'I attended for just over a year, then abandoned it.'

'Good heavens! Why?'

'I met a man . . .'

Catherine glanced at Louisa's ringless finger, and bit back her cry of delight.

'He is a painter, too . . . only he is a real painter. He has vision and commitment . . . I began to see that my poor dabblings had little to do with the essentials of art.'

'But why?' Catherine exclaimed. 'You used to do the most exquisite flower paintings. One wanted to reach out and pick them! Miss Edwards was most insistent that art was the only career you should consider.'

'I know.' Louisa looked wistfully down at her hands. 'I suppose that is why she merely teaches art, instead of practising it. I now realise that true art has to be an expression of emotion. My own little talents are illustrative, not creative.'

'What nonsense!' Catherine said robustly. 'My father is a professional painter. He spends his life trying to keep emotion out of his work. He says you should be detached and paint what you see – warts and all.'

'But he is an academician, and a portraitist. He has a connection, and he is painting to satisfy his clients. There is no room for real creativity in what he does.'

'I would not agree with that for a moment,' Catherine said, nettled.

'I am sorry,' Louisa said contritely, 'I did not mean to criticise. But he is part of the establishment that is hostile to Ben's ideas.'

'Ben?'

'Ben Fowler – my friend. I should like you to meet him, Catherine. He really is very nice, when you get to know him.'

Catherine looked at Louisa more critically. Her coat was at least a year out of fashion, her hair had been perfunctorily screwed up into a bun, and she was wearing no jewellery whatever.

'I was really wondering if you could help him.'

'Help him?' Catherine's burgeoning sympathy was checked.

'He is exceedingly talented, but his temperament is against him. He does not express himself with the forbearance that he ought to show. He becomes impatient. You see, his work is rather *avant-garde*; people need time to appreciate it . . . We

12

had hoped that an art dealer would take him up, but he seems to be too far ahead of his time.'

'But, how on earth do you think I could help him?'

Louisa's eyes dropped to her hands again. 'Ben does live in the City of London,' she said with a note of pleading in her voice. 'I have often read the *City Press*, and I know that you have occasionally written articles about people and places in the City that might be of general interest.'

'But they have been people actually working in the City,' Catherine said dismissively.

'Ben does work here. His studio is in Plough Court, off Fetter Lane. And, apart from his pictures, I have persuaded him to do some murals – rather in the Pre-Raphaelite manner. He demurs, but one must live.'

'So the public are able to see his work?'

Louisa smiled wanly. 'Not the public as such. The commissions I have so far obtained are in men's haunts, such as clubs.'

'Huh!' Catherine snorted. 'And, no doubt, they are somewhat lacking in delicacy.'

'Oh no! Ben would never lend himself to the salacious,' Louisa said emphatically.

'Well, I must see some of his work, before I can even consider writing an article,' Catherine said firmly. 'We have never done anything quite like that. I am afraid that the editor sees his paper as a detached commentary on the ebb and flow of the commercial tides that govern the destiny of nations! I had great difficulty in getting him to accept my article on the College of Arms – and the Heralds have been in the City since the fifteenth century!'

'If you were to come down to Plough Court, I could show you some canvases,' Louisa said hesitantly.

'Now?'

'Why, yes. It is not far. We could easily walk there.'

Nevertheless, Catherine insisted on taking a passing cab. It might, indeed, have been quicker to walk, because they were soon swallowed up in the plodding evening traffic. However, it allowed Catherine to observe her companion covertly. She was restless, continually taking off her gloves and fiddling with her bag. Such remarks as she made, were uttered in a bright, hard voice, totally foreign to the Louisa she had known. She found herself speculating about the man who had brought this warm and intelligent girl into a state of brittle tension. She would never allow anyone to do this to her! she told herself . . . But perhaps she was unable to feel the kind of love that seemed to have ensnared Louisa; perhaps she was too aloof, too cerebral. She put the thought from her as they turned into a narrow, rutted street. The buildings were old and neglected, a mixture of artisans' dwellings and small manufactories. Louisa pushed up the trap-door in the roof, and called directions to the driver. The horse came to a halt in the middle of a soot-blackened terrace. The façade was totally devoid of ornament, the windows grimy and curtainless. As they got down from the cab, Catherine could see that there was a casual ward next door. A line of ragged men was already forming, huddling together in the bitter wind, waiting defeatedly to suffer the condescending charity that would provide them with an enforced bath, and a bed for the night.

A defensive look settled on Louisa's face, as she led the way down the area steps and unlocked the basement door. They stepped into a large room that had evidently once been the kitchen of the house. Under the window was a small table littered with tubes of paint and brushes. An empty easel stood close by, and several canvases were propped along the wall. In the centre of the room was a rickety gate-legged table and some chairs; the floor was covered in cracked linoleum. A handful of coals glowed in the iron range, at the back of the room. To the left of the fireplace, a door led to a scullery with a chipped, stoneware sink. Catherine could see there a small oil-stove, that seemed reasonably new. Louisa opened the door of the room on the right of the fireplace and went in. It had once been a storeroom, Catherine thought; the iron double-bedstead almost filled it. Louisa took off her coat and, crawling over the bed, removed an old sheet from a rail of hooks. She hung her coat with the rest of her clothes, and replaced the sheet over them. Glancing round, she saw Catherine watching her, and her face set defiantly.

With a sudden access of compassion, Catherine put her arms around her. Louisa gently pushed her away.

14

'It's all right, really it is,' she said quietly.

Catherine turned in embarrassment to the canvases and picked one up.

'I would hardly have called this *avant-garde*,' she remarked.

Louisa smiled. 'That is not Ben's work! They are canvases which I bought for a song, yesterday. I was supposed to clean them this afternoon . . . We cannot afford new ones.'

Then the door swung open, and a man stood on the threshold. He was powerfully built, with an untidy shock of dark hair and piercing blue eyes. He glanced in Catherine's direction without acknowledging her. Louisa took a step towards him, hands outstretched, but he brushed past her and went towards the scullery.

'I want a drink,' he called over his shoulder, in a hectoring voice.

'I bought some tea this morning,' Louisa said timidly.

'Tea!' His head appeared round the door. 'I cannot work on tea, woman!'

After a few moments, he emerged with a large tumbler of red liquid in his hand.

'This is the elixir that unlocks my art,' he said, taking a gulp.

He set the glass on the table and, removing his overcoat, flung it on to a chair. Then he picked up one of the canvases.

'You did not strip them, I see,' he said belligerently.

'I had to go out,' Louisa said quickly. 'I shall be able to do them tonight.'

'Do not fail me. I shall need them in the morning.'

He picked up the glass and drained it, then took it back to the scullery.

'You are falling behind with my nectar,' he said, coming to Louisa. 'You know I cannot work without it.'

'I do wish that you would wean yourself away from it,' Louisa said pleadingly.

'Nonsense! . . You should be pleased. I have spent another day bowing down to mammon, for your sake.'

'Did they give you any money?' asked Louisa.

'Money, woman? You are no better than they are! All you think about is money. They buy genius for the price of a box of matches, and with as little regard . . . Because of your machinations, I am wasting my life on an excruciatingly platitudinous mural; not because they can appreciate it, or will ever look at it, but because they find the serenity of a bare wall disconcerting.'

'Is it going well, dear?'

'No, it is not going well,' he mimicked her savagely. 'The back leg of the horse is not right. The wretched animal is a monster! One of the clerks had the gall to draw my attention to it. What did he expect? I am not a rude mechanical. If they wanted a technical exercise, devoid of emotion, they should have gone to Burne-Jones. He enjoys that kind of thing.'

'Burne-Jones would have cost them a great deal more,' Louisa said with asperity.

'No doubt, now that he has pawned his meagre talents for a baronetcy.'

Catherine felt like a spectator at the zoo, watching the skirmishing of wild animals oblivious of her. Indeed, she felt herself start as Fowler's gaze swung round and fastened on her face.

'And who is our guest this evening?' he asked, with sudden geniality.

'Catherine Marsden, a reporter on the *City Press*. She is going to help us.'

Fowler advanced towards her, his eyes locked with hers.

'And what do you know about painting, Miss Marsden?'

Catherine tore her glance away. 'A good deal. My father is William Marsden, the artist,' she said stoutly.

'Ah! Wiliam Marsden RA,' he said with heavy sarcasm. 'The sugar-plum fairy himself! He will magic up a simpering sylph from a shapeless mound of flesh – and all for a thousand guineas a time! How is the daughter of William Marsden proposing to help us, Louisa? Will she ask that paragon of the Academy to show me how to churn out their costive little canvases?' He smiled fiercely at Catherine. 'Will he get them to accept me back into their schools, so that they can teach me how to paint their befrocked yokels and marzipan cottages? . . . Well, thank you, but no!'

He turned away and took up a position with his back to the fire.

'Catherine may be able to get an article about you published in the newspaper,' Louisa said in a placatory tone.

'Pah! You deceive yourself, if you think that the *City Press* will recognise my talents. Its readers are the chief supporters of an art that has sold its soul for thirty pieces of silver.' He thrust his head forward. 'Art does not exist to make you feel cosy!' he said fiercely. 'It is not to titillate your intellect, as you unravel the clues to a supposed story; depicting a fallen woman by an apple on the floor, and a letter on the table. For God's sake, painting is not literature! It is the hot blast from the furnace of emotion. A picture should take you by the throat, shouting "feel this experience in your guts, if you dare!" It should not toy with your emotions, it should overwhelm them!'

'You appear to scorn my father's portraits,' Catherine said evenly, 'but he goes to great lengths to keep sentimentality out of them. He tries to be objective, and paint what he sees.'

Fowler yawned and appeared to be losing interest.

'Then he ought to be a photographer,' he said. 'If I paint someone, the likeness is unimportant; the picture crystallises my emotions. It says: this is how I feel about X; not "see", "feel"!'

'But you will let Catherine help, if she can?' Louisa asked in a wheedling voice.

'Do as you like . . . I am going to bed.' he crossed to the bedroom, then looked back. 'You will strip those canvases tonight?'

'I promise,' Louisa said, as he closed the door.

An uncomfortable silence grew between the two women. At length: 'What was it that he drank?' Catherine asked.

'Laudanum.'

'That is made from opium, is it not?'

'Yes. He believes that it releases his creativity. He will sleep now for eight hours. Then he will get up and paint his dreams.'

'Dreams?'

'Not such as we would experience. He describes them as vortices of sensation, which threaten to swallow him . . . but I believe it is really the accompanying music that he paints.'

'So painting can be music, if not literature,' Catherine said acidly.

'Please do not dismiss him,' Louisa said. 'He was not always like this. When I first met him, he was just an amusing iconoclast . . . It has all come with the laudanum.'

'Has he taken it for long?'

'For six months . . . but now he takes far too much.'

'How much?'

'He drinks two half-pint glasses every day. He has me make it for him, because he says that the laudanum from the druggist is too weak . . . If only he could gain recognition, he would be able to wean himself from it, I am sure.'

'I gather that you are his mistress,' Catherine said bluntly.

'Yes . . . For two years now.'

'What on earth would you do, if he got you with child?'

'That is one thing that I no longer need to worry over. The laudanum seems to have dried him up inside.'

'But, what is going to happen to you?'

Louisa looked up. 'I love him,' she said steadily, 'and I shall stay with him, whatever happens.'

'But you were not made for this life! What would your parents think?'

'I can only hope that they will not find out. They still think that I am at art school . . . Without the allowance I receive from them, we would have had nothing to live on for the last two years.'

'But surely you have been to see them?' Catherine asked incredulously.

'Of course!' She smiled. 'They take my rather threadbare appearance as the bohemianism of a true artist!'

'I wish that I could help you,' Catherine said pointedly.

'You can only do so by helping him.'

'In that case, I would like to have some of his work to show to my editor.'

'And, no doubt, to your father also.'

'Yes, certainly. I know nothing about the technicalities of painting . . . and you may be sure that he will be fair.'

'You will keep my secret?'

'Of course.'

'Then, I will let you take my portrait.'

'Surely not! It may be three years since you met my parents,

18

but they could well recognise you.'

Louisa began to laugh. 'I do not think that there would be much danger of that!'

She went into the bedroom, where Fowler was snoring loudly, and brought out a canvas from under the bed. She held it for Catherine's inspection. There was nothing recognizably human in the picture. It was principally a bold swirl of red tones, with irregular blotches of primary colours.

'So that is Louisa Sommers?' Catherine remarked dubiously.

'He would say that it represents how he feels about me.'

Catherine shivered. 'In that case, I certainly do not envy you,' she said.

2

Sir Fergus Jardine snapped his watch shut irritably. He half wished that he had not consented; he had more important things to do than play at medieval merchants. He had arrived for the meeting precisely at the time appointed and been left by the beadle to cool his heels in an ante-room. His sponsor, the chaplain, had just chatted to him briefly, but it was more than probable that some of the officials had still not arrived. He listened at the doorway, and could hear breathless voices below in the vestibule. The trouble with the City of London was that it lived on its past. It expected the rest of the world to bow down to it, as the pre-eminent commercial centre. Like the British aristocracy, it did not expect to have to exert itself to maintain its God-given privileged position. It had been good to get back to Scotland, not only because it was his native country, but because Glasgow was urgent, thrusting, vibrant. People there were prepared to work hard, to be ruthless, to fail if they had to, but to strive . . . He smiled at the thought that he was about to extend his involvement with the City's ossified institutions. But he needed them. At the moment, they would support him because, in principle, they were in favour of trade. The more he belonged here, the more they would see the coming struggle as an attack on the City itself. He walked across the room, to where an ornate parchment was framed in a glass case. He screwed up his eyes to decipher the medieval script . . . A charter from King Richard the Second, dated 1395. And on that five-hundred-year-old bit of sheepskin, a great edifice of position and power had been built . . . The Great Seal looked impressive enough, anyway. Yet it somehow seemed incongruous, dangling by its slender ribbon. What would happen if it became detached? Would the charter become invalid . . .?

'Excuse me, Sir Fergus.' A black-robed figure appeared at his elbow. 'I am the clerk. I just wanted to be sure that you know what to expect.'

Jardine smiled. 'I think so,' he said.

'As it is not a regular meeting, it will not take long. There will be a short address by the master, to which you will no doubt reply.'

'Briefly, I assure you!'

'Yes, sir. Then there will be the loving-cup ceremony. Has your proposer explained that to you?'

'Yes. It is the same as the Mercers'.'

'Good. The renter warden and the chaplain will be your supporters. After that, the master will present you with your certificate, and you will then withdraw.'

'Do I come back here?'

'Yes, sir. After a few moments, the other members will join you, for sherry.'

'That sounds most civilised.'

'The beadle has put your box on the table, near where you will be standing. Now, if you will follow me . . .'

They walked with measured tread along the landing and into a large, opulent room. The walls were lined to shoulder height with a plain wainscot, painted and gilded. Above its cornice, the wall was divided into panels by ribbed pilasters, which merged with the elaborate frieze. The ceiling, too, was encrusted with rich plaster-work. Jardine followed the clerk across the deep-red Turkey carpet, towards a long table with two spurs. He was guided into its hollow, then the clerk bowed and retreated to the end of the top table. There was only a handful of men seated there. The chaplain smiled at him reassuringly, and he nodded his head in acknowledgement.

'Sir Fergus Jardine,' the master had risen to his feet, a complacent look on his chubby face. 'It is with great pleasure that I welcome you to the Worshipful Company of Saddlers. It is one of the most ancient institutions of the realm, having existed for many years prior to the Norman Conquest. In former times, as a craft guild, we held jurisdiction over the saddlery trade throughout the length and breadth of England.'

He smoothed the fur-trimmed edge of his robe, as if to recreate the sensation of ancient power.

'Nowadays,' he went on, 'our concerns are mainly educational and charitable, together with the maintaining and supporting of the City of London and its privileges.' He smiled at Jardine. 'From time to time it is our custom to elect, as honorary members of the company, men who are distinguished users of the saddle. Your own prowess as a rider and race-horse owner is well known; and your influence has reached beyond Britain to its far-flung colonies, to the great advantage of the saddlery trade in the mother country . . . Having been thus elected as a yeoman of the company, you will be entitled to the same rights and privileges as any other member to the company. I am delighted, as master, to welcome you into our fellowship.'

He sat down amid murmurs of concurrence.

Jardine composed his features into a mask of solemn deference.

'I am very sensible,' he said gravely, 'of the great honour which has been bestowed on me this day. I engage myself to uphold the traditions of this noble institution, and to participate, as fully as my commitments allow, in its ceremonies and other activities. As a mark of my gratitude, master, I would like, with your permission, to present to the company a ballot box, which was made in 1619 for the Honourable East India Company, and was used in times past for the election of its officers.'

He gestured towards the box, and there was a murmur of approbation and satisfaction.

'That is most generous of you,' the master said, then leaned forward and nodded to the renter warden, who was seated some places from him. He rose and went to a side table; then took a decanter and poured some of its contents into a two-handled, silver loving cup. He placed the cover on the cup and set it before the master, who gravely inclined his head. Then the warden walked with ecclesiastical solemnity around the spur table until he was facing the master. He lifted the cup, then went over to Jardine and took up a position with his back to him. At the same time the chaplain walked round the other spur and came behind Jardine, forming a short line. Then the warden turned on his heel and, bowing to Jardine, held out the cup. Jardine removed the cover and the warden drank. He then wiped the rim of the cup with a napkin attached to one handle and held out the cup so that Jardine could replace the cover. The warden passed the cup to Jardine, then swung round to face the master. Jardine turned to the chaplain, who removed the cover from the cup. Jardine took a deep draught of the spiced wind. It was revolting – at once cloying yet bitter . . . It caught at his throat . . . suddenly, it was difficult to get his breath. He fumbled with the napkin, his head swimming. He raised the cup towards the chaplain . . . then blackness enveloped him.

Bragg and Morton walked briskly down Lower Thames Street to the Custom House. They were directed to the laboratory, which occupied a long room on the top floor, with a view of the Thames from Charing Cross to Wapping. A man in a white coat looked up as they entered.

'What can I do for you, gentlemen?' he asked.

Bragg took out his warrant-card. 'We are police officers,' he said. 'We are looking into a report that some tea in the warehouse of Cassell Smith & Co has been poisoned.'

The man whistled. 'I missed that,' he said. 'My name is Samuel Pawson. I am a chemist by trade and, for my sins, I am in charge of this laboratory. I would be glad to help you, if I could.'

'We understand that you take samples of tea that comes into the docks. Constable Morton saw a chest of tea at Cassell Smith's which bore a Customs stamp.'

'Very likely, they are one of the major importers. I will check the files, but I cannot hold out much hope of being able to help you.'

He took a manila folder from a drawer in his desk, and ran his finger down sheet after sheet of paper.

'I have checked back to the middle of 1893,' he said. 'Every sample from Cassell Smith's that we have tested has been cleared.' He replaced the file in his desk and picked up a pipe from an ashtray, then, taking some tobacco from a tin, pushed it over to Bragg.

'You look like a pipe-man,' he said. 'Try this – a special Dutch blend, beats anything I ever smoked . . . Of course,' he went on, 'the fact that we have passed the samples is not conclusive, so far as your problem is concerned.'

'Why is that?' asked Bragg, carefully packing tobacco into his pipe.

'Our concerns are specific and, though it may seem odd to you, they do not extend to whether the tea is poisoned or not.'

'So, what are you after?'

'It is not Customs work at all, really; we are here to detect adulteration, and it is mere convenience that leads us to make the examination at the point of entry.'

'Surely poison is adulteration?' Morton said.

'I could hardly quarrel with that!' Pawson smiled. 'But it is trade adulteration that we are after. You must realise that Britain is the largest market in the world for tea. It is the only country where tea is now the staple beverage of high and low. Consequently, it is an important trade. We now import over two hundred million pounds weight a year. The duty on that lot is knocking on for five million.'

'That's a hell of a lot of money,' Bragg grunted.

'Indeed! And you can imagine that the populace expects the government to make sure it is getting value for money.'

'To hear Cassell Smith's manager,' said Morton, 'you would not believe that adulteration existed.'

'Well, they do trade at the top end of the market, but even they cannot afford to be complacent. It is in the China teas that adulteration most frequently occurs.'

'Who gains from it?' asked Bragg.

'Why, the producers. They adulterate in two ways, but with only one end in view – to push up their profits. One of their tricks is to bulk up the tea by adding foreign matter, such as oxide of iron, silica – we have even found iron filings!'

'Perhaps giving the dust to the foundlings is not such a laudable gesture, after all,' Morton said with a grin.

'The other ploy is to mix in spent leaves, or foreign vegetable matter.'

'But surely that would stand out a mile,' said Bragg.

'Not to your ordinary tea drinker; they go to some length disguise the fact. Where black tea is concerned, they mix leaves with powdered plumbago, which is the black-lead fou in pencils. It is called "facing" the tea, and it gives it a smoo glossy appearance. It is easily detectable by anyone in the trad but a merchant stuck with a chest would have to be a saint no to pass it on.'

'It is not poisonous then?'

'No. The most you would find, was that the tea was weaker than usual.'

'And what is the second way?'

'That involves green teas only. You must appreciate that it is the same leaf as the black, but the green has been dried more quickly. Nevertheless, it is a tricky process. If the temperature in the pans is allowed to get too high, or if the leaf starts to ferment through being kept too long, the resulting tea could not be sold as green. So our resourceful oriental friends colour it artificially. I will show you!'

He went to a table at the other end of the room, which was covered with rows of labelled packets, and selected one.

'This was shipped as a Twankay, which is a high-quality green tea. Now watch.'

He dropped some tea-leaves from the packet into a glass of water. After some moments, he shook it and a perceptible greenish tinge appeared around the leaves.

'The tea has been made saleable by colouring it with a mixture of turmeric, Prussian blue and indigo.'

'Good God!' exclaimed Bragg. 'That is fraud!'

'Indeed! And I cannot pretend that we intercept every doctored chest. But we take several samples from most shipments. If we find evidence of adulteration, we can condemn the whole shipment, so we keep it within reasonable bounds.'

'And none of this foreign matter is poisonous?' Morton asked.

Pawson pursed his lips. 'If I were honest, I would have to admit that we assume it is not. After all, it would not be in the interests of the planter to poison his customers. But this is not a pathology laboratory; we are concerned only with the physical condition of the tea.'

'When was the previous sample of teas consigned to Cassell Smith's taken?' Morton asked.

Pawson referred to his file. 'The twenty-eighth of January.'

'That is over six weeks ago . . . I imagine that the whole of that shipment has been disposed of now. And the recent one?'

'The eighth of March. It came in on the ss *Kowloon*, if you are interested.'

'What was the name of the Customs officer that took the sample?'

'That I do not know. I can find out for you, if it is important.'

'We can leave it for the moment. Thank you, anyway. And thank you for the tobacco . . . Smuggled, was it? Or were you testing for adulteration?'

Pawson laid his finger to his lips. 'Sssh!' he said with a smile.

'You know,' said Bragg, as they made their way out of the building, 'it all seems too hit-and-miss for my liking. They can't be out to poison a particular person – unless it's Pixley. I expect he drinks his own tea! To my way of thinking, it all comes down to somebody wanting to ruin Cassell Smith's business. If that be so, why should they run the risk of actually poisoning the tea, when they can get the same result by getting the *Echo* to spread a story to that effect?'

'So, you will not want me to interview the Customs officer who opened that chest?'

'Not for the moment, lad.'

'I wonder if Miss Marsden could discover the source of the *Echo's* information,' said Morton.

'It would do no harm to ask her . . . Yes, why not? You seem to be well in with her these days.'

Morton grinned. 'In professional matters, she can be somewhat prickly, but I will try!'

When they arrived back at Old Jewry, Bragg found an urgent message on his desk, requiring him to report to the coroner. Leaving Morton to write up his notes on the tea case, he took a hansom to the Temple, where the coroner – who was also a distinguished barrister – had his chambers. When Bragg was shown into his room, Sir Rufus Stone was leafing through a

book of law cases. He turned his leonine head and stared coldly at Bragg.

'You took your time, Bragg,' he said truculently. 'It is now two hours since I sent for you.'

'I was out on a case which the Commissioner regards as of some importance, sir,' Bragg replied placidly.

'Bah! Some stolen handbag, no doubt, or a clerk making off with the petty cash. Sometimes, I regret the convention that a coroner should use policemen for his investigations. It has led to the decline of the office. Pay him a pittance, so that he must use the police, and the coroner can be controlled. That is the thinking of those shiny-elbowed clerks in the Home Office. Well, I will not be manipulated, Bragg!'

'No, sir.'

Sir Rufus rose from his desk and took up a position with his back to the fire, legs a-straddle. He glared at Bragg for some moments.

'I suppose it is beyond your capacity, Bragg, to deal with a matter in a politic manner?' he said.

'Well, if you wanted something covered up . . .' Bragg replied slowly.

'Covered up! You know perfectly well that it is not in my nature to conceal anything. Moreover, had I wished to do so, I would have appointed someone else as my officer!'

'So it's a case, is it?' Bragg smiled.

'Indeed it is, Bragg, and a case of some delicacy. I should tell you that the police have not so far been involved in it.'

'Treasure-trove, then?'

'No, it is not,' said the coroner scornfully. 'I have no time for transcendental divinations about whether a man lost, or buried, his treasure. No, Bragg, it is a case of unexplained death and, if you will cease interrupting me, I will give you a résumé of the facts as I know them. He seized the lapel of his coat and threw back his head. 'An apparently healthy man, in early middle age, was attending a function this morning at the Saddlers' Hall. He seems to have been taken by a seizure of some description, for he suddenly collapsed on to the floor. The other people present acted with commendable promptitude, and had him conveyed to St Bartholomew's Hospital. However, by the time he was examined by the doctors, he was already dead.'

'I see.'

'By a recent act of delegation, I have empowered the authorities at Bart's to carry out post-mortem examinations, in such cases, without referring to me first. As it happened, our own chief police surgeon, Professor Burney, was in the hospital and, with his insatiable appetite for autopsies, he officiated himself. The essence of his preliminary report is that he does not yet know the cause of death, but that the man did not die from natural causes.'

'Hmn. Interesting.'

'You will find it the more interesting when I tell you that the dead man is Sir Fergus Jardine.'

Bragg looked blank.

'Do you take no interest in what goes on around you, Bragg? Sir Fergus is – was – the principal of Jardine Matheson, the biggest opium dealers in the East. Now you can appreciate why we cannot have the police blundering about in their usual manner.'

'An important man, was he?'

'Do not try my patience! Even you must appreciate that the prohibitionists will celebrate his demise as divine intervention on their side.'

'I pay no attention to that lot.'

'To close one's ears is almost as reprehensible as to close one's mind, Bragg. The point I am labouring, somewhat unsuccessfully, to make, is that his death has a political dimension. The Royal Commission set up last year into the opium trade, has already heightened public sensitivities. If the case is handled badly, the interests of justice could be eclipsed by political manoeuvring. I want the truth to emerge, but not to become a political football. Moreover, the Jardines are Scotch. And the Scots are apt to boast about the alleged superiority of their own legal system. I intend to demonstrate that justice operates smoothly and effectively in England also.'

'Then, I had better have a word with Dr Burney, sir.'

'Yes, Bragg. I will rely on you to keep in touch with the progress of his researches. Above all, you must keep the wretched politicians in ignorance.'

'I will do my best sir.'

'That is not good enough, Bragg! You must succeed!'

Bragg took his leave of Sir Rufus, and went in search of the pathologist. He had left St Bartholomew's for the day, and Bragg was directed to the Golden Lane mortuary. He trudged over, in light rain that threatened to turn to sleet, but Burney was not there either. He was glad to get back to his room in Old Jewry, where Morton had a good fire going. He had just given him an account of his interview with the coroner, when the Commissioner poked his head round the door.

'Ah, Bragg,' he said disarmingly. 'I was wondering how the Cassell case was coming along.'

'Cassell?' Bragg affected to be at a loss.

'The tea merchants.'

'Ah, yes. Well, sir, we have been to their premises, and we have also been to the Customs.'

'Customs?'

'You may not realise it, sir, but the Customs do their own tests on the tea that is imported. We confirmed that they had tested the last couple of shipments to Cassell Smith's, and that the results were satisfactory.'

'I see. I did not know that. So you think there is nothing to worry about?'

'Pixley is sampling every chest in his warehouse, just to be on the safe side; but to my mind, it is just a rumour put about by someone who wants to ruin them.'

'A competitor, you mean?'

'That would be the obvious explanation.'

'Well, I hope that they do not succeed. I doubt if anyone else would supply the blend they make for me . . . So, what are the next steps?'

'We are hoping,' said Morton, 'that we can persuade Miss Marsden to find out the source of the report. We shall know what credence to place on the rumour, then.'

'The young newspaper reporter? I am not wholly happy with that connection of yours, Bragg. I know that she has been useful to us in the past; but suppose some mishap should befall her. There would be a public outcry at the police's using a woman in that way.'

'She is one of the new breed, sir; thinks she is as good as any man – and I don't know that I would want to dispute it with her!'

'Well, I only hope you can clear up this business quickly, it is rather worrying.'

'You will be aware that I have a new case from the coroner,' Bragg said stolidly.

'I had forgotten that . . . I must say that I am increasingly irritated by the way this coroner nominates the people he requires to act as his officer.' The Commissioner's face had flushed a deep pink, and his resemblance to the Prince of Wales became more pronounced. 'His predecessor was content to allow us to allocate whomever we thought fit. It was a great deal more flexible . . . However, he seems to be within his rights – though whether he is justified in demanding that his cases take precedence over all others, is another matter.'

'They are generally murders, sir,' said Bragg.

'Hmn. What is the latest one?'

'Sir Fergus Jardine. Collapsed this morning, at a meeting.'

'I had heard a rumour that he'd died. Is there some doubt about the cause?'

'Dr Burney did the post-mortem, sir, and he is satisfied that it wasn't natural.'

'Well, you had better proceed with caution. We are deep into City politics, here. There will be any number of people looking to carve up his empire. It would hardly be too fanciful to suggest that one of them had disposed of him. You had better keep me closely informed on this case, Bragg. The coroner always wants to blunder on, regardless of the pressures we face. He may be a law unto himself, but we certainly are not.'

3

Bragg and Morton mounted the grand staircase of the Saddlers'
Hall, and were met on the landing by the clerk. He was dressed
in morning-coat and striped trousers, and his fingernails had
been carefully manicured. Not as downtrodden as his title
implied, thought Bragg. Indeed, he looked more like a partner
in a prosperous firm of solicitors.

'I understand that you are police officers,' he said in some
perturbation. 'Is it in connection with the sad events of
yesterday?'

'The coroner asked us to have a quick look round, sir,' Bragg
said. 'Now, if you could show us the room where the meeting
was being held, and so forth, it would be a great help.'

'Yes, of course . . . Sir Fergus was being admitted as a
yeoman member of the company, so he waited in this
ante-room while the preliminaries were gone through.'

Bragg poked his head through the door, noting the rich
carpet, the antique chairs disposed around the walls.

'He was all right when he left here, I take it?'

'Indeed! I myself escorted him into the meeting, so I can
positively confirm that.'

'Where did you take him?'

In reply, the clerk led them through an adjoining doorway,
into the main hall.

Morton gasped in surprise. 'What an extraordinarily splendid
room!' he said.

'Yes.' The clerk smiled. 'We are rather proud of it.'

'Was it arranged, yesterday, as it is now?' asked Bragg.

'Exactly as now.'

'So, where did you take the deceased to?'

31

'Into the hollow of the tables, more or less precisely in the centre.'

'And what was he doing? Just standing there?'

'No, sergeant. We were beginning the loving-cup ceremony, with which we welcome new members. Sir Fergus had just drunk of the cup, when he pitched forwards.'

'Where is this cup?'

The clerk led them to a glass-fronted cabinet at the back of the hall, which was filled with salvers and cups. He unlocked the door and took down a wide two-handled cup, with a cover like a steeple.

'Here it is,' he said. 'Unfortunately, the cup has been slightly deformed by his falling on it.'

'A pity, that,' said Bragg sardonically. 'A bit of silver is more important than a human life, after all.'

The clerk flushed. 'I will ignore that remark,' he said, 'except to tell you that it is one of a few items of plate in England to have survived the Civil War.'

'And I suppose you were so concerned about that, you didn't think it might be better to leave the cup unwashed?'

'I . . . No, I am afraid I did not. After all,' he added spiritedly, 'when we put him into the cab, none of us thought that he was going to die.'

'He was dead before he got to the hospital, and that's not half a mile away.'

'Well, had we known, we might have acted differently; though, at the moment, I cannot think what else we could have done.'

'Was he unconscious?'

'Deeply so. We decided against calling a medical practitioner, on the basis that it was better to get him to Bart's as quickly as possible.'

'Who went with him?'

'The beadle.'

'Right, I will have a word with him later. Now, can you show us where the deceased fell?'

The clerk frowned at the repetition of the word 'deceased', then led them back between the tables.

'He was standing there.' He indicated a spot on the carpet

with the toe of his boot.

'The constable will stand as he stood, and we will see if we can get him to fall as he did.'

Morton stepped forward.

'No. He was facing the back of the room at the time.'

Morton pivoted round. 'Is this better?' he asked.

'That is as he was standing.'

'What next?' asked Bragg.

'You must understand that I was sitting at the end of the top table. Moreover, I was far from giving the ceremony my full attention. I had seen it many times before.'

'Then do your best, sir.'

'He seemed to crumple up, falling both sideways and forwards.'

Bragg nodded his head, and Morton slumped to the floor. 'Like that?' he asked.

'Yes, yes. He did not collide with the chaplain, who was standing in front of him. It must have been just like that.'

Bragg walked round Morton's body, frowning.

'And the cup?' he asked. 'Where was that?'

'It was under the body . . . Sir Fergus's body, I mean.'

Bragg looked searchingly at him. 'Are you sure that he was still alive when you packed him off for his little trip to the hospital?' he asked coldly.

'He was certainly still breathing when we lifted him on to those chairs, if but shallowly. I cannot say that we continued to verify the fact. Our concern was to get him to medical help, with the minimum of delay.'

'That cup – was there still wine, or whatever, in it?'

'Most certainly. The chaplain had still to drink of it.'

'So some wine must have spilled out. Where, I wonder . . . Up you get, lad!'

Bragg dropped to his knees and began passing his hand over the surface of the carpet.

'Here we are – a damp patch. Hello! Someone's cleaned it! See that thread of rag in the pile?'

'I would not have thought that unreasonable,' said the clerk. 'Would not you remove spilled wine from your carpet?'

'It might surprise you to know, sir, that some people have

neither wine nor carpet. And, not having your instinct for skivvying, I am left wondering why everybody here was so keen to get rid of the evidence of what was in that cup.'

The clerk stood dumbfounded.

'Who prepared the wine?' Bragg asked roughly.

'The . . . the beadle.'

'Where will I find him?'

'He will be down in his room, I expect.'

'Thank you, sir. I would be glad if you would wait here, in case we need you again.'

Bragg and Morton found the beadle in a large butler's pantry, on the ground floor. He was a thick-set grey-haired man, with an anchor tattooed on his arm. He put down the glass he was polishing and gestured them to sit.

'I hear that you took Sir Fergus to the hospital yesterday,' Bragg began amiably.

'That's right.'

'We hear that he was dead before the doctors got to him.'

'I dunno, mate. I propped him in the corner of a growler, and held him so's he wouldn't fall over. Then, when we got to Bart's, I legged it for help. He was still leanin' in the corner, when they came for him.'

'He must have died during the journey. Have you no idea where it might have happened?'

'I told you,' his voice rose in protest, 'I was just holding him up.'

Bragg paused. 'Why did you wash the cup in such a rush?' he asked.

'I didn't.'

'Who did, then?'

'I mean I didn't do it in any rush. It was on the table. I just brought it down, and washed and polished it automatic, like.'

'Was it the same with the carpet?'

'No. Mr Alexander told me to do that.'

'For what reason?'

'Look here, mate, he's a warden. I didn't ask him, I just done it. I'm on a nice little number here, I ain't goin' to rock no boats.'

'What was in the cup?'

'Spiced wine.'

'Do you make it yourself?'

'No, we get it from Brett's in Idol Lane.'

'And, yesterday, were you using up an opened bottle?'

'No, I drew the cork myself, and filled the decanter. Then I took it upstairs and put it with the cup, on the side table.'

'Where is the decanter?'

The beadle reached up to a cupboard and took a heavily-cut decanter from the top shelf.

'So that has been washed as well. What did you do with the wine in the decanter?'

'I poured it back in the bottle, of course.'

'Can I see it?'

The beadle stooped and took a bottle from a rack. It was less than a quarter full.

'Now, here is a conundrum, and no mistake,' said Bragg, tugging at his ragged moustache. 'That decanter won't hold more than half a pint, and you say that you emptied some back. How comes it that there's so little left in the bottle?'

'I have to try it when I open a bottle, in case it's gone off,' the beadle said defensively.

'Come on!' Bragg grinned. 'You've been swigging it, haven't you?'

'Well . . . I needed something when I got back from that bleedin' hospital; and there was nothing better open . . . It's not nice,' he added in exculpation.

'How do you feel?' asked Bragg solicitously. 'Have you had any dizzy spells? Are you passing blood?'

The beadle blanched. 'Here, give over! How was I supposed to know the bloke had been murdered?'

'Who said anything about murder?'

'Well, the way you're going on, it couldn't be anything else!'

'Then, you should thank your lucky stars that you are not as stiff as Jardine.'

Bragg and Morton went back upstairs. They found the clerk staring vacantly out of the window.

'Well, sir, that has tidied things up a bit,' Bragg said genially. 'Now, I want you to take me through the events leading up to Jardine's collapse.'

'The actual ceremony, you mean?'

'Yes.'

'Very well . . . The master had welcomed Sir Fergus, and he had replied. At that point Mr Alexander, the renter warden, poured wine into the cup and placed it before the master.'

'Is that the same Mr Alexander who ordered that the carpet should be cleaned?'

'We have only one Mr Alexander.'

'I see . . . Go on.'

'In the normal course, the key warden would take the cup from the table and bear it to the line.'

'Key warden?'

'That is the title of the most senior warden.'

'Right.'

'This was a rather hurriedly arranged meeting,' the clerk went on, 'because Sir Fergus was returning to the East shortly. As a result, all the officers could not be present. Consequently, the renter warden took over the function of the key warden also.'

'Did you say there was a line, sir?' asked Bragg, peering at the carpet.

'No, no. You misunderstand me. When we administer the loving cup to new members, it is generally to several at once.'

'And this key warden goes to which end of the line?'

'To the front.'

'And the chaplain is at the rear?'

'Not normally. That is the role of the quarter warden. Since he also was unable to be present, the chaplain stepped into his shoes. It was appropriate, since he proposed Jardine's admission.'

'How long ago was it arranged that Sir Fergus would become a member?'

'Well, he was elected at the last meeting and proposed at the previous one, so it was common knowledge some two months ago.'

'And when was the actual meeting arranged?'

'No more than a week ago. His ship docked on the tenth, and he had to go up to Scotland first.'

'Who knew when it was to take place?'

'As it was not a regular meeting, we did not notify the membership formally. All the officers were told, of course, and a handful of members who might particularly have wished to be present.'

'Can you give me a list of them?'

'Of course. I will have it ready for you tomorrow.'

'Now, you say that you cannot tell me precisely what happened before Sir Fergus collapsed, because you were day-dreaming. Presumably this renter warden chap will be able to?'

'I would think not. He would have had his back to Jardine at the time.'

'What about the chaplain? He was close enough, by all accounts.'

'Yes, he would have seen precisely what happened.'

'Where can we find him?'

'He is the vicar of St Lawrence Jewry church, by the Guildhall . . . the Rev. George Rylands. You will find him most helpful.'

When Bragg and Morton arrived at the church, a service was in progress. A cluster of assorted matrons was in the front pews, murmuring self-consciously. They stood and looked about them. It was one of Wren's churches, wide and airy, with mellow woodwork and rich decoration. Although Morton's taste inclined to soaring Gothic vaulting and glowing stained glass, he had to admit that it was impressive. It was a preaching church, not a liturgical church. It did not seek to lift the spirit to ineffable heights. In its reassuring interior, the impact of the sublime upon the things of this world could be discussed as between gentlemen.

'They've finished,' Bragg growled. 'Let's grab the parson, before he skedaddles off to his port and cigars.'

They approached the choir stalls, where the vicar was sorting out his books.

'Mr Rylands?'

He looked up with a smile. 'That is so.'

'We are police officers,' said Bragg, showing his warrant-card. 'We would like to have a word about the events at Saddlers' Hall, yesterday morning.'

'Ah, yes. A sad business.' Rylands came down the steps to them. He was in his fifties, wiry, with a shock of grey hair.

'I understand that you are the chaplain of that livery company.'

'Indeed so, though I have no great claims to be connected with saddlery myself.'

'How did you come to be their chaplain, then?'

'Custom is a powerful element in City life, sergeant. The vicar of St Lawrence Jewry has been chaplain to the Saddlers' for hundreds of years. When I succeeded to the one, I inherited the other also. And I must say that I find it very congenial.'

'Are those campaign ribbons on your stole, sir?'

'Yes, they are.' Rylands smiled warmly. 'I spent much of my career as an army chaplain. It was a very rewarding experience, and enabled me to see a good deal of the world. But one grows old, and less tolerant of extreme climates. When the first batallion of the Argylls came back from Hong Kong, in 'eighty-two, I decided to come with them.'

'And how did you land this job?' asked Bragg.

'St Lawrence Jewry is regarded as the parish church of the Corporation of London. They have, in recent years, tended to present ex-service chaplains to the living. Since the City has become relatively depopulated, the work is not onerous, and is therefore well suited to someone beginning parish work in later life. But I like to think that there are positive aspects to the tradition. After all, the City is a great international trading community. It could be that they gain a little from clergy whose experience of the world extends beyond the parish pump! However that may be, it has its advantages for me. I get invitations to all the official functions of the Corporation. Being a bachelor, I find that very handy. My housekeeper's fare is very plain indeed!'

He rummaged in his cassock pocket and produced a well-worn tin box.

'Have a lozenge,' he said. 'They are good for keeping the tubes open this cold weather. There is very little difference between the various colours, though I can recommend the yellow.'

Bragg placed a yellow one in his mouth and, in a moment of

whimsy, Morton took one of deep purple.

'We have had a chat with the clerk, on behalf of the coroner,' said Bragg. 'Unfortunately, he didn't see what happened, because the renter warden was in the way. It seems that you are the only one who can tell us.'

'What is it that you wish to know, sergeant?'

'I am a bit foxed by this loving-cup business. If you could take us through the ritual, as it happened yesterday, we might understand it better.'

'I suppose that it is a debased form of the Eucharist; a joining in a common cup, signifying the bonds of brotherhood.'

'Or perhaps of mutual self-interest?' Morton suggested.

'That too,' Rylands acknowledged with a smile. 'Indeed one important aspect of the ceremony is that it is not only inclusive, but exclusive also. That is best seen when there are many participants. Normally, all are seated except for the man who has just partaken, the actual drinker, and the man about to drink. Having drunk, a member passes the cup to the next in line, then turns round – as it were to defend him from attack at the vulnerable moment of drinking. At the same time, the man on the other side of the drinker rises to cover his rear.'

'But with only one person to be presented, there would merely be three people, all standing.'

'That is so.'

'When were you asked to stand in for the . . . is it the quarter warden?' Bragg asked.

Rylands smiled. 'That is correct. These antique titles have a strange ring nowadays . . . Let me see. It was during the early evening of Monday.'

'The day before yesterday?'

'Yes. The quarter warden had intended to be present, but withdrew at the last minute.'

'Hmn . . . Now, if you could describe what happened, sir.'

'The renter warden would hold out the cup to Sir Fergus, who would take off the cover.'

'Would he be holding the cup by both handles?'

'Almost certainly. The renter warden would drink, wipe the rim of the cup with the small napkin appended to it, then hold it so that the cover could be replaced. Jardine would then take the cup from the warden, who would turn round to face the master.'

'Now, you saw everything from then on?' asked Bragg.

'I did. Sir Fergus turned to face me and proffered the cup. I took off the cover with my right hand. He drank and lowered the cup. Then he removed his right hand from the cup and took hold of the napkin. He seemed to be making rather a business of wiping the rim, and I glanced up at him. He had a strange dazed look on his face, and his mouth was half open – as if he was trying to say something . . . Then he gave a kind of gasp and sank to the floor.'

'Did he clutch at any part of his body, as if it was paining him?'

'No. One moment he was trying to wipe the cup; the next he was crumpled up on the floor.'

'You must have seen a lot of dying people in your time, sir. Was there anything different about this one?'

Rylands considered for a moment. 'No, sergeant. I do not believe so. It seemed just the same as any other seizure.'

'I gather that you nominated the deceased for membership of the Saddlers' Company, sir?'

'That is true. Jardine Matheson are based mainly in Canton and Hong Kong, and Sir Fergus has spent many years out there. We became good friends, during my tour of duty in Hong Kong. He was a passionate supporter of everything to do with horses – a founder member of the Hong Kong Jockey Club, and so on. Once I had become chaplain of the Saddlers' I determined that I would propose him at the first opportunity. When he told me that he would be coming to London this month, I put him forward for election.'

'I see, sir.'

'Now, unless there is anything else you wish to ask me, I must rush away. I have a diocesan meeting this afternoon.'

'I confess I was wondering what was the point of having a lid on the cup. It seems just a nuisance, to me.'

Rylands laughed. 'I suppose that, in more recent times, it has served to allow a certain elaboration in ceremonial, but its original purpose was much more practical. We are told that, in medieval times, you had a cover on your cup so that no one could put poison into it, while you were not looking!'

After a quick lunch in a pub, Bragg and Morton made their way to Jardine's office in Great Winchester Street. They were shown to the room of the London manager, a craggy-featured Scot, who greeted them with mild alarm.

'I had no idea it was a police matter,' he said.

'We are just having a look round, on behalf of the coroner,' said Bragg reassuringly. 'In any case of unexpected death, he gets notified.'

'I see, I see . . . Well, it was unexpected, that's for sure.'

'When did Sir Fergus arrive in England?'

'The ss *Rome* docked on the morning of the tenth of March, which was a Tuesday. He came in here early in the afternoon, and we had a discussion which lasted into the evening. Next morning he went to Scotland, which, as you will know, is where the business of Jardine Matheson is based.'

'And when did he return?'

'He had a meeting arranged in London, for Monday morning. I expect he came back again on the Saturday – he would nae travel on the Sabbath.'

'I imagine his hotel would know. Where was he staying?'

'De Keyser's Royal Hotel.'

'Very nice! Who was he meeting on Monday?'

'The manager of the Colonial Bank, in Bishopsgate Street Within.'

'Was that all day of a job?'

'I believe it was expected to last for the whole of the morning.'

'What did he do in the afternoon?'

'I would nae know. I am not his keeper.'

'At least, he had no business appointments?'

'No.'

'Perhaps he took his wife round the shops?'

'Sir Fergus had no wife.'

'But I looked him up in *Who's Who*,' Morton protested. 'He was shown there as married.'

'Ah well,' the manager said reluctantly, 'the truth is they split up, years ago. I think she went back to her family in Edinburgh.'

'Did you see him yesterday morning?' asked Bragg.

'He was in here at nine o'clock, as was his wont, and he stayed here till the cab arrived to take him to Saddlers' Hall.'

'Did he see anyone, other than staff?'

'Aye, he did.' A look of outrage flitted across the manager's face. 'Sir Fergus had scarcely got his feet under the desk, when a man stormed in demanding to see him. I told him it was out of the question, without an appointment, but he insisted. So I went and told Sir Fergus, and he said he would see him.'

'What was the man's name?'

'Volkes.'

'Did he give an address, or say what he wanted to see Sir Fergus about?'

'No. But I gained the impression that Sir Fergus knew of him.'

'Was Jardine irritated to be interrupted like that?'

'No. He was in a very amiable frame of mind . . . Odd, isn't it, when you think he had only hours to live?'

'Was there anyone else?'

'Yes, a Josiah Coaker, at quarter-past ten. He used to work here, so I made the appointment while Sir Fergus was in Scotland. I was sure he would not mind.'

'And were you right?'

'I think he was a little taken aback, at first, but he was pleasant enough about it.'

'Can you give me Coaker's address?'

The manager opened a file and gave a letter to Bragg. It was the brief note written by Coaker, requesting an interview.

'Right,' Bragg tucked the letter in his pocket. 'Now we would like to have a quick look at his room.'

The manager took a key from his desk and, leading them down a corridor, unlocked a door. The room beyond was opulently furnished, but had the air of being little used. There were no books in the bookcase and, although everything was clean and well polished, it was more like a furniture display than a room to work in. The only sign of occupation was a tantalus and a tray of glasses, on a side table.

'Did anyone take refreshment, yesterday morning?' Bragg asked.

'Now, I could not tell you that myself. I will have to ask the office junior.'

He went to the door and bellowed 'Jamie!' In answer, a slight lad of fifteen or so entered.

'Were there any empty glasses here, yesterday, after Sir Fergus's meetings?' the manager said sharply.

'Yes, sir. There were two.'

'What did you do with them, son?' Bragg asked kindly.

'I washed them up, and put them back.'

'Do you know what they had been drinking?'

'It smelled like whisky.'

'Did you bring the visitors to this room, yesterday?'

'Not the first one . . . but I brought that Mr Coaker.'

'Was it a friendly meeting, do you think?'

'Well, they shook hands, if that is what you mean.'

'Right, off you go.' Bragg turned to the manager. 'I'm afraid I shall have to borrow that decanter of whisky for a short while, sir,' he said.

The manager bridled. 'You had better make sure we get it back. It's on the inventory, and it is a valuable piece.'

'I expect you will, sir. Good day.'

Bragg and Morton took a cab to the address on Coaker's letter. It was a large terraced house in a dismal street in Southwark. The door was opened by a middle-aged woman, grasping a scrubbing brush.

'Mr Coaker?' she repeated. 'Yes, he's in . . . The top room at the back.'

They laboured up the narrow stairs, and found Coaker huddled over a small gas fire. The room was scantily furnished, but the whole floor was encumbered with bolts of cloth and great cardboard boxes.

'Mr Coaker?' Bragg asked, picking his way towards the fireplace. 'We are police officers. We understand that you called on Sir Fergus Jardine, at his office, yesterday morning.'

'I saw he'd died,' Coaker said dully. 'I won't say I am sorry, it would be a lie.' He was in his mid-fifties. His face was careworn, his nails bitten down to the quick.

'May I ask what you went to see him about?'

Coaker gave a derisive laugh. 'Are you thinking that I had a hand in it? I only wish I had – I would have done some good in my life, then.'

'So you had a row, did you?'

'No. Nothing so human. The bastard just played with me, to amuse himself for a spell, then kicked me out.'

'You used to work for him, didn't you?' Bragg asked quietly.

'Yes. But once you leave, it's never again.'

'What happened to make you take a job elsewhere?'

Coaker took a deep breath, and expelled it in a sigh. 'Jardines import all kinds of things from the East,' he said, 'silk among them, as you can imagine. I was in charge of fabrics for them. Between you and me, it was my knowledge and skill that made their profit for them. So I wanted to better myself – naturally. I had a wife and five children to provide for. Periodically I used to ask for a rise, and they sometimes gave me one . . . but it was very little. I would have liked promotion, but there was no scope for it, unless I would go to Glasgow. My wife would not even consider the possibility, so there seemed no way forward.' Coaker stared gloomily at the hissing flames.

'So, what did you do?' Bragg prompted him.

'I decided to strike out on my own. I had a good relationship with some of Jardine's biggest customers – wholesalers, you understand. And there are other importers . . . I didn't tell Jardines, of course, when I left them. They even gave me a silver watch as a leaving present!' He laughed mirthlessly.

'Anyway, for a start it went smoothly. I could undercut Jardines and still make a nice profit. Several of their customers switched to me, and I was doing very well – until Jardines found out what was going on . . . I still had friends in the office. They said Sir Fergus went wild. It was just my luck he was over here at the time. Anyway, he persuaded three of my biggest customers to go back to him. How, I don't know. Perhaps he gave them a special price. Whatever it was, they cancelled orders and left me with a lot of goods on my hands. When the time came to pay for them, I couldn't borrow enough money and the importers would not extend my credit . . . They made me bankrupt, and so I had to let down my other customers.'

'How long ago was that?'

'Three years. My wife and children went to relations in

Sunderland. I worked as a clerk, till I had paid every penny I owed. Since then I have been trying to scrape a living, selling at market stalls. It looks easy, when you watch them, doesn't it? But it isn't . . . Do you know?' he asked bleakly, 'I have not seen my youngest daughter for upwards of eighteen months.'

'So, what happened yesterday morning?' Bragg asked gently.

'Last week I decided I'd had enough; so I would go and eat humble pie and ask for my job back. Sir Fergus seemed very affable, offering me a drink and asking after the family; but the bastard was only playing with me. When I asked if he would take me back, he smiled and said there was no opening for me. Me, with my experience! . . I begged him. I said I would do anything, go to Scotland if need be. I practically grovelled, and he relished every second of it. Then he said they had a policy of never taking back people who had left the firm. It was a lie, and he knew it. I mentioned several people who had gone back; but that was in the past, he said – now it was different. And all the time he smiled and gloated . . . I could have throttled him! Then he said he had an important appointment, and he had to go. And, you may be sure, he let me know he thought talking to me was a nothing . . . So I was bundled out.'

'Was that the last you saw of him?'

'It was, sergeant. If he was knocked off, I didn't do it. But I would like to shake the hand of the man that did!'

'Ah, Sergeant Bragg – and Constable Morton too! I thought I might see you soon.'

Burney put down his scalpel on the chest of the corpse whose throat he was dissecting, wiped his hand on the apron draped across his stomach, and held it out.

'I have not seen you since . . . last December was it?' His cherubic face lit up, and his slack mouth gaped in a grin.

Morton took refuge behind Bragg, so that he would not have to grasp the proffered hand.

'We've come about the Jardine case,' Bragg said.

'Yes, indeed. Most extraordinary! And therefore most interesting. I can quite truthfully say that I have never met anything comparable – nor have my colleagues at Bart's.'

'I gather that you don't think it was natural causes.'

'One's first assumption was that it was routine, apoplexy perhaps – another man brought down in his prime through high living. But no. There was no sign of degeneration in the vascular system, indeed, the internal organs were like those of a man half his age.'

'So, what did he die of?'

'At the moment, it is still a matter of speculation. I am loath to believe that a physically healthy man would suddenly cease to live, without some outside intervention. The obvious assumption would be that he had been poisoned. I have sent the stomach contents to the pathology laboratory at Bart's, for them to do tests. He seemed to have consumed a large breakfast, some hours earlier, and there was also a reddish tinge, suggesting the ingestion of wine.'

'He was certainly taking a drink at the time. Would it have been possible for something to have been put in the wine, which would act within seconds?'

'One can certainly postulate the existence of such a poison. After all, hydrocyanic acid or strychnine can kill in that kind of time-span, if taken in sufficient quantity. Not that either of them was used in this case.'

'If so, he was killed in a very public way. It must have been like a stage play. He was standing in the middle of the Saddlers' Hall, drinking from their loving cup, when down he goes like a ninepin.'

'If one assumes a murderer,' Burney remarked, 'his mentality must be quite extraordinary.'

'The trouble about the loving cup,' said Bragg, 'is that it was filled from a decanter, prepared by the beadle before the meeting. Now, he admits to sampling the wine when he opened the bottle, and he had a swig from the decanter after he got back from taking Jardine to Bart's. So if it was done at Saddlers' Hall, it was only the wine in the cup that was poisoned.'

'Is there any of that wine for me to examine?'

'I am afraid not, sir. It was spilt on the carpet. We have another possibility, though.' Bragg took the decanter from his coat pocket and put it on the bench.

'So you have forsaken the hip-flask for something more

46

capacious – and more elegant, too,' Burney quipped. 'I always told you that ardent spirits would be your downfall!'

'We took this from Jardine's office. It seems probable that he drank some whisky from it around half-past ten that morning.'

'Excellent! It will be most useful. I will take it to the laboratory myself immediately. And I will get my report out as soon as I can possibly do so.'

'Good . . . Oh, by the way, Jardines would like their decanter back!'

Catherine Marsden sat down at her dressing table to tidy her hair before dinner. She looked at herself critically. She was looking pale, she decided, and her face was a little thinner. The thought was disconcerting; her face looked long enough already! She needed a little plumpness in the cheeks. She wondered if she should apply the slightest trace of rouge to her cheek-bones, to counteract it. With an absurd feeling of guilt, she applied a little with her finger-tip. It looked ridiculous! Conventional wisdom declared that it would transform her into a woman of easy virtue. Instead, it gave her the semblance of a peg doll! She took some cream and removed it, wondering idly what James Morton's reaction would have been, had he seen her. It was difficult to predict what men would feel, even someone as urbane and tolerant as he. They all shared the same prejudices; would interpret a trace of lip-salve as a declaration of wantonness. She sighed. It was part of the price she had to pay, she supposed. Not for her, languishing in a hot bath, or plastering her skin with unguents. She was up with the lark, carrying the fight for women's rights into the citadel of the enemy. She had to forgo the pampering indulged in by women whose only interest – whose only avenue of social fulfilment – was in marriage. But was it too high a price to pay? . . . Could she detect a hint of mannishness in her face? God forbid! Yet they said that adversaries came to resemble one another . . . Was it mere coincidence that she had not seen James for some weeks?

Less than a year ago, she had been the toast of London; courted by society hostesses, pursued by the Prince of Wales himself. During that time, James had seemed to distance himself from her, his agreeable dalliance replaced by a sardonic amusement. Once she had withdrawn from society, he had resumed his somewhat possessive friendship with her – doubtless on the basis that he had saved her maidenhood, if not her life. But he did not seem to want their relationship to develop into anything deeper. Throughout the previous autumn he had seen her frequently, calling at the office to escort her home, or taking her to dinner at the Savoy. She was sure that all her acquaintances expected an engagement to be announced, but he made not the slightest sign of wanting to settle down. He was behaving just like any other man-about-town, she thought peevishly. No, that was unfair. Young men of his affluent, upper-class background, spent their days drinking and womanising. He, with a splendid eccentricity, had joined the City police as a constable . . . Perhaps he was waiting for a sign from her, content that she should make the running. Well, that she would never do! She had too much self-respect to go fishing for a husband. Anyway, it was for the man to propose, and for the woman to consider and decide. Would she accept him? she wondered. Certainly, she would take no one else she had met . . . And she would not give up her job for any man! That she was determined on. She wondered if he would want her to. They had never come remotely within distance of discussing it, even obliquely . . . It need not be necessary, she decided. They could live in his rooms at Alderman's Walk. It was even nearer to the *City Press* office than was her parents' home. And she was sure that Mr and Mrs Chambers, who looked after him, would accept her. There would be no difficulty in the world. And, after all, it was possible to postpone having children nowadays. Not that that could go on for ever. With only a paralysed brother between him and the baronetcy, he would want to have an heir.

She recalled, with a pang of anxiety, that she had only seen him once since Christmas. He seemed to go down to The Priory much more frequently than before. Perhaps someone in Kent had caught his fancy. There would be scores of young women in the Maidstone area tumbling over themselves to secure such a prize. Well, she would not demean herself by competing with them . . . but she wished she did not look so careworn. Hearing the gong, she settled her pendant round her neck and went downstairs.

There were no guests to dinner, and her parents were chatting about domestic matters. Throughout the meal, Catherine found her concern about James haunting her thoughts. She was forced to acknowledge that she had developed a possessive attitude herself; thinking of him as someone she could marry, had she the inclination. She had unconsciously assumed that his attentions reflected similar feelings in him, feelings that she could bring to an avowal of love, if she so chose. But what if she had deceived herself?

'You seem preoccupied this evening, Catherine.'

'I am sorry, papa. I am a little concerned about an article that I have been asked to write.'

'That seems unlike you!'

Catherine laughed. 'But I am out of my depth, even though I am your daughter. I have been asked to do a piece on a painter living in the City.'

'Your editor is spreading his wings!'

'It is not Mr Tranter who has proposed it, but a friend of the painter. I would like your advice, papa, if you will help me.'

'Do I know the painter?'

'I doubt it! But I have secured a specimen of his work for you to see.'

'Then let us get to it! You will excuse us, my dear?'

Mrs Marsden smiled assent, only too willing to get back to her novel. Catherine took the picture to her father's studio and unwrapped it. He was momentarily taken aback, but suppressed a smile of incredulity and placed the picture on his easel with the utmost gravity.

'It is not exactly an Academy product,' he remarked.

'I gather that the painter was ejected from the Academy school.'

'That could be a recommendation in itself! What is his name?'

'Ben Fowler.'

'Hmn. The name rings no bells with me.'

'The idea is that I should write an informative article about

49

his work, in the hope that it might stimulate public interest.'

'And therefore the sales of his pictures,' her father said lightly. 'Do not misunderstand me, it is something any struggling painter would seize on – and it is only just that newspaper reporters should themselves be used, on occasion!'

'I am well aware that it is a delicate matter, but I would like to help him, if I could.'

'And Mr Tranter can be relied on to take care of the newspaper's interests, eh? Very well, let us consider it dispassionately, and see if you get any ideas from that.'

'Thank you, papa.' Catherine got out her notebook and pencil.

'At first sight, it is outside any current stream of development in painting,' Mr Marsden said reflectively. 'It has some of the technical elements of a Pissaro or a Monet, but, of course, it is entirely different in approach. Has it got a name?'

'It is a portrait of Louisa Sommers.'

'A portrait!' He puckered his brow. 'That name seems familiar.'

'Louisa? Yes, she was at Cheltenham with me. She stayed here several times.'

'The plump girl, with the beautiful brown hair.'

'Yes.'

'She was a talented water-colourist, as I remember.'

'That's right.'

'Hmn . . . And here she is, translated to canvas.'

'Fowler says that the function of art is to express emotion. If all that you want is a representation of the subject, then you should go to a photographer.'

'There is something in what he says,' her father remarked. 'Art certainly should not be devoid of emotion; the difficulty is in discrimination between the genuine thing and an insipid sentimentality. In my own field, I have decided that the trick is to catch a nuance of the sitter's character that the lens cannot reproduce.'

'As in the portrait of me that you exhibited last year?' Catherine said reproachfully.

'I still say that it was not in the slightest degree sensual!'

He bent forward and examined the surface of the painting.

'How old is the artist?' he asked.

'I suppose that he is in his early thirties.'

'He has a promising technique, indeed the whole canvas is interesting. It is bold in execution, without being crude. Look how sensitively the gradations of colour are employed in the central whirl. And the great blotches of blue and yellow are very effective in giving counterpoint to it . . . It was Walter Pater who said that painting had more to do with music than with representation, wasn't it?'

Catherine smiled. 'I do believe that your sympathies are with the modern movement, papa!'

'I would not arrogantly claim, with them, that art must exist for it's own sake, that art can only be judged by artists. If we pursued that line to its ultimate, we would all end up painting for each other, and no one would pay us!'

'So far, I have not got anything very concrete from you,' Catherine objected. 'Please be more specific!'

'Well, let us try to get this painting into perspective. Let us approach it on the basis that it is what Whistler described as "an arrangement of line, form and colour". So we should concern ourselves to evaluate the impact it makes on us – acknowledging that this might be widely divergent between one observer and another.'

'But is it art?' Catherine asked.

'There are no immutables in art,' her father said with a smile. 'Art is what we define as art. So paintings, even the paintings of the old masters, are seen as an adjunct of our experience of life. Only a fanatic would make a journey to Florence, to see the work of primitives like Cimabue. That is because the ecclesiastical restraints, within which they worked, have no relevance to modern times. We leave it to the Pre-Raphaelite brotherhood, to satisfy our craving for the medieval!'

'Certainly, this picture has nothing in common with Rossetti,' Catherine said with a smile.

'Indeed! The other side of the coin is that art must grow out of the past, if it is to be accepted. If you start by using a dramatically new style – as here – you are liable to be regarded as a self-indulgent crank. May I suggest that you get a transcript of the case of Whistler *versus* Ruskin? It is almost twenty years ago now, but in that case the whole essence of the problem is encapsulated. Ruskin accused Whistler of "flinging a pot of paint in the public's face", when he painted his nocturnes. Whistler won the case, but Ruskin still represents the attitude of the picture-buying public.'

'You do not think that the readers of the *City Press* would be interested in buying pictures such as that?'

'I fear,' said her father, 'that they would view them with derision.'

'Then there is no point in my going further?'

'I am sorry, my dear, but that is my opinion.'

4

Bragg and Morton ran the renter warden to earth in a set of chambers in Serjeants' Inn. His name appeared halfway up a board that was headed by a judge. He did not have the magical QC after his name but, to all appearances, he was a junior barrister of some standing in influential chambers.

The clerk let it be known that they were fortunate to find him in, and unengaged. Even so, he was dubious about interrupting Alexander without an appointment. Eventually he showed them into a small room on the second floor. Alexander was sitting at a modest desk, looking through a brief. A mahogany bookcase was crammed with legal volumes and red-taped bundles of papers were littered everywhere.

'Good morning, gentlemen,' he said, holding out his hand. He was about forty-five, Bragg decided, of athletic build, and handsome; but his chief attraction seemed to be a carefully cultivated, mellifluous voice.

'I have been expecting you,' he went on. 'I heard that you had been to the Saddlers' Hall; though what you hoped to find, I cannot imagine.'

'We don't hope for anything, sir,' said Bragg stolidly. 'We are just looking into the circumstances of Sir Fergus Jardine's death on behalf of the coroner.'

'Well, perhaps you ought to sit down.' Alexander cleared the papers from a couple of chairs and motioned them towards them.

'You don't look much like a horseman, sir,' Bragg began. 'How does it come about that you are in the Saddlers' Company? Is your family connected with the trade?'

Alexander looked down his nose reproachfully.

'In modern times, sergeant, it is not necessary to have involvement with the trade. I would think that far more of the present roll of the Company are members by redemption, than by patrimony.'

'Redemption?'

'By payment of a fee.'

'Oh,' said Bragg sardonically, 'you can buy your way in, can you?'

'I would say, rather, that the practice enables men of standing and ability to be of service to the City, without having to be formally connected to the craft and mercantile guilds.'

'That is good for the City, is it?'

'Indeed! The liverymen, that is the senior members of the livery companies, elect the Lord Mayor and the other City officers.'

'The Lord Mayor being a liveryman himself?'

'Yes.'

'And you are a liveryman of the Saddlers' Company?'

'Yes.'

'I see . . . Well now, can you tell me when you first knew about the ceremony for making Jardine a yeoman of the company?'

'Thursday of last week, which would be the twelfth.'

'You seem to be a very busy man. Why did you bother to go? It's not as if it was a regular meeting.'

'I felt it was my duty to do so.'

'It sounds to me like a pastime for people with nothing better to do.'

'Well,' Alexander hesitated. 'I must confess that I was originally disinclined to attend. However, when the master asked me to take the place of the key warden in the ritual . . .' he twisted his mouth wryly. 'There is something of the actor *manqué* in every barrister. I confess that I enjoy these antiquated rituals.'

Bragg smiled. 'Did you know Jardine before that morning?'

'I had met him, but we were not intimately acquainted.'

'May I ask where you met him?'

'In the course of my duties.'

'Hmn . . . Did you see him before the meeting on Tuesday?'

'No.'

'Now, I would like to get clear in my mind what happened in the loving-cup ceremony. Start from where Sir Fergus was brought in by the clerk.'

'When Jardine was in his place, I went to the side table and poured a little wine from the decanter into the cup, then placed it before the master.'

'How full was it, would you say?'

'No more than one quarter full – after all, there were only three people to drink from it.'

'Right, carry on.'

'Then, in my role as substitute key warden, I took the cup from in front of the master to where Jardine was standing.'

'You were facing him at that point?'

'Yes – and the chaplain, deputising for the quarter warden, was by then at his back.'

'What next?'

'I held out the cup, so that he could remove the cover.'

'Did you instruct him what to do?'

'No. I understand that he was already a liveryman of the Mercers' Company. He knew what was expected of him.'

'Why would he want to be a member of both?' asked Bragg.

'Most people connected with the City, would regard it as a considerable honour to be made a yeoman of the Saddlers'.'

'Very well. Jardine has just taken the cover off.'

'I took a sip from the cup, wiped the rim, and held it out for him to replace the cover. Then I passed the cup to him, and turned to face the master.'

'What happened then, to your knowledge?'

Alexander pondered. 'Jardine clearly turned towards the chaplain, because I heard the cover being removed. Then came the noise of his falling to the floor. I turned as the chaplain dropped to his knees.'

'What happened then?'

'The chaplain opened Jardine's coat and felt his heart. He said that he was alive. By then the others had gathered round us. Someone said that we should get him to hospital, and I volunteered to get a conveyance. As I left the room, the others were lifting him on to some chairs . . . In the event, the beadle got a cab and I instructed him to take Jardine to St Bartholomew's Hospital.'

'Why did you do that?' asked Bragg.

'It seemed more appropriate that the beadle should go.'

'Hmn . . . Who carried Jardine downstairs?'

'The beadle took his legs, I took one shoulder and the master took the other – he was quite a heavy man.'

'And he was still breathing when you got him to the cab?'

'I believe so.'

'What happened then?'

Alexander frowned. 'Nothing,' he said at length. 'The meeting was clearly over; no one was disposed to conversation, so we dispersed.'

'But you stayed behind.'

'I?'

'You waited until the beadle returned.'

'Did I? I do not recollect . . .'

'You told the beadle that he must clean the carpet, where the wine had been spilled.'

'It is possible,' said Alexander dismissively. 'I am, after all, an officer of the company.'

'Why bother?' Bragg asked. 'It was a red carpet. A bit of wine wouldn't show.'

'It is not a wholly red carpet; there is some beige in the pattern.'

'So, in the face of the collapse and serious illness of this eminent man, you have the presence of mind to remember a bit of beige wool in a carpet?'

'It is not at all as you represent it,' Alexander said coldly. 'I remember now that I did linger in the hall until the beadle returned. I wished to know if there were any developments regarding the condition of Sir Fergus.'

'And were there?'

'No. The beadle had returned as soon as the hospital staff had taken Jardine from the cab.'

'So when he got back you told him to wash the cup and scrub the carpet.'

'I do not recollect doing either.'

'As a legal man,' said Bragg smoothly, 'you will appreciate

that we must consider the possibility that Sir Fergus did not die from natural causes.'

'Great heavens!' Alexander exclaimed.

'It could be that he was poisoned; and the poison might have been in that cup.'

'But I drank from the cup, also!'

'Exactly, sir . . .'

Alexander looked at the policemen warily. 'Then since I am a lawyer,' he said carefully, 'you will not read into my declining to answer further questions anything more than a proper prudence. Now, I must ask you to leave. I have work to do.'

Bragg was silent, slumped in the corner, as the hansom trotted briskly towards Ludgate Circus. Then he roused himself.

'And what do you think of our joker?' he asked.

'Alexander?' Morton pondered briefly. 'I would certainly regard him as ambitious. He must clearly have reasonable expectations of being made a Queen's Counsel. That, in itself, would fully satisfy most men. Yet he is apparently determined to get his foot on the ladder which could lead to his becoming Lord Mayor, and acquiring a title thereby.'

'You are getting as uncharitable as I am,' Bragg said with a smile. 'For all that, it is difficult to get past the fact that Alexander himself drank from the cup, just before Jardine.'

'We have assumed that, if poison was involved, it was in the wine. But from what we have learned, that seems increasingly improbable. If Alexander had put poison into the cup, after he himself had drunk, he would have had to do it in the full sight of Jardine.'

'Perhaps he is an amateur prestidigitator, as well!'

'Not necessarily. Suppose that Alexander wanted to get rid of Jardine. He could have smeared the poison on part of the rim of the cup, before the start of the ceremony.'

'Wouldn't that be a bit risky? He might end up drinking from the wrong side himself.'

'No. The arms of the company are engraved on one side, while the name of the presenter of the cup is on the other. He would easily have been able to distinguish them.'

'That's a point, lad. But what if Jardine had drunk from the same side too?'

'It could not happen. It is a two-handled cup, remember. Alexander would hold it out with both hands, and Jardine would take it as presented to him. It would be in the highest degree unlikely that he would turn the cup round, before drinking.'

'And, if he had not collapsed,' Bragg mused, 'Jardine would have presented to Rylands the side that Alexander had drunk from.'

'So no one else would have been in danger, and the cup could not be suspect as the method of poisoning.'

'It sounds possible, doesn't it? . . . So Alexander is our man?'

'If we postulate means along those lines, then Alexander certainly had the opportunity – indeed, no one else could have maintained sufficient control over the situation, to ensure that it was Jardine who was poisoned.'

'But why would he do it?' Bragg objected. 'From what he said, he hardly knew the man. Still, it will bear thinking on . . .'

Morton hurried through the congested streets towards St Paul's churchyard. During the morning, the cold wind had dropped and a bright sun was tempting everybody to stretch their legs, in the lunch hour. He should not have spent so long chewing over the Jardine case with Bragg. By the time he had extracted the list from the clerk of the Saddlers' Company, it was already half-past twelve. With her passion for punctuality, Catherine would even now be in the teashop, fuming elegantly. He dashed across the road under the noses of a pair of van horses, and was roundly sworn at by the driver. He pushed through the throng by Queen Anne's statue. Why was it that everything conspired to hinder you when you were in a hurry? And the list had done nothing to lift his spirits. It had some fifteen names on it, only two of which he recognised. He foresaw a dreary round of interviews ahead of him. Well, it was his own fault. It was entirely his own choice that he was a flat-foot. He had to take the humdrum with the exciting. And he found it fulfilling, except on occasions like this, when his inclinations ran counter to his duty. It was a good thing that Catherine was a working girl, with no liking for the vapid socialising that constituted the life of most upper-class women. He had little time for that himself. Suddenly, he realised that he had not seen her since January – worse, that he had not even been in touch with her. His brief note, yesterday, would have seemed conceitedly presumptuous. He pushed open the door of the teashop. Catherine was sitting alone at the far end of the room. She looked up and smiled warmly at him.

'James! How pleasant to hear from you. You look rather jaded. May I pour you a cup of tea?'

Morton could not detect any irony in her tone, but, nevertheless, he decided to proceed warily.

'Yes, sir?' A waitress was standing at his elbow.

'A roast-beef sandwich, please.'

'That seems very little for a vigorous young man,' Catherine remarked.

'I am going out to dinner this evening. It is bound to be a heavy meal.'

'I see.' The acid in her tone was unmistakable.

'It is a society of Kentish men, living in London,' he explained.

'Exiled across the wide waters of the Thames? . . . I have the firm impression that these male occasions, where men try to recreate their schooldays, are very stuffy and boring.'

'Having been educated at home, I have to bow to your superior knowledge of boarding school,' Morton said lightly. 'However, I am by way of being a guest of honour.'

'Ah yes, the foremost cricketer of the county. How irritating it must be for you, not only to have the game monopolise the whole of your summer, but impinge on your free time in the winter also.'

'It is rather a nuisance,' Morton agreed diplomatically.

'And how are your parents?'

'Well, thank you.'

'I had a letter from Emily last week. She told me that you were well.'

Morton decided that penitence was the only refuge.

'I am sorry,' he said. 'It must seem that I have neglected you woefully. I plead guilty to presuming that our friendship is of such a sturdy growth, that it would easily survive a little enforced neglect.'

'But only if it is cherished subsequently!' there was a hint of triumph in her smile.

'Am I forgiven?'

'Let us say that you are on probation.'

'I hope I shall give you every satisfaction, mum,' Morton said in a high falsetto.

' 'Tis devoutly to be wished,' Catherine smiled. 'Am I being too cynical in suspecting that you invited me to lunch so that you might ask a favour of me?'

Morton screwed up his face wryly. 'As a matter of fact, I did wonder if you could do something for us.'

'I thought as much. Well, as my father said last night, it is only fair that reporters should themselves be used, on occasion.'

'We are looking into a report that the tea in an importer's warehouse has been poisoned.'

Catherine's face lit up with interest. 'Is this in the City?'

'Yes, the firm in question is Cassell Smith and Co. We have interviewed the managing partner and looked over the premises, and we frankly cannot see how the chests could have been interfered with. Some tests have been done by the Customs laboratory and, though they are not in themselves conclusive, they have been satisfactory.'

'What led you to institute your enquiries?'

'A report in last Saturday's *Echo*.'

'I missed that. What did it say?'

'It amounted to the reporting of an alleged rumour to that effect. If there is any substance in the report at all, it could be a false rumour put about by a competitor.'

'I see.'

'Rather than waste more police time, we were wondering if you could possibly find out the basis of the report . . .'

Catherine pursed her lips. 'It would not be easy. I have no acquaintances on the paper, and journalists are intensely suspicious of each other.'

'The *City Press* is not regarded as a competitor in gutter journalism, surely?'

'I can try, without any great hope of success – but only if you reciprocate.'

'In any way you propose.'

'I would like you to buy a picture . . . as an act of charity.'

'Does that mean irrespective of its artistic merit?'

'Possibly.'

'Some wooden portrait, obscured by old varnish, perhaps?'

Catherine smiled mischievously. 'I had to return it to the painter's studio, but papa has seen the painting and thought it had merit . . . After all, it may be valuable one day.'

'How much is asked for it?'

'That would be left to your discretion.'

'I normally avoid this kind of request. I prefer to give continuing support to charities in the Ashwell area, such as the church and alms-houses for the elderly.'

'But you do not live at The Priory yet, James. You live in London.'

'There are many rich people in London, but only our family in Ashwell.'

'I am sorry, James. No picture – no source!'

Morton grinned. 'It is the first time that I have been blackmailed in the cause of charity! Very well. Who or what is to be the recipient of my munificence?'

'The painter – a man called Ben Fowler.'

'Not charity, then, but patronage – I do not recognise the name.'

'Promise me, James, that you will buy the picture, even if you do not like it.'

'I promise.'

'Then, we just have time to go there if we hurry.'

They chatted cheerfully during the journey, and Morton was sorry when the cab pulled up outside the dejected terrace in Plough Court. While he paid the cabby, Catherine went down the area steps to the basement door.

'Wait there a moment,' she called.

The door was opened and Catherine went inside. He heard women's voices, then Catherine emerged and beckoned him.

'This is my friend, Louisa Sommers,' she said as he went in.

Louisa gave a startled cry. 'James! Oh! . . .'

'Whatever are you doing here?' Morton asked in astonishment.

'I live here,' she said defensively.

Morton looked around the room, noting the painting gear, the man's hat thrown carelessly on a chair.

'Good God, Lou!' he said. 'I never thought to find you in a place like this.'

Catherine began to feel out of her depth. 'How do you come to know each other?' she asked.

'We were brought up virtually in the same parish,' Morton replied. 'We have been friends since childhood.'

At least, Catherine thought, they had not been close in recent years.

'I did not realise that you two were aquainted,' Morton said.

'We were at school together,' Louisa said simply.

'Do your parents know that you are living in this way?' Morton asked in concern.

'No! Nor must they. Promise me, James, that you will say nothing to anyone.'

Before Morton could answer, the bedroom door burst open and a man appeared, unshaven and tousled.

'This place is getting to be like Paddington station,' he said in a harsh voice. 'Who are these people?'

'They are friends of mine.' Louisa looked towards James. 'This is Ben Fowler . . .'

'Ah, the daughter of the lollipop man,' Fowler sneered. 'Please ask your friends to go away.'

'I must be allowed some contact with my acquaintances,' Louisa said chidingly.

'Not at the expense of my art! You know this is my creative period.'

'But James wants to buy my portrait.'

'Then, get your haggling done elsewhere, woman.'

'No, Ben. This is where I live, I will not give in to your every whim.'

'Then, if they won't go, I will.' He grabbed the hat and rammed it on his head. 'I will prostitute my talent on one of your disgusting murals, while the spark still lives.' He strode to the door and banged his way out of the house.

'Ben is the painter of the portrait,' Catherine said foolishly, to break the silence.

'He is not always like that,' Louisa said. 'He can be kind . . . But he has taken up this fashion of drinking opium to stimulate his imagination. It is not good for him. I hope that, if he sells a picture, his confidence will be restored, and I can wean him away from it.'

'I am concerned for you,' Morton said in a troubled voice. 'You look thin and careworn.'

'I am all right . . . really I am.'

'Well, let me see this portrait.'

Louisa went into the bedroom and brought the picture from under the bed. Morton looked at it with a stony face.

'I would like to buy it,' he said finally. 'I will pay one hundred pounds for it, at a rate of five pounds each week – to be given to you personally.' He took out his pocket-book and handed her a five-pound note.

Louisa hugged him with affection. 'You are just as kind and thoughtful as ever, James,' she said warmly. 'I promise that you will not lose by it.'

'I will bring the money to you each week. When is the best time to come?'

Louisa smiled. 'In the late evening. Ben is usually fast asleep by then.'

'Very well.'

'Could I ask a favour of you, James?'

'Of course.'

'As you have guessed, we are in need of money, and Ben is not very careful when he has it. But he would feel slighted if the money for the picture were paid to me, not to him. It would be easier for me if you did not take it with you now. I can say that you were not interested. Then, in a week or so, when Ben has forgotten all about it, I will bring it to you.'

'Fine. Now, take care of yourself, Lou.' Morton gave her a brotherly peck on the cheek and hurried out. Catherine followed, thinking of nineteen late-night errands of mercy . . . and that Louisa had not needed to ask for James's address.

Once outside, Morton hailed a passing cab for Catherine. As for himself, he would walk. For once, it was worth incurring

Bragg's wrath at being late. The walk might clear his mind . . . Louisa living in those conditions! And clearly by her own wish. Yet the man was plainly a boor! . . . Women never ceased to amaze him. Obviously, she was Fowler's mistress, so she had thrown away any chance of making a suitable marriage . . . He smiled grimly. His mother had thought of Louisa as a possible daughter-in-law, at one time. They had certainly been close as children, but somehow she had been too compliant, too malleable. Her eagerness to please had made her somehow insipid. Then he had gone up to Cambridge, and they had seen little of each other thereafter . . . Well, they said adversity was a great stiffener of the sinews, and she seemed well able to stand up to Fowler. The question was how far anyone had the right to interfere in what was clearly her free choice . . . But was it? Once she had been deflowered, she had little alternative. Even if she left him, there was always the danger that the liaison would become known. She could not rebuild her life on such shifting sands . . . Unless the man she married was already aware of her predicament . . . His eye was caught by a newsboy's placard.

SUDDEN DEATH

IN LONDON

OFFICE

He bought a copy to distract his mind, and scanned the front page. Halfway down the short paragraph he checked, then started to run. He hurried into the Old Jewry building, ran up the stairs and burst into Bragg's room.

'Have you seen this?' he gasped.

'What?'

'This afternoon's *Echo*?'

'I don't bother myself with that rag.'

'Look at the front page! A man was found dead in his office this morning.'

'What is so special about that?' Bragg said uninterestedly.

'He was the Secretary of the Royal Commission on the opium trade.'

'Opium, eh?' Bragg read through the paragraph, 'And

Jardine was involved with opium . . . Kind of the *Echo* to give us the address. Come on, lad!'

They took a growler, and it set them down before a new office building in Queen Anne's Gate. Most of the tenants appeared to be accountants and commercial people. Indeed, the only reference to the Royal Commission was a small printed card, pinned to the occupiers name-board. To Bragg's great delight there was a hydraulic lift, and they rose serenely to a small suite of offices on the top floor. The first room was occupied by a young man, well dressed and somewhat flustered. When Bragg presented his warrant-card, he seemed on the point of exploding.

'Why on earth should you involve yourselves in all this?' he asked irritably. 'Things are complicated enough as it is. A new Secretary to the Commission will have to be appointed. He will know virtually nothing of what went on, and I can only tell him what little I have picked up in the past week.'

'And who might you be, sir,' Bragg asked.

'My name is Ross. I am acting as Mr Hewitt's secretary.'

'I see . . . the secretary to the Secretary. Well, I can't see what all the fuss is about. It is the Commissioners that are important, surely?'

Ross seemed about to contradict this subversive suggestion, then flopped wearily into his chair without replying.

'I did not expect to find you in a place like this,' Bragg remarked, staring out of the window over the bare trees of St James's Park. 'Why are you not in one of the government offices? There are enough of them around here.'

'We are independent of the government,' Ross said sharply, 'and it is important that the fact should be made plain.'

'Ah . . . I didn't realise that. What did Mr Hewitt do, before he was given the job of Secretary to the Commission?'

'He was a senior official in the India Office.'

'And you?'

'I am a somewhat less senior one.'

'So you are both seconded from the India Office?'

'Yes.'

'And that suddenly makes you independent of government policy, does it?'

'We exist to serve the empire,' Ross said dogmatically. 'We are always independent of any particular administration.'

'It's all a bit subtle for me,' Bragg smiled. 'But I don't suppose it matters. Have you known Mr Hewitt long?'

'Not intimately.'

'Where is his residence?'

'The family home is at Brandon House, Chelmsford.'

'In Essex? That's a long way.'

'Yes. In fact he was in the process of building a new house in Highgate . . . he was somewhat exercised over whether he could afford to meet all his wife's wishes in the matter.'

'So he had expectations, out of this job?' Bragg asked sardonically.

'The outcome would certainly have had a bearing on his future career, yes.'

'Did he travel in from Chelmsford, then?'

'No. During the week he stayed at his club.'

'Which is where?'

'It is the Orleans Club, in King Street, St James's.'

'Just over the park?'

'Yes.'

'Now, where is the body?'

'I believe that it was taken to the Westminster mortuary.'

'Right. Did you find him?'

'No. His body was discovered by a cleaner, at half-past six this morning.'

'Is she still around, would you know?'

'I would think not. However, I did speak to her, when I arrived. Mr Hewitt had been taken away by then, but she told me what she knew.'

'What time would that be?'

'Half-past nine.'

'So, what did she find?'

'When she went into his room,' Ross nodded towards a door in the corner, 'she found him slumped over his desk. At first, she thought that he must have fallen asleep, and tried to rouse him. But he was dead, and quite cold . . . She said that he looked peaceful, as if it had come very suddenly.'

'Could we have a look in his room?'

Ross demurred. 'I cannot understand your interest in the matter,' he said.

'We have reason to believe that Mr Hewitt's death might not have been natural, sir.'

'You mean, that he might have been killed?'

'Exactly so. There may be information in his papers that could have a bearing on it.'

'But I cannot possibly agree to that!' Ross exclaimed. 'All the papers relating to the hearings of the Commission are in his room. They are highly confidential, and must remain so, whatever your interest.'

'We are hardly likely to waste time with them. But he probably has some personal papers here – particularly as he was only staying at a club.'

'I am sorry, but it is out of the question.'

'Then I shall get a warrant to take the lot.'

'They are crown property!'

'I hardly think,' Morton interjected, 'that crown exemption would extend to documents belonging to an arm's-length commission.'

A baffled look crossed Ross's face. 'Very well. On condition that the official papers remain inviolate, you may do what you wish with the others.'

'Then you had better come in, to see fair play.' Bragg said, opening the door at the back.

He found himself in a somewhat larger room, with a carpet instead of linoleum. The middle of the room was taken up with a large mahogany desk and chairs. Along one side were several presses, and cardboard boxes of documents were stacked in the corner.

'If there are any private papers, they will be in his desk,' Ross said.

'Would that be where he was sitting?' Bragg asked, nodding towards the swivel chair by the desk.

'I presume so. Everything has been disarranged by the men who came for the body.'

Bragg looked briefly at the chair and the surface of the desk, but there was nothing of significance. He could imagine the charwoman giving everything a good going over, to get rid of the aura of death.

'Empty one of those boxes, lad, and we'll put the stuff from the drawers in it.'

Ross looked on uncertainly, as the contents of the desk were packed up.

'When did Mr Hewitt return to England?' Morton asked, to distract him.

'I am not wholly sure. I was only appointed to assist him last Thursday. I do know that he came back from Bombay on the ss *Rome*. Is it important?'

'You never can tell, sir. Well, we will leave you in peace. Good day.'

Bragg was jubilant as their hansom rattled back to the City again.

'That's one in the eye for the Met!' he said. 'We've swiped everything from under their noses!'

'You seem to be making a considerable assumption, sir,' Morton replied. 'His death might be innocent, or, even if not, it may have nothing whatever to do with Jardine's.'

'Oh no! I have that feeling in my bones, lad.'

When they reached Old Jewry, he rushed up to his room, and had the contents of the box strewn over his desk before Morton had hung up his hat and coat.

'Here's his diary. You skim through the rest, lad.' He settled back in his chair. 'It looks as if he started work last Thursday. There are no entries before the twelfth . . . The appointments for Thursday and Friday seem to be meetings at the India Office.'

'No doubt, he was receiving instructions as to how the colonial service, at least, thinks the report should be slanted.'

'You are getting cynical.' Bragg said with a grin.

'You will have realised, sir, that both Jardine and Hewitt returned from India on the same ship.'

'The ss *Rome*, yes. I don't know quite what to make of that yet, but we must bear it in mind.' He flipped over a page of the diary. 'Hello!' he said triumphantly. 'Look what we have here! An appointment for nine o'clock last night.'

'With whom?'

'Guess!'

'I have no idea.'

'Someone called Volkes. Now there's an unusual name!'

'The one who called on Jardine, you think?'

'More than likely, I reckon.'

'Was the appointment at the office?'

'It doesn't say – but there is a number after the entry. Do you think it could be a file number?'

'I have not seen any folders with numbers on them . . . Six five nine three. Could it be a number on a telephone exchange?'

Bragg bounded across the room and seized the telephone instrument. 'Try six five nine three for me, will you Bill?' he said.

He waited a moment then: 'Hello!' he bellowed. 'Who is that? . . . Sorry, I got it wrong.'

He replaced the ear-piece with a fierce smile. 'Get your coat on, lad. That was the Holborn Viaduct Hotel!'

When the cab drew up, Bragg leapt out, leaving Morton to pay the fare. As he entered the foyer of the hotel, Bragg was banging on a bell to attract attention. Becoming impatient, he marched off towards the dining-room and, finding a waiter, despatched him for the manager. Soon a short, dapper man appeared.

'I am sorry to have kept you waiting, gentlemen,' he said unctuously. 'We do not have a full complement of staff on duty at this time of day.'

'Police,' said Bragg, showing his card.

The deference evaporated from the manager's manner. 'Oh, yes?' he said. 'What is the matter?'

'We understand you have a man, name of Volkes, staying here.'

'Let me see.' The manager opened the register. 'We did have, but he left this morning.'

'When did he first come?'

'On this stay, do you mean?'

'Yes.'

'He registered on the evening of Tuesday, the tenth of March.'

'Had he been before?'

'I cannot tell, without going through the book – I was merely trying to be precise.'

'Never mind. Where did he go?'

'He said that he was travelling to the north country. He did not say where. But he did intimate that he would stay here again, on his return.'

'If he does, I want you to let me know, at Old Jewry – we are on the telephone system now.'

Bragg elected to stroll back to the office, sombre and deflated. He sat down at his desk and picked up a pipe from the ash-tray.

'What do you make of it?' he asked, feeling in his pocket for his tobacco pouch.

'We certainly have a growing area of coincidence,' Morton said thoughtfully. 'As you will remember, Jardine's manager said that the ss *Rome* docked on the tenth. We know that Jardine and Hewitt disembarked on that day. Do you think that Volkes was on that same ship? He registered at the hotel on the evening of the tenth.'

'So it is not opium that is the connection, but the ship?'

'Unless Volkes is also involved in opium.'

Bragg struck a match and laid it carefully across the bowl of his pipe.

'We had better not start jumping to conclusions or we shall cloud our judgement,' he said, puffing till the smoke curled blue around his head.

'There is another entry for last night,' he went on. 'Someone called Painter. It was earlier – at seven o'clock. This time, it's in pencil. I wonder if that means it was not as definite as the ink one.'

'Ross might know.'

'Make a note of it, will you? Now, give me some of those papers.'

For a time the two men read in silence. Then Morton chuckled.

'Hewitt gets more interesting by the minute – and perhaps more human! Look at this. A letter in a woman's hand – on scented notepaper, moreover!'

He laid it before Bragg.

*It is so good to know that
you are back in England.
After so many months! I am
longing to see you.*

> *Till tomorrow.*
> *J M*

'When was it posted?'

Morton retrieved the envelope from his desk. 'Monday the sixteenth, at nine in the morning,' he said

'So the meeting was for Tuesday, the day before he died . . . Well, it might have some connection. Will you follow it up, tomorrow?'

'If I can locate the address!'

I had better let the Commissioner know about our interest in Hewitt before he goes home. We don't want him queering our pitch with some chance remark to the top brass of the Met.'

Morton put more coal on the fire, and settled down to a gentle browse. It seemed that most of the papers related to a period before Hewitt's appointment as Secretary to the Royal Commission. No doubt they had been left in the cupboard in the India Office, and retrieved on his return. Morton was idly turning the papers in a file marked 'New House', when he froze in incredulous surprise. It was a letter signed 'Louisa Sommers' and undoubtedly in her writing.

> *29, Plough Court,*
> *E C.*
> *17 March 1894*

Dear Sir,
Thank you for your enquiry concerning the advertisment. Mr Fowler will be delighted to attend your office at seven o'clock, tomorrow evening, to discuss your requirements.

> *Yours faithfully,*
> *Louisa Sommers*

It must have been addressed to Hewitt. There was no shadow of doubt about it . . . So this was the painter in the diary. But why on earth need it imply that Louisa was connected with his death? Or Fowler either, for that matter. There was not the slightest indication that Hewitt had met either of them before. The last thing that Louisa needed, was to be involved in a police enquiry. Apart from the stress, there was always the danger that a zealous newspaper reporter might follow their trail. Then, her name could be spread across the *Reynolds News* some Sunday. It would ruin her . . . Anyway, Hewitt's death might still prove to have been from natural causes. It was time enough to risk her reputation, when it was certain that there had been a murder. He folded the letter and put it in his pocket. In the meantime, he could ask her about it himself.

5

Next morning Bragg went back to the Saddlers' Hall. He felt he
was being distracted from the main problem. It was tempting to
assume that the Hewitt case was linked to Jardine's death. But
at the moment it was, at best, a side issue. Suppose that Hewitt
had not died from natural causes, where did that get them? It
would be folly to make the assumption that it must therefore be
linked with the Jardine business. What could be the motive?
Suppose that there was a madman, knocking off people
involved with opium; what about the thousands of pharmacists
dispensing opium every day, the doctors prescribing it?
Dammit, Hewitt was not even connected with opium – he was
just an innocuous colonial servant who had been unlucky
enough to be drafted as secretary of a board of enquiry. No,
speculation was all very well, but it mustn't get out of hand. It
was best to rely on methodical police work.

He pushed open the heavy door and went into the vestibule.
He looked around, but could find no one. He determined to go
over the ground again, to see if it would yield any new ideas . . .
Jardine must have come in at this entrance. Perhaps he was met
by the beadle or the clerk, perhaps not. At all events, he knew
enough about livery halls to go straight on upstairs. After all,
there were only servants' quarters on the ground floor. Bragg
began to mount the stairs, looking about him carefully, letting
his mind absorb every detail. It was massive and heavily carved,
but surely it was mahogany? That didn't sound like a medieval
staircase . . . He tried to remember when mahogany had first
begun to be used in England. He had only a sketchy grasp of the
subject, but it must have been after King James's time. Oh well,
it had no bearing on his problem.

The stairs gave on to a wide landing, running the whole width of the building. Directly opposite him was the large double-doored entrance to the hall itself. On either side was a smaller doorway, less elaborately carved. The one on the left was the ante-room they had been shown. Perhaps he should see what was in the other . . . A man was working by the door, his step-ladder obstructing the entrance. He had a painter's palette in his hand, and he was daubing away at a mural. Bragg stood back and looked at the picture; he had not realised that it was unfinished . . . It was its stiff, wooden look that had made him think it was old. Still, it was nicely done. It couldn't have been easy to paint a hunting scene round those three doorways. The spaces between them were occupied by two medieval hunts-men, their horses equipped, naturally enough, with magnificent saddles. To the left of the ante-room, pale beauties in wimples looked on. To the right, a pack of hounds in full cry pursued a boar. It was all quite jolly, with streaming pennants and bright colours . . . and yet there was something not quite right.

'Can I get into this room, please,' Bragg asked the painter.

The man looked down belligerently. 'Will it not wait?' he snapped.

'I won't be more than a second.'

'Damnation, man! One minute you are badgering me to finish the wretched thing, the next you keep wanting me to move. Which is it to be?'

'Please.'

With a scowl, the painter came down the ladder and flung his palette on the twill sheet covering the carpet. Then he stalked over to the window and glared out of it. Bragg moved the step-ladder to one side, and entered the room. It was similar in size to the ante-room, but was furnished as an office. There were presses and bookcases along the walls, but no means of commuication with the main hall. He went back to the landing, and set the step-ladder by the doorway again.

'Thank you,' he said.

The painter flung himself round petulantly, picked up his palette and mounted the ladder. Bragg stood back to watch.

'That boar is going at a hell of a lick,' he observed pleasantly. 'Is it supposed to be a hunt?'

'Don't be a clod,' the painter sneered. 'Of course it is!'

'I am a bit of a clod,' Bragg said amiably. 'A real country bumpkin, I am . . . Are the horses galloping after it?'

'What the devil else do they do, on a hunt?'

'Well, I can see the wild eyes and the flaring nostrils. You have caught them a treat . . . Yes, the body is galloping all right. The trouble is, the legs are trotting . . !'

He turned and went into the hall, following the route that Jardine must have taken. The damp patch, where the carpet had been scrubbed, was dry now. He stared at it, remembering how Morton had lain, crumpled up – with an imaginary cup under him. He glanced towards the side table. In his mind he re-enacted the ceremony, retracing the movements of the cup from the point where it was filled, to where it was dropped to the floor. Apart from one moment, it was in full view of at least two people all the time. That moment was when Alexander poured in the wine from the decanter. His back was bound to screen what he was doing from the rest of the people in the hall. Perhaps there was something in Morton's theory, after all. No one would suspect someone who had drunk from the cup, seconds before. The wine would not be given a moment's thought. But if it had been the rim that was poisoned . . .

Bragg went out of the hall. The painter was nowhere to be seen, though his equipment still littered the landing. He went downstairs, and found the beadle in his pantry. He nodded perkily at the policeman.

'Not given up, then?' he asked.

'Just chewing things over in my mind. You know the loving-cup ceremony?'

'Yes.'

'It seems that, after each of them has drunk, he wipes the rim of the cup with a little napkin.'

'That's right.'

'Have you got the napkin that was used on Tuesday?'

The beadle opened a drawer and took out a small square of linen, freshly starched and ironed.

'There you are,' he said.

'Are you sure this is the one?' Bragg asked.

''Course I'm sure. Got it back this morning, from the laundry.'

'Damn and blast it!' Bragg muttered. 'Why is it that every single thing I want to examine, has been washed and scrubbed and polished? The trouble with you, mate, is you're too good at your job.'

'That's right, guv, I told you I have a nice little number here. How about a glass of spiced wine, to steady your nerves?'

'No thanks! That's an odd chap upstairs – the painter, I mean. Have you noticed he's got the horse's feet wrong?'

'Me? No!' The beadle grinned dismissively. 'I know more about boats than horses . . . But he is a queer 'un, and no mistake. Comes in at all hours; sploshes on a bit of paint, then goes off in a huff. You can't talk to him, without he bites your head off. He nearly came to blows with the clerk, last week. I reckon he's a loony.'

'What was it about?'

'Oh, he wasn't getting on fast enough. He'd promised it would be finished a fortnight ago.'

'Was he here on Tuesday morning?'

'Yes, he was. I had a job to get him to pack up, in time for the meeting.'

'Was there any row on that occasion?'

'No. He just stamped off, muttering, "They'll be sorry"!'

'What is his name?'

'Let me see . . . I don't have all that much to do with him . . . Begins with an F . . . Fowler, that's it. Something Fowler.'

Bragg left the Saddlers' Hall and took a hansom to the Temple. He walked briskly through the mellow courtyards to the chambers of Sir Rufus Stone. He spent some moments kicking his heels in the waiting room, then was ushered into the presence.

'Ah, Bragg. You have come to report progress, no doubt.' Sir Rufus took up his customary position a-straddle the fireplace.

'Report, sir?'

'The Jardine case, man! I am opening the inquest on Wednesday.'

'Ah, yes. Well, that one is still in the hands of Dr Burney, at the moment. You saw his preliminary report.'

'Huh! Unknown poisons! Sounds like a penny dreadful. In heaven's name, how does he expect the prosecution to prove its case, with that kind of material? Not even Burney will cut much ice as an expert witness, if he cannot identify the agent he proposes as having killed the man!'

'You won't be any better pleased, when I tell you that our prime suspect has to be a barrister,' Bragg said with a grin.

'Good God! That is inconceivable! We cannot have you going around, under my authority, accusing members of the bar of murder . . . Who is he?'

'A man called Alexander.'

'Alexander who?'

'John Alexander. He has chambers in Serjeants' Inn.'

'He is not at the chancery bar, at any rate,' Sir Rufus muttered. 'Is he a silk?'

'I would rate him as a senior junior, sir.'

'Hmn . . . And why is he a suspect?'

'He was the last person to handle the loving cup, before Jardine drank from it.'

'Not only an unknown poison, but an instantaneous poison,' the coroner said disagreeably.

'I really came to see if you could do something for me,' said Bragg.

'You wish to involve me in one of your dubious stratagems, no doubt. No, Bragg. More and more, I feel that deviousness merely confuses the issue. Let us proceed with openness and decisiveness.'

'Very well, sir . . . You may have seen in yesterday's *Echo* that a man called William Hewitt died in his office, the night before last.'

'So?'

'He was the Secretary to the Royal Commission on the opium trade. From all accounts, his death was as unexpected as Jardine's, and somewhat similar.'

'Where did he die?'

'In an office in Queen Anne's Gate.'

'That is out of my jurisdiction, Bragg. I could not possibly interfere.'

'I'm not asking you to do anything irregular, sir. But it is interesting that Jardine and Hewitt both came back to England on the ss *Rome*, on the previous Tuesday.'

77

'You think that they might have eaten something that disagreed with them, but which manifested itself only after the effluxion of a week?' asked Sir Rufus sceptically.

'Not that, no sir. But, in my experience, there is often something in coincidences.'

'And what is the coincidence you claim to have discovered?'

'Not just the travelling back together, but that both were, in a way, involved in opium.'

'Pah! Your imagination is running away with you, Bragg. There are at least half a dozen witnesses to that.'

'How do you mean, sir?'

'All the British members of the Royal Commission also came back on that boat. They had been taking evidence on the Indian sub-continent. Why are they not dead, eh?'

'I can't say, sir. Maybe there is something special in their case.'

'Or in the cases of Jardine and Hewitt. To have been murdered is not yet the norm, thank God!' Sir Rufus said ironically.

'Anyway, sir, I think you would be interested in what I propose.'

'Very well, Bragg, what is it?'

'I would merely like you to use your influence, and arrange for Professor Burney to be present at the post-mortem on Hewitt.'

The coroner pursed his lips. 'I might well go as far as that, Bragg. The Westminster coroner is a friend of mine . . . Yes, I will write to him immediately.'

He sat down at his desk and scribbled two notes, then bellowed down the corridor. A fresh-faced youth appeared, looking wary.

'Barnes, take this note – personally, you understand – to the Westminster coroner's office and give it into his hand. The second is for Professor Burney at Bart's. Understand?'

'Yes, sir.' The youth darted through the door again and Sir Rufus resumed his pose.

'You have not explained,' he said thoughtfully, 'the part which the Metropolitan police are playing in your melodrama, Bragg. Have they been relegated to the role of interested spectators?'

'I wouldn't know, sir,' Bragg said stolidly. 'My enquiries have been made purely as your officer in the Jardine case. The Met may not even be officially aware of Hewitt's death.'

'You must think that I am as naïve as you are devious, Bragg. It is in the highest degree probable, that the Westminster coroner will appoint someone from that force as his officer – if, indeed, he has not already done so.'

'I hadn't thought of that, sir. I shall be interested to find out who it is.'

'Please do so. I do not wish your machinations to sour the relations between me and my fellow-coroner.'

'Very well, sir.'

'You know, Bragg,' Sir Rufus said ruminatively, 'I do not know what all this fuss is, about opium. It has been in common use for centuries, and I cannot see that it has done any great harm. I could not get through a Hilary term without my Collis Browne's Chlorodyne, to keep the coughs at bay.'

'Next thing, the do-gooders will be saying you're an addict,' Bragg said straight-faced.

'Pah! What they should be asking themselves is what the poorer classes can drink for a cordial, if they cannot get laudanum. The people who object to opium can afford to turn to whisky as their restorative.'

Morton picked up the letter sent to Hewitt by JM, and wondered what kind of person he would find. It was a warm letter, without doubt. Yet, since Hewitt had a family home in Essex – and therefore a family – his relationship with JM had to be illicit. He had always thought of civil servants as being too stuffy and colourless to have mistresses. But perhaps India Office men had more dash about them. Would it be a chubby, homely matron of his own age? Or might it be a young 'actress'? If he knew where they were going to meet, he would have a better idea. A dollymop would be unlikely to have lodgings where she could entertain her admirers. Though, obviously, a prostitute would. But the letter had an air of real affection. Something in between, then . . . a *demi-mondaine* perhaps;

though a public servant would hardly be able to afford that level of solace, out of his salary. No, more than likely it was a dollymop, whom he would be taking out to a restaurant. Come to think of it, there was a certain archness about the letter that might denote a young woman. If so, he could be wasting his time. He lifted down the gazetteer. The only street with the initials YGP, that he could find, was off Hampstead High Street. It sounded like a good address, too good, in some ways . . . Perhaps an elderly widow lived there, who took in lodgers that were skittish.

He took a cab which dropped him, half an hour later, in Hampstead. He strolled, in the sunshine, past the great houses of bankers and merchants, built in the confident days of half a century ago. It was interesting to see that, even out here, people were no longer keeping their own carriages, preferring to go into London by train and use cabs for local journeys. Here and there, the mews of such a house had been turned into cottages – perhaps for servants to live in . . . Life rushed on at such a hectic pace, he thought. Nowadays, things were no sooner created than they were out-of-date. He wondered if there would still be a place in his children's world for Ashwell Priory a great jumble of a house reaching back to medieval times, surrounded by vast tracts of not-very-fertile land. An enormous dinosaur of a house, which had become a part of him. He was suddenly struck by the thought that he should keep his own children away from it. Not allow them to be seduced by its subtle dissonances, its guileless charm. Then they would be able to be objective about it, sell it to some brash brewer, turn it into a girls' boarding school . . . He thrust the thought from his mind, and looked around him. This was the centre of the old village as it had existed for centuries, before being engulfed by the mansions of London's rich. Here the houses were on a more domestic scale, their warm yellow brick golden in the sunshine. And there was Yorkshire Grey Place, a small cul-de-sac within a stone's throw of the heath. There was no sign of the hostelry that must have given the street its name. Instead, there was a group of new shops on the corner. Morton went into one, and bought a newspaper.

'I am looking for someone who lives in Yorkshire Grey

Place,' he remarked to the buxom young woman behind the counter.

'Who might that be?' she asked with a smile.

'I have been very stupid, I am afraid. I left my bit of paper, with the lady's name on it, behind in the office. The only thing that I can remember with any certainty, is that her initials are JM. It looks as if I shall have to go back and retrieve it.'

'No need for that, sir. It must be Mrs Morell, at number four. She's the only one with those initials, in the street.'

Morton thanked her and went back into the sun. Number four was a small brick cottage, standing alone. It had every appearance of being well cared for; the paintwork gleamed, the lawn was bordered by a profusion of daffodils. He rang the bell, and the door was answered by a maid in starched apron and cap.

'I would like to see Mrs Morell, if possible,' he said. 'Is she in?'

'She's in, all right,' the maid said in a slow countryfied voice. 'But I don't know if she is receiving.' She half-closed the door and disappeared. A few moments later, she returned and showed him into a parlour. It was furnished in traditional style. There were heavy drapes at the window and mantelpiece, the furniture was solid, the walls covered with pictures. He went over to the mantelpiece and took up a photograph.

'My late husband,' said a vibrant contralto voice. A young woman stood in the doorway, smiling quizzically.

'My name is Morton, I am a police officer.' He held out his warrant-card.

She took it, and scrutinised it with mock seriousness.

'And I am Jane Morell. Well, Constable Morton, would you like some coffee?'

'Thank you.'

'Coffee, Maud,' she called to the maid, and closed the door. Her smile became provocative as she returned his card.

'This is an exciting new experience for me, constable,' she said. 'I have never been investigated by a policeman before!'

Morton felt his pulse quicken. 'We think that you might have some information which might help us,' he said in as matter-of-fact a tone as he could muster.

She held up her hand, as the maid brought in the coffee and poured it into elegant china cups. Mrs Morell was a well-formed young woman, Morton thought, from a good background. And there was an effervescence about her that was almost irresistible.

'Now, constable,' she said, as the maid closed the door behind her, 'what is this information you refer to?'

'You are aware that William Hewitt died on Wednesday night?' he asked quietly.

A cloud passed over her face. 'Yes, I saw the report in the newspaper.'

'We found your letter to him in his desk . . . I am sorry.'

'Do not look at me so intently, Detective Constable Morton. You make me feel as if you are seeking out evidence of the fallen woman in me!'

Morton dropped his eyes in embarrassment. 'From your letter,' he said, 'it appears that you had an appointment with him for Tuesday night. Did you keep that appointment?'

'Yes. He came here for dinner. We had a pleasant, intimate evening.'

'You were close to him?'

'Yes, Mr Morton, I was close to him!'

'How did that come about?'

Her mischievous smile faded. 'I must literally be something of a *femme fatale*. Most gentlemen of my acquaintance die young . . . So be warned!' The smile flickered briefly. 'Had my father lived, I am sure that my life would have been very different. But he died, leaving my mother and a large family. He left little enough money, so, when Mr Morell began to pay court to me, mamma encouraged him. There was no apparent alternative for me, so I accepted him . . . I have been my own woman, since I was eighteen.'

'Your own woman?'

'I would not have you think that I am wanton, Mr Morton, but my husband was a disappointment to me. He was twenty years older than I and, I suspect, hoped that our marriage would regenerate his fading desires. For a time it was so – for a few months. Then he began to neglect me. If I pressed my affections on him, he would become angry and retreat to his club. I felt desolate. For me, it was like being given vintage champagne, then told that I could have it only at Christmas . . . Our relationship was dead long before he died.'

'What was your husband's profession?'

'He worked in the India Office, under William Hewitt . . . That was how I regained my independence – in spirit, at least. I suppose you will not remember but, some years ago, when the Tories were in power, the opposition succeeded in forcing through a resolution which was critical of the trade in opium between India and China. It had little practical effect at the time; but there was always the possibility that a future liberal government would feel compelled to enact restrictive legislation. The India Office decided to be forearmed, and sent my husband out to China to investigate the position there. I was fortunate enough to be allowed to accompany him.'

'When was that?'

'In the summer and autumn of 1882. It was an unimaginable wonder for me and, for a time, I was distracted . . . By the time my feeling of desolation returned, fate had already prepared the antidote. It had been arranged that we would go up-river from Hong Kong. We were to stay for a few days at the house of a British merchant, in Canton; then he was to accompany my husband, on horseback, into the interior. As it happened, our host fell from his horse the day before they were due to leave, so he had to stay behind. Mr Morell set out with a Chinese guide, who succeeded in getting lost repeatedly. So when he returned he was some weeks late and exceedingly angry . . . Of course, I had been left with our host. And, since his injuries mended remarkably quickly, I had a wonderful time!'

'Am I to assume that you became intimate?'

'Let us say that I regained my freedom . . . Are you shocked?'

Morton could feel a stirring in his loins. 'No, not shocked,' he said. 'What happened after that?'

'I suppose that my brief dalliance had restored my self-esteem. My husband was suspicious when he returned, but he was hardly in a position to challenge his host! When we returned to England, we took up our life again – except that I no longer needed to feel confined and cheated.'

'You have had other men friends, then?'

'There is no need to feel embarrassed, constable! How old are you?'

'Twenty-seven.'

'I am only thirty, myself, yet you make me feel positively old! . . . I have had a few other friends. People were anxious to assist, when my husband died.'

'When was that?'

'In 'eighty-five. He died from typhoid, quite suddenly. William Hewitt was very solicitous, and secured a small annuity from the service for me. We have been close ever since.'

'Did he tell you about his private affairs?'

'To some extent.'

'No doubt you saw a good deal of him, since he was virtually living at his club.'

'We met at least once, almost every week.'

'Did he introduce you to his friends?'

'No. I had no wish to prejudice his marriage. Almost always, he would come here.'

'You knew where his office was, though?'

'Yes. He gave me the address, in case I needed to contact him.'

'Did he say anything about his trip to India?'

'Only generalities . . . We had not met for four months!'

'Yes, of course.' Morton tried to ignore his growing concupiscence. 'Did he ever say anything to you about enemies he might have had?'

'No, constable. I do not think so. However, I have kept diaries throughout the period of our acquaintance. If you like, I will go through them, and you can call again . . .'

Morton swallowed hard. 'One other thing, what was the name of the man who entertained you in Hong Kong?'

'It was Fergus Jardine – later Sir Fergus.'

'And now the late Sir Fergus Jardine.'

'Yes,' she said soberly. 'I told you that all my men die young.'

'Your own private peeler to see you, miss,' the office-boy announced with a grin. 'Shall I send him in?'

'Yes, please, Tom.'

Catherine swiftly rearranged the jumble on her desk, so that it looked efficient and purposeful.

'Ah, James,' she said with a sparkling smile. 'Are you being *gallant*? Am I to be escorted back to Park Lane? That would be pleasant!'

Morton smiled ruefully. 'As a matter of fact,' he said, 'I was wondering if you had made any progress on the tea case.'

'I do not understand.'

'The report in the *Echo* . . .'

'Ah. The tea chest! Yes, James, I have made progress, though I had to go further in flattering a revolting reporter called Stubbs, than I would have wished.'

'I hope you did not go too far!'

'Because you desire the end, James, you cannot therefore determine the means. It was important to you, so I did what was necessary . . . He is a particularly nauseating person, in a profession that seems to turn men into unfeeling louts.'

'But you succeeded?'

'In the ultimate,' she said lightly, 'any man is susceptible to a woman's charms.'

Morton grinned. 'That does not sound like a feminist!'

'I am not a feminist,' Catherine retorted sharply. 'Merely a woman who is successful.'

'That sounds uncharacteristically smug . . . I hope that you do not neglect to be successful as a woman!'

'We shall see, James, shall we not?'

'So, what did you discover?'

'The basis for the report was a printed anonymous letter, delivered by hand to the newspaper's office in Catherine Street.'

'Did you see it?'

'No. Stubbs was somewhat defensive about it. Not many journalists would base an unqualified report, such as that, on an anonymous source – nor newspapers print it.'

'I dare not think what you would have to do, actually to gain sight of it!'

'No gentleman would ask a lady to go further.'

'Not even if she were a distinguished journalist?'

'No, James,' she said firmly. 'It is now up to you.'

'Very well. Thank you for your help . . . Now it is my turn to be defensive, and, alas! I have no secrets you would wish to probe.'

'Enough of this badinage,' she said sharply. 'What is it that you want now?'

'I am going to see Louisa Sommers. I wondered if you would come also.'

Catherine felt a sudden pang of jealousy. 'Why on earth should I?' she exclaimed.

'No real reason. . . except that I would like you to be there,' Morton said lamely.

'I have no desire to be involved in your past.'

'Please . . .'

What possible purpose could she serve? she thought angrily. Was he deliberately setting out to humiliate her? No, that would be out of character. Did he wish to demonstrate that there was no liaison between him and Louisa? . . . In that case dare she reject the offer?

'Very well,' she said and, putting on her hat and coat, followed him down the stairs.

It had begun to rain again, and the flaps of the hansom gave scant protection as the wind drove it into their faces. Catherine felt that she was becoming more sodden and dishevelled by the minute. She was relieved when James was at last handing her down in Plough Court. She hurried down the steps and rang the bell. There was some delay, then the door was opened and James reached her side.

'Oh . . . Come in.' Louisa seemed tense and troubled. 'I will not be a moment, I am busy making something.'

She went to the kitchen, and Catherine and Morton crossed to stand in the doorway. On a shelf, opposite the window, stood a row of large earthenware jars. Morton counted ten in all, each with a label bearing annotations. Louisa was filtering the contents of another jar into a bowl.

'What are you making?' Catherine asked.

'What Ben calls his nectar.'

'Laudanum?'

'Yes . . . It is a rather involved chore, because the opium has to macerate for seven days before it can be used. And Ben is drinking so much of it.'

'How much?'

'I suspect that he is taking more than a pint a day, now . . .' She added a generous amount of a colourless liquid to the bowl.

'What is that?' Morton asked.

'Proof spirit . . . and a little rough red wine, to give it a better appearance . . . There we are!' She poured the contents into a jar and set it aside.

'How much opium is in that?'

'One and a half ounces of powder to every pint.'

'That seems a very great deal,' Morton said, perturbed.

'Do not be so disapproving,' Louisa replied spiritedly. 'Lots of artists have used opium to stimulate their imaginations. What about De Quincey and Coleridge?'

'Someone said of De Quincey that he merely chewed over the regurgitated remnants of an imperfect classical education,' Morton remarked. 'And as for the *Ancient Mariner*, surely it is little more than doggerel? . . . If you ask me, the use of opium is merely an exercise in self-deception.'

Louisa flinched. 'It is easy for you to say that, James. You have never needed to succeed in anything, the whole of your life.'

Catherine intervened. 'Where is he now?' she asked.

Louisa went into the main living room and gestured towards the other door. 'In there,' she said flatly. 'He came back again about noon. He was very upset. It appears that some officious person where he is working had criticised his painting. I tried to stop him taking more laudanum then . . . but he only does the murals for my sake.'

'Was he very unpleasant?' Morton asked solicitously.

'I stay with him, because I love him . . .'

Morton looked abashed. 'There was something I wished to ask you about the murals,' he said.

'What is that?'

'We found this letter, in the papers of someone we are interested in. Am I right in thinking that it was written by you?'

Louisa scrutinised the page. 'Yes . . . Mr Hewitt. He was one of the few to answer the advertisement.'

'Which was that?'

'When Ben agreed to try murals, I put an advertisement in the *Morning Post*. That was in the middle of January.'

'How did Hewitt get in touch with you?'

'I received a letter on Monday morning . . . I still have it, somewhere.'

She went into the bedroom, and they could hear Fowler's slow, deep breathing. She came out holding a handbag and, rummaging in it, produced an envelope which she handed to Morton.

'Posted in Chelmsford, on Saturday. That explains it. His wife must have seen the advertisement, and given it to him on his return . . . He had been abroad,' he added.

'We had given up hope of receiving any further replies.'

Morton took out the letter. It was signed William Hewitt, and the handwriting matched that on the papers from his desk. In it he referred to the advertisement, said that he was contemplating having a mural in his new house in Highgate, and suggested that Mr Fowler should call on him at seven o'clock on Wednesday the eighteenth of March, at the Queen Anne's Gate office.

'And, did Fowler keep the appointment?'

'I think so. He certainly left here in time to keep it.'

'Did he not tell you about the meeting, when he returned?'

'No. He was in a state of great excitement, and was even aggressive towards me. When I mentioned the meeting, he refused to discuss it. At the time, I thought it very strange. I begin to feel that he no longer trusts me . . .'

6

'Sorry to be late, sir,' Morton said breathlessly. 'I thought that I would call on Ross before he became involved with the new Secretary to the Commission. They have moved with commendable speed in that area, at least. A man called Baines has been appointed to succeed Hewitt.'

'Where did you get that gem from?'

'This morning's *Times*.'

Bragg grunted. 'Well, I have been going through Hewitt's papers. I can't say I am much wiser. They are mostly ages old, but you had better cast your eye over them again, sometime. Well, what did Ross have to say?'

'I asked if the Volkes interview would have taken place at the office. He said almost certainly it would. When he left in the evenings, he was under instructions to leave the outer door of the building open. Apparently Hewitt had come to an arrangement with the janitor, that he would lock up at night.'

'So anybody might have got in,' Bragg grunted.

'Ross was careful to add that he was not saying the Volkes meeting had taken place. He did not know whether it had or not.'

'Is he slippery, or just careful?'

'I think merely pedantic.'

'What about the interview with the painter?'

Morton busied himself with hanging up his ulster. 'He knew nothing about that appointment. Indeed, he was inclined to feel that it was provisional, since it had merely been pencilled in.'

'Hmn . . . Anything else?'

'I also asked if any ladies had called, but he could not help me.'

'Ladies?'

Morton sprawled in the chair by his desk. 'My visit to the mysterious JM yesterday was most illuminating! As we supposed, it is a lady – Mrs Jane Morell. Indeed, she is a most delectable young widow of thirty.'

'His mistress?'

'Not exactly, for she has several men friends; but certainly not a prostitute . . . I would describe her as a middle-class voluptuary. Her almost innocent sensuality was a delight!'

'I bet she makes her living by her body, all the same.' Bragg said sourly.

'Come now, sergeant, you are being puritanical!'

'And none the worse for that! What about her and Hewitt?'

'He was her late husband's boss – though they seem to have been of much the same age. When her husband died, nine years ago, he was solicitous and she grateful . . .'

'He was stuffing her, was he?' Bragg asked coarsely.

'Could so indelicate a phrase ever apply to such a beautiful and radiant young lady?'

'Stop bloody roasting me, lad! We are not playing society weekends.'

'She was happy to admit that they were intimate. She has a small colonial service pension; supplemented, no doubt, by Hewitt, amongst others.'

'On the surface, she had nothing to gain by his death?'

'Indeed not. On the other hand, she did not seem either grief-stricken or concerned about her financial position.'

'A butterfly, is she?'

'That is a much kinder description of her!'

'Had she seen Hewitt?'

'Yes. It was his practice to go to her house in Hampstead, at least once a week. They would have dinner, and then . . .'

'A good shag, for old times' sake, eh?'

'When you meet her, sir, you will realise that you are being unduly censorious. She is a very warm-hearted young woman, who would easily inspire affection in return.'

'When I meet her?'

'She is looking through her diaries, in case there might be a reference to someone who bore Hewitt ill will. It seems hardly likely, but it was a spontaneous gesture of co-operation.'

'She wants to get her hooks into you, lad. That's what it is.'

'Me? A raw detective constable?' Morton grinned. 'Now, a mature well-set-up sergeant would be much more to her taste. You could do worse, sir!'

'Stop piss-taking! Did she go to Hewitt's office?'

'According to her, no. She said that she had no wish to compromise his marriage. She did, however, have the address.'

'So she could have?'

'Yes.'

Bragg looked across at the church tower musingly.

'You know, lad,' he remarked at length, Hewitt couldn't work all the hours that God sends without eating. He would hardly make an appointment for nine o'clock at night on an empty stomach. I bet he had dinner between Painter – if he came – and Volkes . . . Somewhere local.'

'His club was only a few minutes walk away.'

'So it was. We had better check up on that.'

'There was a further interesting piece of information, that Jane gave me. Quite voluntarily, I should emphasise . . .'

'Get on with it,' Bragg growled irritably.

'She is also acquainted with Sir Fergus Jardine – or was, in the past.'

'Jardine?'

'It was he who first seduced her from her marriage vows. I must say that she exhibited neither remorse nor ill-will. Indeed, if anything, she seems to look on the episode with gratitude.'

'When was this?'

'1882.'

'She can't have been much more than a child,' Bragg said in disgust.

'Nineteen, I calculate. It happened when she and her husband were on a trip to China, and were staying with Jardine in Canton.'

'She sounds a right trollop . . . So she knew both Jardine and Hewitt? That's interesting. Had she seen Jardine while he was in London?'

'She merely said that she had seen the announcement of his death in the newspaper. She seemed quite unaffected.'

'Can you see her knocking them off?'

'Unless she is a consummate actress, no . . . Speaking of Jardine, I went last night to Coaker's lodgings in Southwark. I was told that he had left the previous day, and had not said where he was going.'

Bragg looked up sharply. 'That's funny – a businessman not leaving a forwarding address.'

'Perhaps all he expected was bills!'

'Better get the Sunderland police to keep an eye open for him; and find out who moved all his stuff. He can't have carried it himself.'

'Very good, sir.'

'Now then,' Bragg looked up with an ill-concealed smirk of pleasure. 'Just in case you think you are the only one that does any work around here . . .' He pulled some sheets of paper from a drawer, and pushed them towards Morton.

'What is this?'

'The passenger-list for the voyage home of the ss *Rome*.'

'Really! How did you get hold of this?'

'Never you mind. It's unofficial, so don't broadcast the fact.'

'What is the significance of the names underlined in red?'

'They are all to do with opium, lad.'

'Lord Brassey? Surely not?'

Bragg smiled smugly. 'Read on.'

'Fanshawe, Hewitt, Jardine, Lyall, Mowbray, Pease, Roberts, Wilson . . . I recognise Hewitt and Jardine, of course, but who are the others?'

'They are the members of the Royal Commission, coming back from taking evidence in India.'

'Are they, indeed!'

'And, since they are all still alive, it seems we might be wrong about the opium side of it. It could be something to do with the voyage, as you suggested.'

'Someone on board who had a grudge against both Jardine and Hewitt?'

'It's possible.'

Morton riffled through the pages. 'Volkes's name is not on the list. But perhaps he did not travel first-class . . . Ah, here we are, 'Volkes M' in the second-class. So we were right! Is there any way we can trace him?'

'I telephoned the manager of the hotel this morning, but he has not shown up yet.'

'One presumes that since he come to this country he might leave it again. Is there any way to find out if he has booked a return trip?'

'Officially, you mean?'

'Well, yes.'

'Not officially, there isn't. But I didn't work in London as a shipping clerk for nothing. If he books a passage, I shall hear of it.'

'You are a man of great resource, sergeant . . . And I suppose you have noticed the name at the head of the first-class list?'

'J. G. Alexander, you mean? Yes, I thought we might pop in and have a few words with him.'

They took a cab to Serjeants' Inn and, going to Alexander's chambers, sought out the clerk.

'We would like a few words with Mr Alexander,' Bragg said gruffly.

'Mr Alexander? Not here, you can't. He always spends Saturday morning at the Society.'

'Society?'

'He is Secretary of the Society for the Suppression of the Opium Trade – has been for years.'

'And where might they be?'

'Forty-one, King Street, Westminster. You could catch him all right.'

Bragg leaned moodily in the corner of the cab, as it rattled down the Embankment, then he sighed.

'This case is a real sod! We keep going round in circles. First it's opium, then the ship, then opium again.'

'Or the ship and opium combined,' Morton remarked. 'And you will have realised that the address we have been given for the Society's office is in the same street as Hewitt's club.'

'I know, lad, and only a stone's throw from his office.'

'Yet one must wonder what Alexander personally had to gain from the death of either Jardine or Hewitt.'

'Perhaps we shall discover that.' Bragg jumped out the

moment the cab stopped and bounced up the stairs to the first floor of the building. The door gave on to a large outer office, where a sprinkling of young women sat at tables. They seemed to be putting leaflets into envelopes. A tow-headed girl approached them with a warm smile.

'We are preparing for the campaign,' she said in a cultured voice. 'Have you come to join the Society?'

'No, miss,' Bragg said gruffly. 'We just want a quick word with Mr Alexander.'

'I will find out if he can see you. What name shall I give?'

'Bragg and Morton.'

She went towards a door at the back of the room, and Bragg started after her. Alexander seemed about to refuse, then, seeing the policemen in the doorway, assented reluctantly.

'You didn't say anything about being involved with this lot,' Bragg began.

'I would not have thought it necessary,' Alexander replied tetchily. 'It is a matter of public record.'

'No doubt . . . Would you mind telling me why you were on the ss *Rome* on her last voyage, sir?'

'Not at all. I was returning from Bombay.'

'Was it a private visit?'

'No. I had travelled to India to attend the hearings of the Royal Commission on the opium trade.'

'That must have entailed a big financial loss to you.'

'It was more important than anything else I am likely to achieve in my life,' Alexander said pompously.

'Could you not have given evidence in London, last autumn?'

'My purpose was not to give evidence, sergeant, but to see that others did so.'

'I don't understand you, sir.'

'Is it necessary that you should?'

'It could be.'

Alexander sighed theatrically. 'Very well . . . Even you, sergeant, will appreciate that the whole affair of this Royal Commission has been manipulated by the government. The concern of this Society is with the opium trade in the whole of the Orient. Parliament, however, allowed itself to be persuaded that, since China allows the import of opium from India, it was

94

not for Britain to enquire into the affairs of another sovereign nation. Our elected representatives ignored the fact that we had forced the relevant treaty on the Chinese, at the point of a gun, in one of the most discreditable episodes in our history. As a result, the Commission's terms of reference limited it to enquiring into the opium trade on the Indian sub-continent only.'

'That was a blow to you, was it?'

'Indeed! Then the government packed the Commission with members unsympathetic to our cause. Of the nine, two were Indian princes, one a blatant supporter of opium in the House of Commons, and the lawyer and doctor were clearly looking for honorific preferment.'

'I seem to recollect,' said Morton, 'that a member of the general council of your own society, plus a prominent anti-opium Member of Parliament were also nominated.'

'That is true, but they were always going to be outweighed by the others.'

'So the government was cooking the books?' Bragg remarked.

'Undoubtedly. Furthermore, the supporting staff were all allocated from the Indian civil service. In our travels around the country, we were even escorted by the Indian army. How could the Commissioners hope to get a fair picture?'

'But you were not a member of the Commission?'

'No. But it was clearly my duty to assist Henry Wilson, by ensuring that witnesses favourable to our cause were able to appear.'

'And you were not hindered in that?'

'No . . . I imagine that they regarded the result as inevitable. But we shall see.'

'Why should the government bother to manipulate it?' Bragg asked sceptically.

'The usual combination of pressure from interested parties, inertia and electoral considerations.'

'Does that mean that the people of Britain are not behind you?'

'They would be,' Alexander said heatedly, 'if they could see the moral and physical degeneration that indulgence in opium brings. You need not go to the Orient! Even in our own country, this evil drug is bringing neglect of home, of children, of business; causing infant mortality, suicide and insanity; leading to crime and the ruin of countless families!'

'All that through opium?'

Alexander's eyes widened in a stare of incredulity.

'Of course,' he said. 'Opium is a poison, of no possible benefit to man. It is used only for vicious and baneful indulgence.'

'I have heard it said that opium breeds crime,' Bragg remarked, 'but I have never seen much evidence of it.'

'Then go to the East End, or the cities of the north,' Alexander snapped.

'And it is even worse in the Orient?'

'Indeed, particularly in China. Missionaries are convinced that opium is the chief hindrance to the spread of Christianity. You see coolies sprawled in the gutter, while their womenfolk beg for bread . . . or worse. And we are responsible! Do you know that virtually all the opium produced in India is exported to China? We are in the position that all the money the Chinese earn from selling tea, they spend on that accursed drug. Even worse, opium abuse has effectively become a mainstay of the Indian economy. And we, you and I, bear the moral responsibility!'

'I see . . .' Bragg paused to let the tension relax. 'Why did you come back to England on the ss *Rome*?' he asked.

'I have told you, my task was finished.'

'But the Commission stopped taking evidence at the end of January,' Morton said. 'Why did you not come home earlier? There were several sailings.'

Alexander looked disdainful, as at a trick question from a pupil barrister. 'It is my duty to try to influence the members of the Commission, up to the very day they publish their report.'

'When will that be?'

'Probably not before the middle of next year.'

'Do you know a man called Volkes?' Bragg asked abruptly.

'No. Should I?'

'He was on the ship with you.'

'I was not aware of the fact.'

'Ah, no. I was forgetting, the second-class passengers are not allowed to mingle with their betters,' Bragg said sardonically. 'But you knew Sir Fergus Jardine.'

'I have already told you so. I met him on board.'

'Why was he there, do you think?'

Alexander's lip curled. 'I do not need to speculate. He was flagrantly lobbying on behalf of the opium interests.'

'It cannot have been a very harmonious first-class, on that voyage.'

A wary look came over Alexander's face. 'We were all gentlemen,' he said.

'Still, it can't have done your cause any harm, that Jardine has been removed from the scene.'

Alexander smiled. 'Perhaps it is true, after all, that God is on the side of the righteous.'

'Would you object to giving us a specimen of your printing, sir?' Morton asked casually.

'For what purpose?'

'We would like to eliminate you from our enquiries.'

'The usual deceitful formula, eh? Well, officer, there is no reason in the world why I should not give you what you request; nevertheless, I decline to do so. Now, if you will excuse me, I have work to do.'

Once outside, Bragg gave a rueful smile. 'That's a self-righteous bugger, if ever I saw one,' he said. 'But why did you ask him for a specimen of his printing?'

'You remember what he said about the Chinese spending all the money they got from tea, on buying opium.'

'Yes.'

'Were you to re-state that, you could be saying: "If only we can stop the Chinese selling tea, they will have no money to buy India's opium".'

'You mean, the tea poisoning is indeed connected with this opium business? . . . I suppose you could be right, but it's a bit far-fetched, isn't it?'

'Perhaps. But everything about this case is strange.'

Bragg laughed. 'It's a bugger, isn't it? They say that alcohol makes you beat your wife, and solitary vices send you blind; now opium turns you insane! I reckon whatever new pleasure

97

you invented, somebody would found a society to suppress it!'

They took a cab to the Golden Lane mortuary, and found Burney writing out some autopsy notes. For once, the grey slate slab in the centre of his room was empty. He greeted them with his usual grin.

'I was wondering when you would be chasing me again! I take it that it is the Jardine case that concerns you.'

'That's right, sir,' said Bragg respectfully.

'Fascinating, fascinating,' Burney murmured ecstatically. 'I am not yet in a position to make a definitive report, since the laboratory has further tests to do. However, the basic position is clear,' he paused and licked his lips.

'It was poison, was it, sir?'

'You policemen brush aside every refinement in life,' Burney complained. 'The flair of those young men at Bart's is something to marvel at. The test they devised was nothing short of elegant.'

'But it was poison?'

'Yes, sergeant, it was poison. They recovered alkaloidal extracts from Jardine's stomach-contents. When they injected them into rats, the animals promptly died.'

'Did they test the whisky?'

'They did, and it proved negative. The decanter is on the bench, over there, if you want it. Unfortunately, they seem to have required the whole of the contents for the purpose of their investigations . . .'

'I bet they did! So, what poison is it?'

'We cannot say. I am in the process of consulting my colleagues at the other teaching hospitals; but, so far, no one to whom I have spoken has had any experience of it. It is clear, however, that it operates by paralysing the central nervous system.'

'How long would it take to work?'

'That is difficult to say. It could possibly vary according to the strength of the preparation and the quantity ingested. The method of administration might also affect its efficacy. The tests were done by injection into the subcutaneous tissue of the rats; whereas in the human cases the poison was introduced via the stomach.'

'Are you saying that Hewitt was killed by the same poison?'

'Oh yes, sergeant . . . I must say that I am grateful to the coroner for arranging that I could be present at his post-mortem. It was most satisfying and, I think, helpful to my colleague at Westminster.'

'Tell me, sir, did the contents of Hewitt's stomach look like those of Jardine's?'

'Not so. He had eaten a substantial meal, somewhat over an hour before.'

'With red wine?'

'So it appeared.'

'You see, I am wondering if this poison is red-coloured and the only way of slipping it to anybody is in a glass of wine.'

'I would prefer not to comment on that, until my final report.'

'We seem to have a contradiction,' Bragg said gloomily. 'If I am right, Hewitt seems to have taken it two hours before he died; whereas, in Jardine's case, death was virtually instantaneous.'

Burney's mouth dropped open in a shamefaced grin. 'The difference is not necessarily inexplicable,' he said, 'but I am afraid we shall both have to wait.'

'I wonder, sir, if you could help us more generally,' Morton said. 'We need to check the reliability of some information we have been given.'

'I can try.'

'These two cases seem, in some way, to be connected with opium. Can you tell us about the use of that drug?'

'It is widespread, if that is what you mean. I fear that far too many of my medical brethren are casual about prescribing it. They give it to women who are suffering from nothing more life-threatening than monthly pains, or boredom. Even more reprehensible is their habit of teaching their patients to inject the drug themselves. In a situation where a patient can get one prescription dispensed over and over again, it is nothing short of a professional scandal. Addiction used to be a phenomenon of the artistic classes; I am afraid that, nowadays, the typical addict is likely to be a middle-class housewife, with too little to occupy her time.'

'We are told that it is used to commit suicide.'

Burney pondered. 'I would think that, nationally, of the five hundred or so cases of poisoning in a year, no more than one in ten involves opium and its derivatives.'

'What about infant mortality?' asked Bragg.

'They used to say that, in the old days, opium was used to get rid of twins and female babies! Even in the depths of the country that could hardly be practised now – if it ever was. There is no doubt, however, that children consume more opium than one would ideally like – in soothing syrups, cough elixirs and the like. Undoubtedly, some of them become mildly addicted to these preparations. But what is the alternative? No one would leave a child to wail the night through with toothache, if a dab of opium would relieve the pain.'

'So, it is addictive?'

'Inevitably so, I am afraid. However, that does not mean that the dose taken must necessarily escalate.'

'But if the body grows accustomed to it,' Morton said, 'then surely an increasing dose is required?'

'Where extreme pain is concerned, that is undoubtedly so; though in such a case it would be the lesser evil. But if we consider the luxurious use of opium, where people take the drug to stimulate their faculties, or enhance their physical powers, an increase in the amount required is by no means inevitable. William Wilberforce used to take laudanum before his important speeches, to steady his nerves – as I believe, does Gladstone. Neither of them would be denigrated as opium addicts.'

'So, what would be a safe amount to take?'

'The maximum therapeutic dose is normally three grains, given over a period, preferably by quarter-grain injections . . . It is an indication of the human body's amazing ability to acquire a tolerance to the drug, that De Quincey, at the period of his greatest addiction, was habituated to a daily consumption well in excess of four hundred grains – if he is to be believed, that is.'

After a light lunch in his rooms in Alderman's Walk, Morton

took a train to Hollingbourne, in Kent. The day was cold, and a damp wind blew from the south-west. Yet, even so, he was reluctant to arrive at his parents' home before the day faded. He left his bag to be sent up to The Priory by the station trap, and set out to tramp along a lane that partially encircled the estate. He would be able to approach the house from the other side and still arrive in ample time for dinner.

In the middle of February his elder brother's condition had deteriorated. He had taken a chill, which had developed into bronchitis, then pneumonia. Last weekend the illness had reached some kind of crisis. Morton had sat up with him for one night, listening to the mucous rattling in his throat, feeling guilt for years of uncharitable thoughts. It was amazing that Edwin had survived so long. It was nine years, now, since he had been wounded at the battle of Abu Kru, in the Sudan. Hit in the back by a dervish sniper's bullet, he had lain near to death for weeks. Then he had been shipped back home, paralysed from the waist down, angry and resentful. From his youth Edwin had been conscious that, in time, he would succeed to the baronetcy; that his children would inherit the great house, add lustre to the Morton name. It must have been unendurable to have this vision shattered in an unimportant skirmish in a minor colonial war. Yet he had endured. He had shut himself up in his rooms, with only a manservant to look after him. Sometimes he could barely bring himself to allow his mother to see him. Inevitably, perhaps, his corrosive bitterness had soured the relationship between the brothers. By that simple ball of lead, James had become the prospective inheritor of the estate; the Morton line would only survive through him . . . Naturally enough, his parents' concern was with Edwin. They had tried to persuade him that he might be cured; they pretended that he was managing the farms – when, in fact, it was the bailiff who took all the decisions. In doing so, they effectively excluded James from discussion about the future. Even worse, they took umbrage at any remark he made about the present condition of the estate. As a result, he had begun to feel resentment in his turn. So, when he came down from Cambridge, he had joined the City police as a constable. In part, it must have been meant as a snub to his parents, and all they stood for. Yet, though he found the work interesting and satisfying, he had only to come back to The Priory to feel frustration bubbling up in him again. Even now, he thought ruefully, his parents were liable to misconstrue his hike round the estate; in their minds accuse him of wishing Edwin dead. It had been folly to invite that. He turned down a path under the gaunt beech trees and quickened his step.

When he arrived at the house, he saw, with relief, that his bag had not yet been delivered. He found his mother in the small drawing-room, curled up on a settee with a magazine in her hand. He kissed her forehead.

'How is Edwin?' he asked.

'He has improved a little every day in the last week, dear. The doctor says that there might still be a relapse, but he is hopeful that he will make a reasonable recovery.'

'Good! And what about you?'

'It has been a very anxious time, of course, but we have survived.'

'Where is father?'

'He had to go to a Lord Lieutenant's reception in Maidstone. He should be back before dinner.'

'Are there any guests?'

'No dear. Indeed, Emily has gone to stay with the Smiths, at Hoddeston Hall.'

'When is the engagement to be announced?'

'Rueben had wanted it to be at the beginning of the Season, but he quite realises that it would not be in the best of taste, if Edwin is still very ill.'

'That is considerate of him. I am looking forward to having him as a brother-in-law.'

Lady Morton smiled. 'There is small chance of his escaping! Emily is besotted with him. When they are not together, she talks constantly about him. It is a real love-match – on her side, at least.'

'I am sure that he is equally taken with Emily.'

'I do hope all goes well . . . And you, James, have you had a busy week?'

'Yes, and an interesting one. We are involved with a couple of murders that seem to be linked with opium in some inscrutable way.'

'Really? Now, who was it who was mentioning opium? . . . I know, it was at dinner somewhere, just before Christmas. I was taken in by a charming man from the coast, near Romney Marsh. He had recently come back from the East, and was telling me about some official enquiry into the trade. He seemed to be exceedingly well-informed. Whatever was he called? When we were introduced, I remember thinking, "There is a name I shall not forget." But it has gone. I shall probably wake up in the middle of the night with it on the tip of my tongue – then not be able to get back to sleep! . . . I know, he gave me a card. It will still be in my bag. I must settle the matter, once and for all.' She hurried from the room.

Morton threw some logs on the fire and stretched out before the blaze. This room had always been his favourite. Comfortable, even a little shabby, it was a family room and kept inviolate. If ever he proposed marriage, he would like it to be in this room. Not only would his prospective bride have to measure up to the great hall, the French drawing room, all the grandeur of the house; she would also have to feel at home here, be contented in its somewhat raffish domesticity.

'Here we are!' His mother came back in triumph. 'Henry Brocklehurst, of Playden House, Rye.' She handed the card to Morton.

'I see that he is on the telephone,' he remarked.

'We are becoming quite up-to-date in the depths of the country, you know!'

'Could I telephone him from here?'

'Why, yes. Just ask the operator to put you through to the South of England Company's exchange. The line is rather crackly, but you can make yourself heard.'

'I might just go over tomorrow, if things are all right here.'

'Why not? It would do you good to get a breath of sea air.'

Morton laughed. 'We are getting plenty of sea air blowing up the Thames estuary, at the moment!'

'Have you met anyone interesting in London?' his mother asked with a meaningful smile.

'Not really . . . But I will tell you whom I have met . . . Louisa Sommers.'

'Louisa?' Lady Morton's face flushed with pleasure. 'That's nice! She is such a lovely girl. She went to art school there, did she not?'

'Yes.'

'We have not seen her since . . . since you went up to Cambridge, I suppose. She was always so warm and gentle.'

'You used to think that she would make a good wife for me, as I recall it!'

'No, dear!' Her delighted smile belied her words. 'But . . .'

'But what?'

'Well . . . we are all very fond of Catherine, of course, and she and Emily are exceedingly close . . .'

'But?'

'She is very . . . independent; not at all submissive.'

'I cannot remember your being very submissive!'

'Ah, but I had to manage our affairs, with your father away for years at a time. You will not be in that position.'

'Why do mothers persist in wanting for their sons what they would never dream of being themselves?' Morton said lightly.

'It is not that, dear, it is just that Catherine does not seem to be . . . well, a country person.'

'Come! You know her better than that, mother. There is nothing of city society about her,' Morton said warmly. 'She comes from Hampshire stock, and is rather proud of the fact. After all, much the same could have been said about you. Even more so! You were the daughter of the American ambassador to Britain – brought up in Boston and living in Mayfair. Did my father's parents object to you?'

'No, dear. Of course not . . . but your father was rather older.'

'If you want my opinion of Catherine Marsden, it is that she would succeed in anything she set her hand to.'

'Well, yes . . . I suppose you are right.'

'And, at the moment, she is intent on becoming the premier journalist in England.'

'And you?'

'I am content with my bachelorhood.'

'You do not think that Louisa . . .' Lady Morton began tentatively.

'No,' Morton interrupted, with a smile. 'Louisa is not remotely interested in me, nor I in her.'

Next morning, Morton took a train to Ashford, and thence to Rye. He had lunch at a hotel in the town, then hired a trap to take him to Playden, a small village on the outskirts. Playden House proved to be a large villa in ample grounds, surrounded by a shelter-belt of evergreen trees. His ring on the bell was answered by a severe-looking housekeeper.

'Mr Brocklehurst is in the conservatory,' she informed him. 'He said that if you arrived, I was to ask you to join him.'

'Thank you.'

Morton followed her into a heavily furnished study, then through a glazed door into a long, iron-framed conservatory. A man in his early fifties was stooping over an extensive bed of flowers at the far end. As Morton approached, he straightened up and held out his hand.

'Mr Morton?' he asked. 'Glad to see you. I won't be a tick, but I have to finish this job now, or it will be spoiled.'

'What are the flowers?'

'You are wanting to know about opium? Well, that is the fellow – *Papaver somniferum album*.'

'You can grow them here?'

'With a little help from steam pipes! They are a winter crop in India.'

'Why do you bother?'

'Partly as a challenge, partly because the only opium you can get round here is in powdered form. I acquired the habit of smoking the odd pipe, in China; I can extract enough opium gum from these for my needs. It is a pernickety job, because, unless you get the timing right, the morphia – which is what you are after – just vanishes. See . . .' He gestured towards a patch of plants with mature seed-vessels. 'Just before the petals are due to fall, you take them off. Then, a few days later, you can start the operation . . . like this.'

He bent down, and made an incision two-thirds of the way round a seed-capsule the size of a duck's egg. Immediately, tiny beads of white juice appeared in the cut. Brocklehurst treated fifty or more capsules similarly, then straightened up.

'I shall leave them to bleed till tomorrow morning. Then I shall scrape the juice from the skin, and let it mature in the air for a few weeks. It is not as good as Benares opium, but it is acceptable – and it is an amusing hobby.'

'A fairly rare one, I should think.'

'Believe it or not, opium used to be grown commercially in England, earlier in the century. Even now, you will find patches of the poppy in many cottage gardens, in the fens or on Romney Marsh. A good few pints of poppy tea are drunk hereabouts!'

'Why in the fens, particularly?'

'Opium has traditionally been used to keep the ague and rheumatism at bay. There are little old ladies in places like King's Lynn, who can down a dose of laudanum that would have you or me flat on our backs – and never turn a hair!'

'I have been told that it has historically been the ordinary people's medicine.'

'Not only people, animals too. The rule of thumb around here is six drachms of laudanum for a sheep, three ounces for a horse.'

'I suppose that it is logical!'

'You do not want to buy a horse in this area,' Brocklehurst said with an engaging grin. 'Anyone that has a vicious animal to get rid of, will put opium in his last feed, to keep him docile till you get him home! Let us go in and have a snifter.'

He led the way into the study and poured two large glasses of whisky.

'Cheers,' he said, taking a gulp. 'Now, what is your interest in opium? There is nothing illegal about it, so far as I know.'

Morton smiled. 'No. I am merely seeking background information about the trade in the East.'

'I can help you there, all right. I spent a good part of my working life in China. I started off in the Customs department. Then there were the Opium Wars, between Britain and China. Wars! They were nothing more than local skirmishes, if you ask me. Anyway, under the treaties which followed them, traders were allowed to import opium into China, and China was allowed to levy a duty on it. The only odd circumstance was that the duty was to be collected within the treaty ports – which meant that it had to be collected by British Customs officers. So I was seconded for a spell – a spell that turned out to be half a lifetime!'

'Where did you work?'

'At various times, I have been at Shanghai, Amoy, Canton and Foochowfoo.'

'We have been hearing a great deal from the Society for the Suppression of the Opium Trade about the evils of opium use,' Morton remarked.

'No doubt you have. My sister was a member of its predecessor society. In those days, it was run by well-meaning liberals and Quakers. Since then, it has been taken over by the temperance and missionary interests.'

'They certainly make great play of our moral degeneracy in forcing opium on the Chinese.'

'That shows how pig-ignorant they are. China was buying opium from India long before the Europeans came. Even now the Indian opium is less than a third of China's total consumption.'

'Why the misrepresentation?'

'I won't say that we have not pushed the exports to China, we have. But make no mistake, the Chinese want it. They could easily grow more themselves, but theirs is not such good quality.'

Brocklehurst took another swig from his glass and set it down. 'If you ask me,' he said, 'the missionaries are at the bottom of it.'

'In what way?'

'Well, apart from a few diplomats and sailors the only British who have any experience of China are the merchants and the missionaries. Now, the merchants are not interested in informing the people back home about conditions out there. Their concerns are to export the silks and tea, sell them, then go back for more. But the missionaries are different. When they come back to the old country, they go round giving lantern lectures up and down, trying to drum up funds. It's their view of things that the public absorbs.'

'What is wrong with that?'

'First of all, they start from the notion that the Chinese are a nation of savages, who have got to be converted to Christianity. Bloody arrogant, but there it is. When they set about it, however, they do not have much success. It is one thing baptising droves of Africans, when there is a detachment of British troops nearby, and the Union Jack flying from the flagpole. It is quite another trying to convert people in an independent country which had a highly developed religion and culture when we were grubbing for roots in the mud . . . But the missionaries have to justify their poor results to people back home; people who are convinced that Christianity is the only true faith, and must be irresistible. Opium provides a very convenient justification for failure.'

'Are you saying that there is really no opium addiction in China?'

'No. There is addiction in plenty. On any strict view, I am an addict myself. I take a small amount regularly, for various aches and pains – like people here take tobacco or a glass of spirits, and think nothing of it. But addiction does not necessarily mean abuse. You could find opium-sodden derelicts on the water-front of Shanghai – or Hong Kong, for that matter – in the same way as you could find drunkards on the streets of any of our cities. It does not mean that the whole population is degenerate. These do-gooders make me bloody sick!'

'You say that you have been to Canton,' Morton said. 'Did you ever come across Sir Fergus Jardine there?'

'Indeed I did. That was before he was knighted. Now there's an odd mixture for you. A strong supporter of the kirk, he had the reputation of being totally ruthless in his business dealings. He could be dour one minute and charming the next . . . And a real ladies' man. There was a story of some liaison with the wife of a British diplomat, who was staying with him . . . I forget the name.'

'Morell?'

'That's it. Anyway, Jardine's wife left him over it.'

'Did you ever meet an India Office man called Hewitt?'

'The one who died the other day – had been Secretary to the Royal Commission?'

'That's him.'

'Oddly enough, I did meet him. When I came back on my last

furlough, before retiring, I was at a Foreign Office meeting where he was present. It is a pity about him. He was a bright one. They say he was being groomed for the top job . . . A pleasant man, courteous, and his private life was impeccable – it has to be nowadays, if you want to reach the top.'

7

'Well now, Mr Stubbs,' Bragg said, 'I wonder if you can help us.'

'What about?' the reporter asked defensively.

'The *Echo* ran a story on Saturday the fourteenth about some chests of tea having been poisoned.'

'What is that to you?' He was short and running to fat; his hair was red, his pale skin blotchy. When he spoke, his mouth twisted in a sneer.

'We seem to be stuck with a case that has nothing to it,' Bragg said evenly. 'The Customs have sampled the tea, Cassell Smith's have tested every chest, and not a trace of poison can they find.'

'I can't help that. The report was based on information received. If I had to be able to swear to the truth of everything, I would never write a word.'

'Your paragraph amounted to an emphatic assertion that the tea had been poisoned,' Morton said.

Stubbs rounded on him. 'Are you telling me how to do my job?' he asked unpleasantly. 'It is the duty of the press to protect the public against unscrupulous traders.'

'It is also the duty of the press to act responsibly.'

'So, what should I have done? Screwed up my report and thrown it into the waste-paper basket? . . . What would you be saying then, if thousands of people up and down the country had been dying from some mysterious illness? You'd be wanting my hide for not publishing it! If it turns out not to be true, that is everyone's good fortune.'

'Except for Cassell Smith's,' Bragg said dryly.

'What do you mean?'

'Now that you know the tea is not contaminated, are you going to publish that information in the *Echo*?'

'It is the editor who decides what goes in,' Stubbs snapped. 'I just write the copy.'

'Can't you see that you were being used?' Bragg said contemptuously. 'Someone wants Cassell Smith's ruined, and you have been their cat's-paw – willingly or unwillingly.'

'What do you mean, willingly?' Stubbs asked sharply.

'Let's take a hypothetical case, shall we? Suppose a journalist knowingly published a false story – he might even accept money for doing so. Whatever you say about the duty of the press, he could well be conspiring in the commission of a felony . . .'

'Are you accusing me?' Stubbs interrupted.

'I don't know. Am I? . . . And, to my mind, there's not much difference if he published it, reckless of whether it was true or false.'

'Look, sergeant,' Stubbs said with a sneer, 'all I know is that the editor gave me an anonymous letter to look into.'

'The trouble is that you did no such thing. You didn't go to see Cassell Simth's, you didn't go to the Customs . . . Why not?'

'I was up against a deadline. Look, my piece did not say anything about whether it was true or not. It just said there had been a report that the tea had been poisoned. Nobody can get me for that!'

'Don't be too sure. Where is the letter?'

'You can't see that! If we started passing things on to coppers, our sources would dry up before you could say "nark".'

'I can believe yours would. All right, you have a choice. On the one hand you show me the letter; on the other, you don't – in which case, I'll make it my business to frigging well nick you, every time I see you!'

'What for?'

'As a loose, idle and disorderly person, disturbing the peace.'

'You couldn't do that!'

'You read the Police Act, then tell me I can't.'

Stubbs stared at him for a moment, then turned abruptly. He picked up a file from his desk and extracted a letter. Bragg took it. It was a sheet of cheap writing paper. The crudely printed message was brief.

> THE TEA IN CASSELL
> SMITH'S WAREHOUSE
> HAS BEEN POISONED

'And you made a story out of that?' Bragg said contemptuously. 'I wouldn't have soiled my arse with it.'

'Here! You can't take that away!'

'Evidence!' Bragg folded the paper and put it in his pocket. 'I am accepting your version of events – for the moment, that is.'

Bragg winked at Morton, and they tramped solemnly out of the office.

'I can understand why Miss Marsden detested the man,' Morton remarked with a grin.

'We ought to get her a medal for meritorious service!' Bragg flagged down a passing hansom.

'The De Keyser Hotel, cabby,' he directed.

'What do you have in mind?' Morton asked.

'Let's see if we can push the Jardine end a bit, shall we?'

When the cab drew up he leapt out. Morton paused to pay the driver. It would take him half a day to work out his expenses claim, he thought ruefully. As he entered the gleaming marble foyer, Bragg was banging the bell on the reception desk. A clerk came hurrying up.

'Get me the manager,' Bragg said brusquely.

'The manager is off duty at the moment, sir. I am the assistant manager, can I help you?'

'Police!' Bragg shoved his warrant-card under the man's nose. 'Sir Fergus Jardine has been staying here. When did he arrive?'

The man turned back through the register. 'He arrived here on the evening of the tenth of March.'

'When did he go to Scotland?'

The man looked down his nose. 'It is not our practice to monitor the comings and goings of our guests,' he said disdainfully. 'He had reserved his suite until the twenty-sixth, on which date he was to take ship for the Orient.'

'Good! Then we will just have a look through his things. Give me the room key, will you?'

'You may see the room, certainly, but Sir Fergus's effects have been packed and placed in the storeroom.'

'Not above taking two lots of rent for the room, then? Have his things sent over to me in Old Jewry, will you?'

'We could hardly do that, unless we were served with a warrant.'

'I'll see you get one, if it's publicity you are after.'

The assistant manager flinched. 'Surely the obtaining of a warrant would not be a public matter?'

'That's true,' Bragg said amiably. 'But these reporters are a tenacious lot, and Sir Fergus was an eminent person.'

The man looked at him doubtfully. 'Very well,' he said. 'But I don't know what my manager will think of it.' Bragg took the key and marched gleefully over to the lift.

Jardine had occupied a luxurious suite on the river frontage. Bragg prowled around the bedroom and sitting-room for a time, then he darted down the corridor to the housemaid's cubby-hole.

'Well now, young lady,' he said amiably, 'do you look after number seventy-three?'

'I does all them as is on this corridor,' she said. 'What's up?' She was middle-aged, with a hard, thin face. The frilly cap looked incongruous on her, Morton thought.

'We are just having a look at that room – with the manager's permission, of course. Would you care to join us?'

She glanced up dubiously at Bragg's courteous tone, then followed without a word.

'This room was last occupied by Sir Fergus Jardine, wasn't it?'

'Yes.'

'You know that he died?'

'I knows I had the job of doing up his things.'

'Did anything special happen, while he was here?'

'What d'you mean, special?'

'Unusual.'

'He weren't hardly here. Empty more nights than not, it was – still, suits me . . . He was tidy, I'll say that for him. Not like

113

some – clothes all over the place! It's not my job to hang them all up. And these la-di-da women are worst of all. Treats you like dirt, they does. Then, when it comes to tipping, it's a shilling on the table. I used to work at Wood's Hotel. A much nicer class of people – professional gents, mostly.'

'But the money is better here, eh?' Bragg said with a smile.

'Yes.'

'I expect you have a good memory.'

She looked up quizzically. 'It depends . . .'

'I can see there's no point in trying to conceal anything from you, ma'am. The fact is that I am employed by a firm of solicitors. One of our clients suspects that his wife is being, well, a bit flighty.'

'Oh, yes?' Her eyes were watchful.

'We are charged with getting the evidence, one way or the other. After that, it will be up to our client to decide how he uses it.'

'I give evidence in the divorce court, once,' she said ruminatively. 'All I got out of it was my bleedin' cab fare. The bloke said if I was paid, the judge wouldn't take no notice of what I said. Flamin' cheek, I calls it.'

Bragg took a half-sovereign from his pocket. 'I bet you could tell us if Sir Fergus got up to any hanky-panky,' he said.

'I thought you told me he was dead. They can't touch him now.'

'That's right. And, of course, you owe the lady nothing.'

She eyed the small gold coin on Bragg's palm and licked her lips.

'Did he have any lady visitors?' Bragg asked.

'Yes, he did. A young woman came in on the Monday afternoon. He had tea sent up for them.'

'What about Monday night?'

'Yes – a different one. Smart, she was.'

'You are sure of that?'

''Course! And they done it, all right.'

'They enjoyed a sexual conjunction, you mean?'

'Yes, that's what I mean.'

'How do you know?'

'Well, I changes the sheets, don't I?' . . . Anyways, I seen her in the morning, sneaking off. These nobs never think some folk starts work at half-past six.'

'What was she like?'

'Well, I don't want to get nobody into trouble . . .'

Bragg spun the coin in a glittering parabola, and caught it again.

'Mind you, it ain't right for her to play fast and loose . . . She was a young woman, a bit taller than me, with brown hair done fashionable like. And she was pretty, real pretty.'

'Did she have a small mole on her cheekbone?' Morton asked.

''Ere, you knows her! You've been having me on!'

'Jane Morell,' Morton murmured.

Bragg pressed the coin into her hand. 'Thank you ma'am,' he said warmly. 'We will let you know, if we need you. Good day.'

When Bragg and Morton arrived back at Old Jewry, they were greeted by a grinning desk-sergeant.

'I reckon your sins have found you out, Joe!' he said.

'Why is that?'

'A couple of minutes ago, I sent a bloke up to the Commissioner; then, not ten seconds after, he sends down for me to find you two.'

'Either, or both?'

'I dunno. The bloke had "complaint" written all over his face!'

'Then it had better be both – good experience for you, lad!'

They went up the curving Georgian staircase, through the ante-room, and tapped on the Commissioner's door.

'Come in!' Sir William's voice was a staccato bark. He was under pressure . . .

When they entered the room, a large balding man was standing by the window, staring at St Olave's Church below.

'Ah, Bragg. This is Chief Inspector Cotterill, of the Metropolitan police. He has come to see us about the death of a William Hewitt, who was apparently some kind of civil servant. Please sit down, gentlemen.' The Commissioner waved at Cotterill to begin.

'One of my sergeants was appointed coroner's officer, when this man died,' Cotterill said roughly. 'As you already know, his death took place at work – some offshoot of the India Office. We found out that his residence is in Chelmsford, but he lived during the week at the Orleans Club. We collected his things from there but, when we went to his office, we were told that you had been already, and taken away everything private.'

'That is quite correct, sir,' Bragg said evenly.

'Then, we want them back.'

'I am afraid that is not possible, sir.'

'Not possible?' Cotterill's eyes bulged with anger. 'Dammit all, he died on my patch! What right have you to come meddling?'

'I believe that I am acting within the usual arrangement between the forces,' Bragg said equably.

'I shall need some convincing of that! As far as I know, it doesn't allow you to investigate a murder taking place in the Met area.'

'You have made up your mind it was murder, have you, sir?'

A wary look came over Cotterill's face. 'Well, the post-mortem report says death was not by natural causes.'

'I would think that is true enough.'

'Well, then?'

'The trouble from a procedural point of view, sir, is that we are certain he died from a rare posion, which was also present in a death in the City – a death we know was a murder.'

'What the hell has that got to do with anything?'

'This poison is so rare, that the two cases must be connected. Yet, for all our efforts, we have not been able to find a third party with a motive for poisoning them both . . . and our man died getting on for a couple of days before Hewitt.'

'Are you saying that Hewitt poisoned your man, then committed suicide?' Cotterill asked sharply.

'It took me a good bit longer to see that; but, yes, I believe you are right. The only other theory is that Hewitt got some of the stuff on his fingers, and poisoned himself accidentally . . . Anyway, I don't suppose you still pursue suicides as criminals, any more, do you?'

'No fear! We have better things to do in the Met.'

'Then, perhaps you will let us have the effects you took from his club.'

'What?' Cotterill spluttered. 'This a Metropolitan police case! Moreover, it is us that has to report to the Westminster coroner on his death. We aren't going to be turned into mouthpieces for you lot. I insist that you release Hewitt's papers!'

From the unhappy look on the Commissioner's face, Bragg could see that he was vacillating.

'I am sorry,' he said respectfully, 'it's not on. Not only are they evidence in a City murder case, there is also a connection with a much more serious matter. Some would-be mass killer has poisoned a whole warehouse full of tea, in the City.'

Cotterill glared at him in incomprehension.

Sir William cleared his throat. 'So far as the tea business is concerned,' he said portentously, 'it is clear that my responsibilities extend, not only to the community of the City of London, but also to those populations throughout the country who may have been sent chests of tea from that warehouse. It follows that I must decline to release any documents which may have a bearing, however remote, on that investigation.' He rose to his feet dismissively.

Cotterill jumped up in a fury. 'You haven't heard the last of this!' he snarled. 'I shall take the matter higher!'

'With respect, sir,' Bragg said blandly, 'you cannot go any higher in this force.'

Cotterill gave him a baleful glare, then stamped out of the room.

'If I may say so, sir,' Bragg remarked, 'it was a privilege to see how you handled that situation.'

Sir William preened himself. 'Thank you, Bragg. We must not let the Met bully us. We must fight for our independence, eh?'

There was a tap on the door, and a woman came in, carrying a large silver tray.

'Oh,' she said in surprise. 'I didn't know your visitor had gone, sir. I have brought you some tea.'

'Never mind, Mrs Peabody,' the Commissioner said expansively. 'Bring another cup for Constable Morton – we have things to discuss.'

After she had poured the tea and left the room, Sir William

turned to Bragg.

'Forgetting for the moment what you said to Cotterill,' he said with sly smile, 'where do we stand with regard to Jardine and Hewitt?'

'As you know, sir, it was the same poison that killed them both. Our problem is that, so far, Dr Burney has not yet told us how long it takes to work. If, for instance, it acts instantaneously, then, in Jardine's case, the poison was in the loving cup. If, however, it takes time, then it could have been administered as far back as breakfast. It seems fairly clear that, between then and the moment he drank from the loving cup, all he'd had was some whisky in his office.'

'Could it have been in that?'

'We had the contents of the decanter tested, and that was all right. It might have been introduced into his glass; unfortunately, that had been washed up.'

'How does that compare with Hewitt's case?'

'Well, sir, Hewitt had eaten a heavy meal, about an hour before he died. He could have been given it then.'

'We have a theory,' Morton interposed, 'that the poison may have some physical properties which can only be disguised in a glass of wine. Both Hewitt and Jardine had taken wine before their death.'

'In that case,' Sir William observed, 'it would exculpate the whisky in the Jardine case. Have you any suspects?'

'So far as Jardine is concerned, we have several. An ex-employee, named Josiah Coaker, visited him in his office on the morning he died. They had a glass of whisky together, but it wasn't a pleasant meeting. Jardine had deliberately bankrupted Coaker. He admitted he was glad to see Jardine dead, but wasn't accommodating enough to admit that he'd done it. However, immediately after our meeting, he vanished. He'd said his wife and family are in Sunderland, so we have telegraphed the police up there to keep an eye open for him.'

'It sounds suspicious,' the Commissioner murmured.

'We have another vanishing trick on our hands, too. A man named Volkes called at Jardine's office, first thing on Monday, without an appointment. They were together some time, though Jardine doesn't appear to have offered him a drink.'

'What did Volkes want?'

'Jardine Matheson's manager had no idea, but Volkes seemed a bit agitated.'

'Homicidally so?'

'Perhaps. Volkes is supposed to be coming back to London. We have arranged for his hotel to notify us, if he does.'

'Well, at least we are not floundering about in the dark.'

'No, sir. The most interesting of the lot is Alexander. He is the Secretary of the Society for the Suppression of the Opium Trade, and a real bigot. We have discovered that not only did he offer the loving cup to Jardine in the ceremony, but he came back from India on the same ship as him.'

'Do you think he would kill for his beliefs?'

'He might. Lawyers tend to think of themselves as above the law, don't they?'

'Hmn . . .' The Commissioner pondered awhile. 'Are any of them connected at all with the tea trade?' he asked.

Bragg smiled. 'Not really, sir. We feel that the Cassell Smith's business was either a hoax, or a slander put about by competitors to ruin them.'

'Thank God! I doubt if I could remember the details of my blend myself, now – and this is almost the last.' He smiled smugly. 'Do you like it?'

Morton took a drink and swirled it around in his mouth, savouring it.

'It is really quite remarkable,' he said judicially. 'Mainly Pin's Head and Imperial Moyune, I suspect . . . The interaction of their flavours is a sheer delight. But to add the Formosan, as a kind of grace-note, is a touch of genius.'

Gratification and suspicion chased each other across Sir William's face. Then he cleared his throat. 'Yes . . . thank you,' he said gruffly. 'Well, let us get back to the case. Where were we?'

'I think we have dealt with the Jardine suspects,' Bragg said, suppressing a grin. 'So far as Hewitt is concerned, motive is pretty scarce. What is interesting is that two of the people we have mentioned in relation to Jardine were also known to Hewitt.'

'Indeed? Who?'

'Volkes and Alexander. Volkes had an appointment to see Hewitt, at his office, the night he died. The significant thing is that, if the appointment was kept, they must have been together only minutes before his death.'

'That would correspond more nearly to the time-scale of Jardine and Alexander,' the Commissioner remarked.

'Indeed! If it had been Alexander calling on Hewitt, I'd have had no hesitation in nicking him. The nearest Alexander comes to Hewitt is that they both travelled back on the ss *Rome* with Jardine – and, indeed, with most of the members of the Royal Commission.'

'Hmn . . . It is all somewhat tenuous.'

'Yes, sir. And we have to admit that the murderer could be anybody. Hewitt had arranged that the street door of his office should be left open – for his own convenience.'

'More specifically,' said Morton, 'his self-indulgence encompassed the favours of a young lady, who was also known to Jardine. Indeed, it is possible that she spent the night before Jardine died, with him in his hotel.'

Sir William wrinkled his nose in distaste. 'Surely they did not share the girl?' he asked.

'Not knowingly, I would think,' said Bragg. 'However, she knew the address of Hewitt's office. She could easily have gone up and poisoned him. Mind you, it's a long shot. For my money, both deaths were tied up with this opium business, one way or another.'

'But how? Why?'

'I don't know . . . Did you ever go out to the Orient, sir?'

'As a matter of fact, I did, Bragg.' The Commissioner sat forward importantly. 'I had a spell in China as a young subaltern. That was in 'fifty-seven. I went out with Lord Elgin's expeditionary force, to Shanghai. It was all very exciting for a young man. We fought our way to Peking and burnt the Emperor's Summer Palace around his ears, before he would make peace . . . Not that it seems very heroic, at this distance. The European powers had been like a pack of hounds at China's throat – Japan and America too. Her armies were ill-equipped, and no match for modern weapons. She would be forced to give concessions, then, when we withdrew, would repudiate them. Our expedition was basically concerned to teach her such a lesson that she would, in future, abide by the treaties she signed.'

'Was this what the Liberals call an Opium War?' Morton asked innocently.

The Commissioner shifted uncomfortably in his chair. 'It was certainly an example of Palmerston's gunboat diplomacy . . . I suppose that, in some ways, opium was involved. Certainly, one of the terms of the Treaty of Tiensiu was that China would permit the importation of opium on payment of a duty . . . The Chinese would have liked to have a high duty that would have kept the opium out. But, under the treaty, the British had the right to set its level. So they ended up with a moderate duty and a big market for opium.'

'Would you say that Indian opium was being forced on the Chinese?' Morton asked.

'I think it is fair to say that their educated classes regarded opium as a great evil. Their government has been trying to suppress the trade for centuries, but they could never beat the smugglers. At least, that way, they got an income from it.'

'Was there much evidence of opium abuse?'

'It is not easy for a soldier to observe the life of ordinary people, in an enemy country,' the Commissioner replied. 'There were plenty of coolies lying about in a stupor, everywhere you went. I don't know if that constitutes abuse.'

There came hurried steps in the corridor and, after a perfunctory knock, the door was opened by the desk-sergeant.

'Sorry to disturb you, sir,' he said anxiously, 'but I have Mr Mowbray, one of the MPs for the City, who insists on seeing you.'

A wiry sunburnt man pushed past him. 'I do, indeed, Mr Commissioner. It is a matter of the greatest urgency.'

'Very well,' Sir William nodded dismissively to the sergeant. 'Please take a chair and tell me what is troubling you.'

'I demand police protection!'

'Do you indeed! Against what?'

'Against murderers!'

'Have you any reason to believe that you are in danger?'

'Every reason! I am a member of the Royal Commission on

opium. Already two people who came back with us from India on the ss *Rome* have died suddenly. There is a rumour that their deaths were not natural. Is that true?'

Sir William nodded his head gravely. 'These two officers are certainly investigating the possibility that foul play was involved, but no firm conclusions have as yet been drawn.'

'I do not intend to wait until you have drawn your conclusions,' Mowbray said threateningly, 'I want protection.'

'Why do you suppose that you are under greater threat than the other Commissioners, sir?' Bragg asked quietly.

'Because it is well known that I support the opium interests, in the House of Commons.'

'I see . . . It would help us, sir, if you could clear up a point or two for us.'

'Of course,' Mowbray said impatiently. 'What is it that you wish to know?'

'I have heard it said that the composition of the Royal Commission was fixed, in favour of your side. Are you saying that it could be a reason for murdering you?'

'They would have to be fanatics – but there are plenty about.'

'So it was fixed?'

'Not at all! I would say that it no more than reflects the various views on opium, in a balanced way. Lord Brassey, the chairman, is non-political and respected on all sides. True, I make no secret of my sympathies, and Fanshawe is known to favour the continuance of the trade. On the other hand, Arthur Pease is on the council of the Society for the Suppression of the Opium Trade, and Henry Wilson – who sits on the government benches – is rabidly anti-opium. Lyall, the lawyer, and Roberts, the medical man, are both non-party, and seemed genuinely to have open minds on the subject.'

'There were two Indian members, were there not?' Morton asked.

'Not unreasonably so. The Indian government stands to lose income of close on ten million pounds a year, if the abolitionists have their way. That would cause enormous social problems – unless the British taxpayer could be persuaded to put his hand in his pocket to that extent. Your zealots will say that they will gladly do so, but I doubt if the man in the street would agree.'

'At all events, your fanatics could see the Royal Commission as somewhat weighted in favour of opium?' Bragg remarked.

'I would say pro-Indian,' Mowbray insisted. 'The opinion of the public in Britain is largely in favour of continuing the trade in opium; in India it is overwhelmingly so.'

'I can see that some bigot might knock off Jardine,' Bragg said, 'because he was one of the major figures in the trade. But why would anyone bother to murder Hewitt? He was nothing more than a glorified clerk.'

'That shows how little you know about our system of government, officer,' Mowbray said. 'Civil and colonial servants wield great power behind the scenes. Their influence can often be crucial. In the House, our skills are in lobbying and debating. They fight their corner with their pens. They have always to appear impartial, but the whole slant of a document can be changed by the astute choice of a phrase.'

'But why kill him now? Surely his work was done, once the minutes of the evidence had been taken.'

'Not so. His main task was just beginning. He had been charged by the Commission to make a preliminary draft of the report. Have you any idea of how difficult it is to change a document to any degree, once it has been drafted? Particularly one running into hundreds of pages.'

'But the draft would surely have set out to reflect the weight of evidence and the feelings of the Commission?'

'Of course, but it would also have taken account of the views of the India Office. Anyone who was present at a public hearing of the Commission, could have little doubt about where their sympathies lay. Hewitt's interventions were always ostensibly to clarify the evidence given by a witness; but, without exception, their effect was to reinforce the arguments in favour of continuance. He was very clever. He managed to make some of the witnesses drummed up by the Society for the Suppression of the Opium Trade appear as dogmatic idiots; with neither grasp of, nor care for the social implications of banning the trade.'

'It would not take much, to make some people we have met appear as bigots.'

'Indeed! It was almost amusing to watch Hewitt baiting

Henry Wilson; who had totally prejudged the outcome, and announced at the start of the proceedings that he would be writing a minority report, setting out the Society's case.'

'Is this Henry Wilson an impetuous man, would you say, sir?'

'No politician can afford to be impetuous, officer, he would give too many hostages to fortune. Henry is certainly a zealot; but he has too much to lose to go about murdering people.'

Bragg sighed. 'The trouble is, that everybody in this case would have a great deal to lose . . . You seem to be of the opinion that if someone did dispose of Jardine and Hewitt, it is likely that they had attended the public hearings of the Commission.'

Mowbray wrinkled his brow. 'It had not occurred to me in quite those terms, officer, but it certainly seems possible.'

'Could you tell us a little about the voyage home, sir? It does not seem to have been a particularly happy trip.'

'It was certainly not that!' Mowbray replied with a smile. 'I suppose that we were all tired, and had been away from home for too long. And, with the best will in the world, there is bound to be friction when people of strongly opposing views are cooped up together. Even so, I think the most disruptive influences came from outside the members of the Commission.'

'How do you mean, sir?'

'Well, by the end of February, even Henry and I were thoroughly sick of the repeated iteration of the arguments on both sides. We would gladly have forgotten the whole thing for a while. But, of course, Jardine was on board, lobbying hard for the opium interests, and John Alexander was busy on behalf of the Society.'

'Did Alexander quarrel with Jardine?' Bragg asked quietly.

'Alexander quarrelled with everybody – including the doctor and the lawyer on the Commission.'

'Surely not with Pease?'

'Especially with Pease! He had a real up-and-downer with him. He even had a heated debate with Hewitt.'

'So he appreciated the influence Hewitt could have?'

'Undoubtedly.'

'What about you?'

Mowbray laughed. 'He did not waste his time with me, he

knows that I am too far gone, to be converted to his way of thinking!'

There was a pause, and Sir William cleared his throat.

'I have to say, Mr Mowbray, that our enquiries do not suggest that you are in any real danger.'

'Then you must be particularly obtuse, Mr Commissioner,' Mowbray retorted angrily. 'Anyone could safely assume that, when the report comes to be finalised, I shall be supporting the continuance of the trade. If I am removed, the likes of Henry Wilson might even envisage a victory for their side. At the very least, by counting signatures, the pro-opium lobby could be made to appear less extensive than it really is.'

'I am sorry,' Sir William said doggedly, 'there is no way that I can allocate three or four constables, to give round-the-clock protection to someone – however eminent – who merely suspects that an attempt might be made on his life. I will, of course, do so the moment you can give me evidence that you are in danger.'

'I can do better than that, Mr Commissioner,' Mowbray said coldly. 'I am not one of the City's MPs for nothing! I shall go straight to the chairman of the police committee, and see that you are compelled to your duty!' He got up and stalked out of the room.

'You see what kind of pressure I am under,' Sir William said plaintively. 'Every jack-in-office thinks that he should have priority – or else . . . You had better get to the bottom of this, Bragg, and quickly.'

8

The sun shone brightly as the trap bowled along, the air was almost balmy. But the flat Essex countryside was still caught in the grip of winter. It would be a late spring, Bragg thought. The lamb's-tail catkins were only just out. As they approached the hamlet, they passed several old timber-framed houses standing forlornly in the fields, like children's toys left behind on the lawn. By now they must be three miles out of Chelmsford. If you added the train journey to Liverpool Street, and the cab drive to Queen Anne's Gate, it was no wonder that Hewitt preferred to stay at his club. Bragg shrugged off a sense of unease. It was just that he disliked a landscape as flat as a billiard table, and great luminous skies. In Dorset, where he had been brought up, the country was ruckled with low hills. To get anything like a vista, you had to climb to the top of Bulbarrow Hill, overlooking the Blackmore Vale. His was a domesticated countryside, harmonised. Here you felt exposed and vulnerable.

'This is the place, sir,' the driver said, reining the colt in.

It was a large, square Georgian house, as austere as the country around it. It was screened from the road by a high privet hedge. In a paddock, to one side, a couple of hunters grazed obsessively. Telling the driver to wait, Bragg and Morton went through the wrought-iron gates and up a sweeping carriage drive. The gravel was freshly raked, the lawns smooth and moss-free. There was no shortage of money here, that was for sure. And it wasn't kept like this on any colonial servant's salary. Now the front of the house was revealed, severe in its lack of ornamentation. If it had been his, Bragg thought, he would have grown a climber up it – one of those Virginia creepers, that went flame-red in the autumn . . . At least the curtains were drawn back, so the funeral must be over. That was all to the good. This interview would be distasteful enough, without holding it in half-darkness . . . Damn and blast it! He was getting soft, that was the truth of it. Too much of a towny, only at home in grimy streets and fog. He rang the bell and the door was opened by a young maid, her manner suitably subdued. She showed them into an elegantly furnished morning-room. Mrs Hewitt rose from a table, where she was writing letters on black-edged paper.

'I am sorry to disturb you, at this time, ma'am,' Bragg said, holding out his hand. 'May I offer you our condolences?'

'Thank you.' Her lips twitched in a momentary smile. She was over medium height, with a plain, angular face. She was big-boned, too. Bragg could well imagine her putting one of those hunters at a fence.

'Mary said that you are policemen from London . . .' She had the clear, assertive voice that invariably went with money and social position. She seemed calm and self-possessed; but her eyes were red-rimmed and puffy, so she wasn't wholly untouched by her husband's death.

'Yes, ma'am, City of London police.' Bragg proffered his card, but she waved it away.

'I still have not totally come to terms with the fact that William will never again come through that door on a Friday night,' she said.

'Have you any family living near?' Bragg asked solicitously.

'No family. But I have many friends in the area. And, of course, the boys will soon be home for the Easter holidays . . . It seemed rather pointless, sending them back again after the funeral. But I am sure it will be better for them to be with their schoolfriends.'

'Will your husband's death make things difficult for you?'

'Not in a material sense, but it has obviously affected our plans for the future . . . We had intended to move to London, to be nearer William's office. We were having a rather splendid house erected in Highgate,' she said deprecatingly. 'It is exciting to build a house to your own specification; indulging your own whims, instead of putting up with someone else's. We were even going to have a mural of a hunt in the garden room – to compensate me for what I had left behind, so William said . . .' She blinked rapidly, and sniffed. 'I am sorry,' she said. 'It is strange. Our way of life had seemed so perfect. Now he is gone, I feel guilty for letting him spend his week at that miserable club . . . He was so tolerant and indulgent.'

'Why were you going to move at this stage?' Bragg asked.

She smiled briefly. 'William's appointment as Secretary to the Royal Commission was a significant step in his career. It was a sign of the India Office's esteem and confidence in him. And, because of the age distribution in the higher ranks, he could see preferment to the very top – if all went well, that is.'

'With the Commission's report, you mean?'

'Exactly . . . I wish now that he had not been selected for the task. I am sure that the burden of those wretched hearings brought on his illness. And, by his having to go to India, I was deprived of sharing the last four months of his life . . . his last Christmas.' She took a black-edged handkerchief from her bag, and blew her nose delicately.

'Has anyone been to see you from the office?' Bragg asked quietly.

'Yes. Ross, his assistant, came to the funeral yesterday. Apparently the police have taken away all his personal belongings . . . It seems that there will have to be an inquest, but Ross thought that I would not be called to attend . . . He said that William was found sitting peacefully in his chair. So he could not have suffered, could he?'

'I'm sure he didn't, ma'am.'

'But why are you here? Is it something to do with his death?'

'That matter is within the province of the Metropolitan police. Have they been to see you?'

'No. Ross said that he would deal with all such matters.'

'Good. We, in the City force, were interested in certain aspects of Mr Hewitt's work. We had been looking forward to hearing what he had to say about the India trip. His death has left us in something of a vacuum. Did he, by any chance, discuss it with you?'

'We had only one weekend together after his return; but, yes, we certainly talked about it.'

128

'He was not looking forward to it, in some respects, I remember.'

'Well, it was a great responsibility, of course. And, if it had gone wrong, it could have been a setback for him.'

'Gone wrong?'

'Mr Gladstone expected the status quo to be endorsed. He has always been pro-opium; but, because of the radical element in the Liberal Party, he has been compelled to sit on the fence . . . I wonder what Lord Rosebery's attitude will be, now that he has succeeded him as Prime Minister . . . But it is hardly important, now.'

'From what I hear, the majority of people in Britain do not feel strongly about abolishing the opium trade.'

'I think that is true. But my husband was concerned that the findings of the Commission should derive from the evidence submitted, with a high degree of inevitability. Even before the trip to India, while evidence was being received in London, he had become concerned about the submissions made by the Society for the Suppression of the Opium Trade.'

'In what way?'

'He said that he was prepared for them to show emotional commitment, and therefore for a commensurate lack of objectivity. But, in some areas, statements were being made which, he felt, were quite at variance with everyday experience. Take their claims about the detrimental effect of opium on the populations of our cities. Well, William knew from personal experience, that they were wildly exaggerated . . . He was brought up in Birmingham,' she added, in some embarrassment. 'Because of his background, he was sceptical of their claims that to take opium at all leads to addiction. In order to form a personal opinion, soundly based, he even went to the lengths of visiting an opium den, in the East End of London.'

'Where was that?'

'I really cannot remember – but I found a scrap of paper in the pocket of his overcoat, when I was packing it for the voyage. He said it was concerned with an opium den. On a mischievous impulse, I kept it. I am sure that I can locate it. Excuse me, a moment.' She hurried from the room.

'Going to an opium den seems well out of the line of duty,'

Bragg remarked.

'Well, we know that he was prepared to overstep the mark on occasion,' Morton said with a grin.

'Mrs Hewitt is not a woman I can warm to,' Bragg remarked. 'She has put her own selfish pursuits first, and now she is full of remorse for neglecting him.'

'But he made up for it. I know whose bed I would rather be in – Jane Morell's, every time!'

'That's hardly seemly, lad, in a house of mourning,' Bragg reproved him.

'Sorry, sir.'

The door opened and Mrs Hewitt returned with a small piece of paper.

'I was wrong,' she said. 'It was the address of the police station in Stepney, and the name of the officer he was to contact.'

'Who was that, ma'am?'

'Inspector Youdall.'

'Ah, yes. I know him . . . Did your husband say anything about the India trip?'

'I think that he found it a strain. He was looking forward to two months' quiet, in London, drafting the report.'

'What about the voyage back, in the ss *Rome*?'

'He said that his companions were an unappealing conjuncture of pro-opium self-interest, and anti-opium bigotry. He was concerned at the way in which the members of the Commission, and the various hangers-on who had haunted them throughout their journeyings, split into cliques on the voyage home. Lord Brassey, Sir John Lyall and Sir Walter Roberts were all placed at the captain's table, together with high-ranking military men and administrators. Thereafter, they stayed aloof from their colleagues. Fanshawe, Mowbray and a passenger called Jardine made up a pro-opium faction, while Henry Wilson and a John Alexander – who is Secretary of the Society for the Suppression of the Opium Trade – made up an anti-opium clique. Mr Hewitt was most upset at a blatant attempt by Alexander to compromise his independence.'

'In what way?'

'He did not say, but they had a very sharp exchange over it.

My husband spent most of his time with Arthur Pease – who is on the council of the society, but whom William found most congenial.'

'We heard that there had been several quarrels on the way back.'

'I gather that there was a running battle between Jardine on the one hand, and Alexander and Wilson on the other. And my husband said that Alexander had a particularly violent quarrel with Arthur Pease.'

'Did he say what about?'

'No. And I did not pursue the matter. It seemed of little consequence, and my chief interest lay in having my husband back, after so long.'

'I'm sure . . . Before we go, can I ask you a favour?'

'Of course.'

'I would like a photograph of your husband, if you have a spare. It would be nice to have one.'

She smiled, and crossed to the mantelpiece, which was crammed with framed snapshots. She took one down, and gave it to Bragg.

'I am sure that he would be pleased to be remembered by his friends,' she said.

Bragg looked at it. 'Thank you, ma'am,' he said warmly. 'This will do very nicely.'

It was mid-afternoon, before the train pulled into Liverpool Street station. Bragg and Morton had managed to buy a pork pie at Chelmsford station's buffet; but they had not had time for anything to drink. Bragg's throat was parched. He had not even been able to enjoy his pipe on the return journey. Come to think of it, his last swallow had been his breakfast cup of tea. It was one of the quirks of being a policeman. No matter how innocent your enquiries, or how pleasant you were about it, the public never thought to offer you refreshment. He looked at his battered watch, then at the pub opposite the station entrance. A pint or two would not take long. But, by then, the afternoon would be as good as over. Blast this case! You went round and round in circles, getting more information, but making no actual progress.

'We'll tidy up a loose end, lad, before we go back to Old Jewry,' he said, walking over to the cab rank.

A half-hour later, they were mounting the steps of the Orleans Club. Pushing open the door, they found themselves in a narrow vestibule, with a scarred oak counter and pigeon-holes above.

'Yes, sir?'

The porter's uniform was creased, and shiny at the elbows.

'Police. We want to have a word with the secretary.'

The porter looked at Bragg dubiously. 'I'm not sure if he is in or not,' he said. 'I'll go and see. You had better wait in the smoking room.'

He pointed to an open door beyond the hallway and left them. They wandered over to it. Morton thought it one of the most unappealing rooms he had ever seen. There was a dark-brown dado round the walls, the space above being painted a buttercup yellow that had become darkened with grime and tobacco smoke. The velvet curtains had once been bottle green, but were now silvered over with dust. A handful of coals smouldered sulkily in the grate . . . and the place stank of the rank odour of generations of cigars and pipes.

'A far cry from the Carlton Club, I reckon,' Bragg observed sourly.

'I imagine that Hewitt could not afford to stay anywhere better on a regular basis. I think that our top public servants are still expected to have considerable private means.'

'They weren't short of a penny, if their house is anything to go by.'

'No doubt,' said Morton. 'But from the momentary embarrassment Mrs Hewitt showed over her husband's origins, I presume that the money was from her family – and, I imagine, is controlled by her, in these enlightened days.'

'Poor bugger!'

Bragg wandered over to the fireplace and stirred the coals into life with the toe of his boot.

'You wished to see me?'

Bragg jumped back guiltily. 'Are you the secretary of the club?' he asked.

'I am.'

'We wanted to have a word about Mr Hewitt.'

'Your people have taken everything that was here,' the man objected.

'I know. There was just one matter that we wanted to clarify. Did Mr Hewitt have a meal here the night he died?'

The secretary bridled. 'It cannot have been anything he ate here,' he said sharply. 'No one else was taken ill.'

Bragg smiled. 'I am sure you are right,' he said soothingly. 'We are just trying to establish his movements on the night of the eighteenth.'

'It was certainly his practice to have an early dinner, promptly at half-past seven. Then, I believe, he would return to his office for a few hours. As to whether he had dinner that night . . . Just a moment.' He hurried off, and returned with a large book.

'I was wondering if the eighteenth was the night Mr Carruthers stayed with us.' He turned the pages slowly. 'Yes, it was.'

'What has that to do with it?'

'Another member had joined Mr Hewitt at his table, for a glass of wine. An altercation arose between them, and Mr Carruthers complained to me about it. He is one of our oldest members, you see.'

'So, you are sure Mr Hewitt dined here that night?'

'I am certain that he did.'

'Who was the member he had a row with?' Bragg asked.

'Mr Alexander.'

'J.G. Alexander, the barrister?'

'Yes. He is secretary of a society with an office along the street. He often drops in.'

'I see . . . Anyway, Mr Hewitt dined here. That's what we wanted to clear up. Thank you.'

In the cab back to Old Jewry, Bragg was uneasy, grunting to himself and drumming his fingers on his knee.

'Will you be getting a warrant for Alexander's arrest?' Morton asked, to break the silence.

'That's the very thing I've been pondering, lad. At the moment, the evidence against him is purely circumstantial.

Until Professor Burney tells us how long that stuff takes to work, it's nothing more than coincidence. No court would look twice at it . . . Even then, I doubt if a jury could be convinced that a public figure, and an altruistic humanitarian at that, could bring himself to commit multiple murder for his beliefs.'

'So, what will you do?'

'We need a bit more on him . . . One thing, though – he's not likely to run away, if we don't press him. We will let him have a bit more rope.'

They paid off the cab and strolled through the courtyard of the headquarters building, to the entrance.

'Joe! I have a telephonic message for you,' the desk-sergeant called. 'I reckon we shall have to get our number taken out of the book . . . either that, or get somebody to look after the instrument full-time. It's getting to be a pest!'

'Sorry, Bill! What is it?'

'The Holborn Viaduct Hotel rang. A man called Volkes has returned, it seems. They expect him to be in for tea.'

Bragg took out his watch. 'Might just catch him. Thanks, Bill . . . Come on, lad!'

They ran back to the street, but their cab had vanished. They pelted up to the junction with Cheapside. There was not a cab in sight there, either.

'Inspector Cotton would be proud of us,' Morton said with a grin.

'Maybe,' Bragg gasped. 'All the same, I'm not running any further, for all the snotty bastards in Christendom. Volkes will have to sodding wait!'

It was some minutes before they secured a cab. There were plenty on the street but, every time an empty one approached them, some young stockbroker or other would jump out and commandeer it under their noses. Finally, an empty one came trotting along the very street they had sprinted up.

'You see, lad,' Bragg said sourly, 'all this racing about gets you nowhere in the end.'

But by the time the cab pulled up in front of the hotel, he had recovered his breath and his spirits. This time the reception desk was manned by a stooping, grey-haired clerk.

'I am told that Mr Volkes has come back to the hotel,' Bragg said. 'Is he in?'

The man looked up lugubriously. 'He's just gone up to his room, not five minutes ago. Five hundred and twelve.'

'Good! Have you got a lift?'

'No. The stairs are over there.' He gestured towards the rear of the hotel, and turned back to his work.

'They shouldn't be allowed to have hotels without lifts, nowadays,' Bragg complained, as they toiled up to the top floor. 'Now, Volkes's room should be along this corridor . . . We'll treat him gently at first, right?'

He knocked firmly. There came the sound of a wardrobe door being closed, then the rattle of the key in the lock. The man who opened the door was in his late forties, broad and suntanned.

'Yes?' he asked.

'Police,' Bragg showed his warrant-card, pushing into the room.

'What do you want of me?'

'Just a chat. You are Mr Volkes, I believe.'

'Yes.'

'And you came to England on board the ss *Rome*?'

'That's right.'

Bragg sat down on the only chair, so Volkes perched on the bed, leaving Morton standing by the door.

'We understand that you went to the north country, shortly after you arrived,' said Bragg in a conversational tone.

'That is true,' Volkes frowned. 'What is the matter with that?'

'There is nothing the matter. I told you, I just want a chat . . . Would you mind telling me the purpose of your visit?'

'Not at all. I went to Manchester, to see if I could arrange for my tea to be shipped direct. Now the Manchester ship canal has been opened, ocean-going vessels can sail direct to Manchester docks. There is a massive market for tea in the midland counties. As a Lancastrian myself, I am all for cutting out the robber-barons in London! And it looks as if we shall be able to ship it more cheaply, as well.'

'So you were successful?'

'If I can get a few more planters to come in with me, yes.'

'Good. How long have you been in the business?'

'I went to Assam twenty years ago to learn the trade. Then, after five years, I took a stretch of land myself.'

'Wasn't that a risk?' Morton asked. 'After all, tea had been grown in India only for ten years before you went out.'

'That is not strictly true. *Thea Sinensis* is native to Assam, so there is no doubt that it can be cultivated successfully. The trouble is that, in its wild state, it forms a tree some twenty feet high. That is useless commercially. All you can use are the young leaves; and they have to be at a height where the native girls can easily reach them. For the first three years I was clearing the ground and planting new shrubs – and seeing never a rupee back.'

'You obviously needed substantial capital.'

'All borrowed . . . but there is no risk. The bushes in the plantations have to be kept to four or five feet high, by pruning; and the pruning stimulates new shoots. With care, you can get eight or nine flushes of new leaves each year – all of excellent quality. It's like growing golden guineas!'

'You know Sir Fergus Jardine, don't you?' Bragg asked.

Volkes's head jerked round. 'I know of him,' he said cautiously.

'You travelled over here together, on the ss *Rome*?'

'Hardly together. I was in the second-class. I wouldn't waste my money, travelling first.'

'You know he has died?'

'Yes. I read his obituary in the *Manchester Guardian* . . . I'm sorry,' he added unconvincingly.

'You went to see him a couple of hours before his death.'

'I was not aware of that.'

'But you did go to his office, on that Tuesday morning?'

'Yes.'

'What about?'

Volkes took a deep breath, and let it out in a resigned sigh. 'Sir Fergus had a special position, out East,' he began. 'Jardine Matheson are big in China; that makes them the leaders of the China merchants. Now, you may not believe it, but the success of the Indian tea plantations is threatening the China trade. I am by way of being one of the most forward-looking of Indian

136

planters. If Sir Fergus could queer my pitch, he might have hoped to discourage the others. I am sure that was his idea – but he had another think coming!'

'You've lost me,' Bragg said.

'The main purpose of my trip was to raise finance from the Colonial Bank for land that would double my crop. I had got an interview with the manager, on the afternoon of Monday the sixteenth. I must confess that I looked on it as a mere formality. They had lent me the original capital, without any fuss. I had paid the interest on time, and repaid some of the capital before time. So you can imagine that I was flabbergasted, when he turned me down. I couldn't understand it. I pressed him for a reason, but he would not give me one that made any sort of sense. I asked him to reflect on the information I had provided, and more or less insisted on another appointment. He opened his diary to look for a suitable time – and there, above my name for that day, was Jardine's. It was crystal-clear then. Jardine had managed to put the stopper on it. I couldn't fight him, with his influence; so I called on him, next morning, to ask him to change his attitude. He turned me down flat – seemed to enjoy it . . . However, it did not matter in the end. I got the loan from Martin's Bank in Liverpool.'

'And was that the only time you met him?'

'Yes, thank God! I shouldn't think he will be playing any harps, where he's gone.'

'You had a meeting with William Hewitt, the Secretary of the Royal Commission on the opium trade, I believe,' Bragg said casually.

Volkes was suddenly watchful.

'No. That's not quite true. I had hoped to, on the ship, but the first-class and the second-class were segregated, so I was not able to.'

'What about?'

'I had intended to put a submission to the Commission at one of their public hearings in India, but I was unable to get away. But once I heard that the members were travelling on the same ship as me, I decided I would try to approach the Secretary informally.'

'What were you going to say?'

'I look on Britain and the empire as one big family. And, like any other family, I believe we should trade with each other first – keep our wealth inside the empire, encourage members to provide within the family what we are currently forced to buy from outsiders.'

'So?'

'We, in Britain, spend millions of pounds every year buying tea from China, when India could provide it within the family. You would think it was obvious, but no. Mention it to politicians or India Office wallahs, and they suddenly go stone-deaf. The reason? If Britain didn't buy China's tea, China wouldn't buy India's opium.'

'So your proposal was that India would really benefit from banning the opium trade?'

'That's what it would have been.'

'I think it right to tell you, sir,' said Bragg sternly, 'that we found an appointment with you, in Hewitt's diary, for nine o'clock on the eighteenth – shortly before he died.'

'Is he dead too? Christ!'

'So, what did you say to him?'

'I never went . . .' Volkes said agitatedly. 'I got tied up with some people, then I couldn't get a cab.'

'What people?'

'I don't know. Some people in the bar at the Prospect of Whitby.'

'I am sorry,' Morton said, 'but we cannot accept that. We found some jottings on his office pad. They correspond exactly to what you have just told us.'

A stunned look spread over Volkes's face.

'Did you have anything to do with sending an anonymous letter to the *Echo*?' Bragg asked.

'No. I had nothing to do with that,' Volkes said dully.

'But you knew about it?'

'It was gossip in the trade when I arrived.'

'From what you have said, it would be of benefit to you, if China tea was discredited.'

'I don't deny that, but I still had nothing to do with it.'

Bragg stood up. 'Matthew Volkes,' he said gravely, 'I am arresting you on suspicion of the murders of Sir Fergus Jardine and William Hewitt. Anything you say will be recorded, and may be used in evidence.'

'Well, Sar'nt Bragg, what can we do for you?'

Inspector Youdall took a cigarette from a new packet, then offered it around.

'I'll stick to my pipe, if you don't mind,' Bragg said. 'And the constable doesn't – he's only a lad, yet!'

'Suit yourself,' Youdall lit his cigarette and took a powerful draw on it. 'It's a long time since we collared Joe Ramshorn for you, sar'nt. Only see you City lot when you want something. What is it this time? Another desperado?'

'No, sir. We are checking on the movements of a man called William Hewitt.'

'Hewitt . . . that rings a bell. Should I know about him?'

Bragg took out Hewitt's photograph from his pocket. 'That is him,' he said.

'Ah, yes . . . One of the busy-bodies we are lumbered with, I seem to remember.'

'He was appointed to be Secretary of the Royal Commission on opium, last autumn. He said that you found a nice safe opium den for him to visit.'

'Yes, that's right. One of my officers did take him to an opium establishment – we don't call them dens round here.'

'Why not?'

'The chief says its too pejorative – which means it's putting the mockers on.'

'Which establishment did he visit?'

'I don't know. Sar'nt Poole took him – it's his patch. But he won't come on duty for another few minutes.'

'Then, if you could fill in a bit of background, sir, I would be grateful. I gather you are by way of being an expert on the subject.'

Youdall took another drag, so that the glowing ring crept halfway up the cigarette. 'You could say that,' he remarked, the smoke spurting out of his nostrils. 'It's not surprising, either. Of the six hundred aliens in London, three hundred are China-born; and, of them, I reckon ninety per cent live in Limehouse

Causeway and Pennyfields, just round the corner.'

'So that is where the opium smoking goes on?' Bragg said.

'Of course. It's not a crime. They don't make trouble. Opium is part of their culture – like we smoke tobacco or have a glass of whisky. There are about a dozen boarding houses in the Causeway, where Chinese sailors put up. They bring in the opium, so the Pharmacy Act doesn't apply. It's all above board.'

'What is all the fuss about, then?'

'God only knows! For a nation that rules half the world, we are bloody queer with the foreigners living in this country. Anybody would think they might jump up and murder us all in our beds! We have endless do-gooders – like Hewitt – coming down to investigate the degenerative effects of opium. They see a Chinese labouring type – thin because that's how they are built; hollow cheeked, because they don't need false teeth with their grub – and they go back with all their prejudices confirmed. Bloody stupid, it is. And what's worse, the public expects us to keep an eye on these so-called dens. We have to pretend they may be disorderly houses, to give us an excuse to search them now and again. I tell you, Bragg, there are worse things than opium smoking, hereabouts.'

'The impression one gets from *Dorian Gray* and *Edwin Drood* is of squalor, and decadence, and sinister orientals,' Morton remarked with a smile.

'Well, Dickens would always over-egg the pudding, wouldn't he? The truth's too dull to sell many books. But, I'll tell you what, it's buggers like Oscar Wilde that cause us most trouble. Arty people looking for a new experience; West End slummers out for a thrill. They are like children telling ghost-stories in the dark. And when they frighten themselves, they come running to nanny. Me! . . . I think that's Sar'nt Poole now. Half a mo.' He went into the outer office.

'Everyone we speak to gives us a new angle on opium,' Morton said. 'I wonder where the truth lies.'

'Perhaps you should have a pennyworth yourself, lad, then you could tell me,' Bragg replied with a grin.

'Not likely! You would never catch me taking any drug – certainly not for amusement! I will stick to my dull, wholesome way of life, if you don't mind.'

Youdall strode in again, followed by an amiable-looking uniformed sergeant.

'This is Sar'nt Poole,' he said. 'Anything you want to know about the Chinese quarter, just ask him.'

'It would be even more helpful, sir, if we could walk round the area with him,' Bragg suggested.

'That all right with you, sar'nt?'

Poole nodded. 'The shift-change is in ten minutes, we could have a wander round then.'

'Thank you for your help, sir.'

'That's all right, Bragg. Any time . . .' Youdall fumbled in his packet for yet another cigarette.

Poole made a few remarks to the uniformed constables gathered in the charge-room, then they formed up into a line outside the police station. A smart right turn, and the file of men marched briskly along the road as if they were still in the army. It was a stupid system, Bragg thought, as they swung along, stopping every so often to collect a constable who had finished his shift and drop off his replacement. Any villain in the area knew precisely where the beat constable would be at the shift-change times – standing like a dummy at his pick-up point. So far as he could remember, no attempt had ever been made to vary them. It was all of a piece with the whole beat system – a rigid sequence of streets to be walked, set out on the beat card. They even timed the process, so that a householder knew where the constable would be at any given time. Dammit, they actually published the route and times at the station house! All a screwsman had to do was say 'I live at so-and-so. Can you tell me when the constable will pass my house?' and he was quids in! Stupid!

At the last pick-up point, Sergeant Poole sent the men back to the station on their own and, with Bragg and Morton, plunged into the web of narrow streets along the river. On the left was the towering cliff of a dock wall, the creaking clank of the cranes clearly audible. Then down to the Thames itself, oddly luminous as the darkness gathered. Along the bank, Bragg could see the jut of Limehouse pier. In the shadows, he could just persuade himself it was sinister. Then Poole stopped at a crossroads.

'There you are,' he said. 'That's the beginning of the Causeway ahead. It takes you up to West India Dock Road. Pennyfields continues on the other side of it.'

'It's not half a mile, in all,' Bragg remarked, as they crossed.

'That's right, and seething with our yellow friends. Poor buggers, they cram themselves in there because they are scared of us. We treat them like bogey-men because we are afraid of their foreign ways. Queer, isn't it? . . . And it's my job to keep on good terms with them, convince them we mean them no harm.'

'It can't be all that easy, with nosey-parkers and do-gooders hanging around all the time,' Bragg said.

The Causeway was narrow, with a badly-rutted road and broken pavement. The buildings were soot-blackened and decaying, their frontages irregular. In some of the nooks rubbish had collected; in others were the hunched figures of Chinese, squatting passively.

'So that's what opium does to you?' Bragg said with distaste.

'Not necessarily,' Poole replied. 'Opium is a queer substance. Sometimes, when they take it they will be put to sleep. At other times, they will take a couple of pipes then go straight off and work like lunatics for twelve or fifteen hours.'

'Inspector Youdall said that you have no trouble with them.'

'That's true enough – nothing like with the English sailors, coming roaring drunk out of the pubs at midnight.'

'Could you take us to where you took William Hewitt, in the autumn?' Bragg asked.

'If you like. But I can't guarantee that they'll be smoking opium there. These places tend to be lodging-houses. If they are not full, they will give you a bed to smoke a pipe. It means a bob or two in their pocket.'

'I particularly wanted to have a look at that one.'

'Very well.' Poole crossed the road and plunged into a dark alley. Morton could feel the hairs on his neck prickling with apprehension as he followed. Poole stopped by a narrow doorway.

'I don't want to disturb them more than necessary. Just stick with me. They will recognise me, and won't bother us.'

They ducked under the low lintel and found themselves in a small whitewashed lean-to. There was a stone sink in the corner and a table by the window. The flickering flame of a small table-lamp was the only illumination. The air was heavy with a scent like burning cinnamon. An elderly Chinaman stood by the table, holding a pipe. It had a bamboo stem, about eighteen inches long, with a small bowl that seemed to be made of cast iron. The Chinaman looked up expressionlessly and, seeing Poole, nodded to them. Then he took a needle and dipped it into a small basin, so that some of its contents adhered to the end.

'Is that opium?' Bragg whispered.

'Yes. He is preparing a pipe. Watch . . .'

The Chinaman was turning the opium in the flame of the lamp, watching its consistency intently. When he was satisfied, he heated the bowl of the pipe in the flame. Then he transferred the bead of opium through a small aperture in its top. After a moment, he removed the pipe from the flame and sucked at it tentatively. Having ascertained that it was functioning satisfactorily, he took it reverently in both hands, and went into the house. Morton almost laughed. He had seen the same look on the face of the butler at The Priory, when he had been offering some particularly venerable port.

'How long will that last?' Bragg whispered.

'Ten . . . twenty minutes. There is a little lamp, on a table by the bed. As long as you keep the bowl hot enough, you will get the fumes until the opium is burnt up.'

'Hmn. Have you ever tried it, sergeant?'

'What, me? Not bloody likely! I prefer my pint!'

At that moment an altercation began in the house, there was the sound of a door being opened violently, and a strident English voice.

'Here! Johnny! . . Come here, chop chop! This damned pipe has gone out!'

The man banged up and down the ground floor, apparently finding no one.

'I say, you chaps,' he called to some companions, 'I don't know about you, but I think this is a bit of a swizzle!'

'I agree,' another joined in. 'It's a damned swindle. Where

are the slimy yellow creatures?'

'I can't find a damned one,' said the first.

'Let's show them they can't put one over on us,' a third suggested.

'Good idea! Splendid!' they brayed.

Poole strode to the doorway and into the passage, Bragg and Morton following. There was a room at the front of the house, empty save for three beds and tables. As Poole entered, a well-dressed young man was holding one of the tables above his head, about to smash it against the wall.

'Police,' said Poole crisply. 'What do you three think you are up to?'

'Ah, sergeant,' cried the one who had first complained, 'jolly good thing you have come. These people are diddling us! We have paid them a half-sovereign each, and there is so little of the stuff in the pipe that it goes out after the first puff.'

'It takes practice, sir, it's an art, keeping the pipe going.'

'Don't be a chump, officer. We are all smokers. Why should this take practice?'

'Your nursemaid wiped your arse at first, didn't she? There's a knack to everything . . . But this is one that is not worth learning. Now, you just run off home like good little boys, or I shall have to run you in.'

'I say!' exclaimed one of the others. 'Whatever for?'

'Intending to cause a breach of the peace. Now, you just go back to where you came from, and keep out of trouble.'

The three trooped out into the passage muttering 'spoil sport' and 'rotten rozzers'; then with ostentatious slowness they opened the front door and were gone.

'It makes me puke!' Poole exclaimed, 'having to be polite to spoiled brats like that. Sometimes, I think it would be worth getting dismissed the force for the pleasure of giving them a good thump.'

The Chinaman reappeared on the stairs and, seeing all was quiet, came down. He bowed gravely to Poole, then went into the back kitchen again.

'Might as well do the rounds, while we are here,' Poole said.

They went up to the next floor. There was a large room, which appeared to be the living quarters of the proprietors.

Next to it, was one little bigger than a cupboard. In it was a bed, on which a man was sprawled. He was heavily built and wearing European dress. In the corner was a small table with a lamp on it and an opium pipe.

'Roll him over, lad,' Bragg said. 'We'd better check that he's not dead.'

Morton pulled on the man's shoulder, his body flopped over, the head following drunkenly. Morton started back in alarm. There could be no doubt about it . . . the opium-sodden wreck on the bed was Ben Fowler.

9

Jane Morell answered Morton's knock with a provocative smile, which faded as she saw Bragg standing there also.

'Good morning, constable,' she said in her warm low voice. 'Who is your companion?'

'This is Sergeant Bragg, my boss.'

'Do come in. I am afraid it is Mildred's day off,' she said, leading them into the parlour. 'But I could offer you a glass of wine.'

Bragg followed her glance towards the decanter of claret on the sideboard.

'No thanks,' he said hastily. 'It's a bit early in the morning.'

Mrs Morell turned her smile to Morton. 'I have looked through some of my diaries,' she said, 'but without success. I can find no suggestion that William might have had enemies. However, as the ones I have consulted were for the earlier years of our acquaintance, they were always less likely to be rewarding.'

'I understand you know Sir Fergus Jardine,' Bragg said brusquely.

'Knew, sergeant,' she corrected him gently.

'Right. Did you see him on his present visit to London?'

She looked at him steadily, a faint smile on her lips. 'Yes, sergeant,' she said.

'At his hotel?'

'Yes . . . Was that wicked of me?'

'When?'

'On the evening of Monday the sixteenth.'

'What happened?'

Her smile became more coquettish. 'We had some refreshment at the Royal, then went to a show.'

'Which one was that?'

'*A Gaiety Girl*, at the Prince of Wales' theatre.'

'It sounds appropriate, from all accounts,' Bragg said sardonically.

'Thank you, sergeant.' She smiled brilliantly at him.

'Did you stay the night with him?'

'You sound so censorious, sergeant! Do you disapprove?'

'It's not for me to approve or disapprove, ma'am,' Bragg said dourly. 'What time did you leave?'

'I did not sneak out like a woman of the streets! We had an early breakfast together in Fergus's suite . . . I must have left a little after seven o'clock.'

'What did he eat for breakfast?'

'Have you neglected to consult the kitchen, sergeant? That is remiss of you! . . . I did not pay any great attention to the food. But, if my memory serves me, there was crispy bacon – which he loved – devilled kidneys, scrambled eggs, kedgeree . . . Yes, that was it, I think – plus toast, conserves and tea.'

'What dishes did he try?' asked Bragg irritably. 'It may be important.'

'Please do not scold me,' she said with a pretty *moue*. 'Such talents as I have do not lie in the direction of detached observation . . . I do remember that he rejected the kedgeree. He said he had quite enough of that out East.'

'Jardine was one of your protectors, was he?'

She smiled impishly at him. 'Thank you for your delicacy, sergeant, but I am not ashamed of my way of life. Sir Fergus was generous to me – on an occasional basis.'

'And William Hewitt was another?'

'As you well know.'

'Have you been to his office in Queen Anne's Gate?'

'Of course. If we went to the theatre, it was more convenient for me to call on him there.'

'You told Constable Morton that he used to come here.'

'That is so. But in the period from September, when he first occupied the office, to November, when he sailed to India, I called there on several occasions.'

'But not after his return?'

'No.'

'What about last Tuesday night?'

'He came here.'

'You are sure of that?'

She smiled warmly. 'I am hardly likely to forget it!'

Bragg cleared his throat. 'You were with Jardine on the morning of the seventeenth, and Hewitt the same night,' he said gruffly.

'Are you asking a question, sergeant, or commending my assiduity?'

'I am wondering about the coincidence that, within a few hours of your seeing them, they were both dead.'

'That was brutal,' she reproved him, the smile gone from her face.

'Hewitt was going to ditch you, wasn't he?' Bragg demanded roughly. 'He was building a new house, bringing his wife to live in Highgate. There would have been no room for your hanky-panky then, would there? He was going to drop you like a dirty rag, in case you soiled his prospects. So you murdered him.'

'That is not true, sergeant,' she said in a level voice. 'William was not a fair-weather friend. There would always have been opportunities to meet. As for killing him . . . I owed him a great deal. But ours was not a possessive relationship. If he had wished to go, I would not have sought to restrain him.'

'Jardine wasn't a cold fish, though, was he?' Bragg asked harshly. 'When he found out about Hewitt, you knew he was capable of destroying you both.'

She laughed scornfully. 'You little know Sir Fergus's character! Had he discovered my liaison with William, he would have been pressing me to use my influence with him, in favour of his beastly opium.'

'So you admit you are against opium?'

She cocked her head, with something of her former assurance. 'Any woman would deplore a substance which so impairs a man's vital spirits.'

'I shall be keeping an eye on you,' Bragg said truculently.

'Thank you, sergeant!'

'You are not to leave London, without my permission.'

'I had not intended to do so, except to visit my mother in Oxfordshire, next week.'

Bragg looked at her quizzically. 'All right, you can go there. Just put her address on a piece of paper for me, so that we shall know where to find you . . . Better print it – my eyesight isn't too good. Put it in capitals, will you?'

She crossed to a writing table and, taking a piece of paper, printed the address rapidly, in small capitals. From where Morton stood, they bore no resemblance to the printing on the anonymous letter to the *Echo*.

Bragg scanned the paper, then folded it and put it in his pocket.

'That will be all, for now,' he said.

She led them to the door and stood back as Bragg marched out. Then she looked up at Morton and smiled.

'Do not forget, Constable Morton, I shall be looking through the rest of my diaries!'

Catherine Marsden prowled happily around the crypt of the Guildhall. It was one of her favourite places. Somehow it took one back to the very roots of London; the medieval granite pillars, polished by centuries of human contact, the limestone vaulting – and all on a domestic scale. Unlike the great ceremonial hall above, one could imagine the crypt stacked with bales of cloth, or piled with armour for the French wars. She hoped the Corporation would not succumb to the modern craze for installing electric lamps everywhere. The gas light suited the crypt, softening its stark lines – though some of the ladies' dresses would have looked brighter with the aid of electricity!

The room was filling up now, and already there was a hum of excited conversation. The British and Foreign Bible Society, as an unexceptional charity, was sure to be well supported – even at lunchtime. Particularly when the Corporation of London was providing the reception. She made her way to the buffet and took out her notebook. Various cakes, sandwiches, *petits fours* . . . She decided that she would have *foie gras, saumon fumé* and perhaps a *caramel de fruits* to follow – if any were left after she had gathered all the material for her article. From past experience, these exquisite creatures would fall on the food like a horde of starving savages, once the signal was given. But first she must make notes on the people present. On one of her early assignments, she had relied on the guest-list, and had reported someone as present who was languishing in bed after a well-reported hunting accedent! Mr Tranter, the editor, would not look kindly on a repetition of that *faux-pas*. Equally, it was essential that she should mention all the really important people who were present. Not necessarily important on the nation's stage, but influential in the City. The Prime Warden of the Fishmongers' Company, for instance, or an alderman likely to become Lord Mayor. She had already marked them on her copy of the guest-list. Now it was a matter of confirming that they were present. She worked her way to the back of the hall. As she pushed out of the press, she collided with someone hurrying to the back stairs.

'Fowler!' she gasped. 'What on earth are you doing here?'

'Why should I not be here?' he snapped aggressively. His face was pallid, his eyes sunken.

'But you are not on the guest-list!'

'Do not be so stupid! . . . I am gloating over the hypocrisy of savages preparing to convert savages; to sacrifice millions of defenceless natives to their cosy English concept of godhead and their lust for treasure.' His eyes glittered, his voice was excited – almost exultant. 'But man is not mocked!' he exclaimed. 'They will understand . . .' He rushed to the staircase and vanished.

Poor Louisa, Catherine thought, to tie herself to such a man. He seemed to be more outrageous every time she saw him. Perhaps . . . she mentally scolded herself for the thought . . . But if he did go away, Louisa would be able to begin again, find someone more suitable . . . The image of James formed in her mind. No! She could not bear that! She shook her head crossly, and concentrated on checking her list. Then she approached the receiving line, where the Lord Mayor, the Lady Mayoress, the Sherriffs and the Secretary of the Society were standing. The Lady Mayoress was fiftyish and decidedly plump. She had elected to be imprisoned in a formidable corset in an attempt to carry off an hour-glass gown. With the material tight over the hips and hugging the thighs, she seemed oddly immobile; smiling and shaking hands like an automaton. Catherine jotted down *plum velveteen*, *fur trimmings* and closed her notebook. She strolled over to the City Solicitor, who was an unfailing source of information for her.

'Good morning, Miss Marsden,' he said beaming. 'Are you here to chronicle our jamboree?'

'I have four column inches reserved, at the bottom of today's leader page!' she said, with a smile. 'I hope that I can do justice to you . . . Who is that? I do not recognise him.'

The solicitor peered in the direction she was pointing.

'The man chatting to the vicar of St Lawrence, in the doorway?' he asked.

'Yes.'

'That is Arthur Pease. He is a Quaker, and something of a notable. He has recently returned from India – he is a member of the Royal Commission on the opium trade, you know.'

'Excuse me, I must try to have a word with him.'

She pushed through the throng. But while she was fighting her way to the door, Pease had made his way to the receiving line. She skirted the assembled guests, then waited at the end of the line, her pencil poised.

'Mr Pease,' she said urgently, 'have you any comments on the effect of opium on the Indian natives?'

He raised his hands defensively. 'You obviously know,' he said with a good-natured smile, 'that I am engaged in an official enquiry on that very topic. I am afraid that it would be quite improper for me to make any utterance at this stage. I fear that you will have to wait until the report is published.'

A waitress approached him with a tray. 'Would you care for wine, sir?' she asked.

He took a glass and turned away.

'But you are on the council of the anti-opium society?'

He smiled at Catherine. 'I think I may just admit to that,' he said. 'Now, if you will excuse me.'

He walked over to a group of men in animated discussion. Catherine recognised Sir William Sumner among them, together with several members of the police committee. Sir

William seemed less than happy. Perhaps some alterations in the force were in the offing . . . She turned to search for the City Solicitor, he might have heard a whisper. Suddenly she heard a commotion, a woman's scream, then a moment's shocked silence. There seemed to be some activity in the group she had been watching, people were pressing around . . . Now there was a general murmur of speculation. She pushed forward, catching disjointed words as she wriggled through the press . . . dead . . . seizure.

She felt her arm grasped. It was Sir William.

'Miss Marsden,' he said urgently. 'Would you please telephone to the police headquarters. There is an instrument upstairs in the porter's office. Tell Sergeant Bragg and Constable Morton to come here immediately!' Then he turned away and, finding a chair, climbed on to it.

'Ladies and gentlemen,' he called. 'There has been an unfortunate accident. I must ask you to disperse quietly and leave the building. Above all, do not drink any of the red wine. I repeat . . . do not drink the red wine. Thank you.'

Catherine escaped from the sudden hubbub, and ran up the back staircase to the porter's office. She seized the telephone instrument and cranked the handle. Almost immediately the exchange answered and she was passing on the Commissioner's message to the desk-sergeant at Old Jewry. She raced back to the crypt. The crowd had almost vanished, leaving a small cluster of people. At their feet was the outline of a human figure, covered with a tablecloth.

'What happened?' she asked the City Solicitor in a whisper.

'Arthur Pease. He dropped dead, moments after you were speaking to him.'

'Great heavens! Why did Sir William say that it was an accident? And why did he forbid anyone to drink the wine?'

'Goodness only knows. No doubt he had his reasons . . . I thank my lucky stars that I was drinking white.'

With a last glance at the draped body, Catherine hurried away. Would Mr Tranter veto a lurid description of the scene? she wondered.

When Bragg and Morton arrived at the crypt, some ten minutes later, they found Sir William sitting disconsolately by the body, while a phlegmatic porter smoked a cigarette in the doorway. As they entered, Sir William got to his feet.

'I am very much afraid that I acted precipitately, Bragg,' he said in embarrassment. 'I am sure that, as a professional, you would have preferred the doors to be locked, and everyone detained for questioning. My amateur reaction was to get them all away from danger, as quickly as possible.'

Bragg looked at the swathed form on the flagstones. 'Who is it?' he asked quietly.

'Arthur Pease. He had just arrived and came to join our group. He took a drink from his wine glass and, the next moment, he collapsed to the ground. We thought he had fainted. But John Stanley, the Medical Officer of Health, examined him and said he was dead. We were shocked, naturally. Then someone said that he was on this opium commission, and I remembered what you said about the red wine.'

'I'm sure you did the right thing, sir,' Bragg said reassuringly. 'You could hardly have penned up half of London's merchant princes for the afternoon, anyway. Not without telling them what was afoot. Besides, you can bet the person that did it was out and away by then. Can you give me a bit more detail about it?'

The Commissioner pondered. 'After he had shaken hands with the Lord Mayor, and so on, he was accosted by Miss Marsden, the newspaper reporter . . . Perhaps I should not say "accosted",' he added, with an embarrassed smile. 'However, they conversed for some moments, and I distinctly saw him take a glass of wine from a waitress. It was the only glass on the tray, and it was red wine.'

'Would you recognise the waitress, sir?'

'I . . . er, no, Bragg. It did not seem of consequence, at the time. Pease escaped from Miss Marsden, if that is the word, and came towards us. I did not follow his progress all the time, but I am of the opinion that he did not drink from the glass until he joined us.'

'How long was it after he drank that he collapsed?'

'To the best of my recollection, Bragg, it was almost immediately.'

'The same pattern as Jardine, eh?'

'So it seemed to me. I decided that you must be brought to the scene as early as possible.'

'That was quick thinking, sir.'

The Commissioner smiled smugly. 'Thank you, Bragg.'

'All the same, it's a bit of an odd one.'

'In what way?'

'If you are right, sir, and it is another poisoning, it has blown one of our theories sky-high.'

'What is that?'

'We have been assuming that it was all to do with opium. Now, Jardine was an opium trader, and Hewitt was known to favour Jardine's side. But Pease is a prominent figure in the Society for the Suppression of the Opium Trade. So that idea goes down the plug hole.'

'Did they not all return from India on the same ship?' asked the Commissioner.

'They did, sir.'

'Perhaps it all flows from that.'

'Perhaps . . . I would be grateful if you could do one thing for me, sir.'

'What is that?'

'You will be able to get the wheels moving more quickly than I could. Do you think you could notify the coroner, and ask him to appoint me his officer for this one, too?'

'Yes, good idea, Bragg.'

'And perhaps you could arrange to have the body taken to the mortuary . . .'

At that moment the door burst open and a man hurried in. He was vigorous, and the whiteness of his hair only intensified the healthy pink of his face.

'I am Sir Joseph Pease,' he announced. 'I am told that my brother has collapsed here.'

The Commissioner gestured to the body.

Sir Joseph dropped to his knees and pulled back the end of the tablecloth. Then he sighed.

'I had hoped it was not he,' he said. 'He looks as if he had just fallen asleep . . . There is no doubt, I suppose?'

'I am afraid not,' Sir William said. 'Now, if you will excuse me . . .' He hurried away, and Morton followed him.

'I have to tell you, sir, that we must treat his death as suspicious,' Bragg said.

Sir Joseph's head jerked round. 'Why on earth . . ?'

'There have been two similar deaths recently, both unnatural.'

Pease got to his feet. 'But that is absurd, officer. He was one of the most inoffensive men you could wish to meet.'

'You have no idea if he had any enemies, then?'

'I cannot conceive of it! I am sure that his death will prove to be from natural causes.'

'I hope so, sir. But, oddly enough, both the other victims have had connections with opium, and both travelled back from India on the ss *Rome* with your brother. Did he say anything to you about the work of the Commission?'

'No! He was a man of great integrity, officer.'

'Did he, perhaps, mention to you any quarrels he had on board?'

'I have not seen him socially since his return. I have been busy in my constituency.'

'Where is that?'

'Barnard Castle, in Durham.'

'But you have met him?'

'Yes. We were both at a meeting of the committee of the Society for the Suppression of the Opium Trade, on the fourteenth . . . However, I had to leave early.'

'You are on the council, as well as your brother, I gather.'

'Indeed! I was one of the society's founders.'

'I see . . . Well, the coroner has been notified, so the whole matter is in his hands now. There will have to be a post mortem examination. Has he any family?'

'I will break the news to his wife, officer. I would be glad if I could be notified at the House of Commons when the body is released.'

'I will see to that, certainly.'

'Thank you, officer.' Sir Joseph picked up his silk hat and strode out of the crypt.

Bragg sat down by the body and slowly filled his pipe. It didn't make any sense. Yet Sir Joseph had confirmed what

Hewitt had told his wife. Arthur Pease was a refined, cultured man – not the most likely candidate for murder . . . Bragg struck a match and applied it to his pipe. On the other hand, he was a member of an extreme organisation . . . Could it be a revenge killing? One of Jardine's people evening the score? . . . Not if it was the same poison, that was certain.

'Ah, Brutus contemplating the body of Caesar!' Morton came back clutching some sheets of paper.

'That's enough of that, lad. What have you got there?'

'The guest-list for the reception. I thought it would be informative.'

'And is it?'

'Since it is in alphabetical order, one needs not read far, before encountering a most interesting entry.'

'Stop pissing about! Give it here!'

Bragg took the papers and began to read, puffing contentedly on his pipe. Then he stopped.

'J.G. Alexander, eh? That's interesting . . . Well, we know it could not be Volkes that did it, because he's in clink; and, so far as we know, Coaker is not within two hundred miles of here.'

'I am relieved to see that Mrs Morell does not appear on the list!'

'No, but how would it be, if Pease was another of her acquaintances?'

'How splendid!' Morton laughed. 'He, Jardine and Hewitt coming back on the same ship, and all in ignorance of their common connection! No, it seems too fanciful, even for me.'

'Then we are left with Alexander . . . It wouldn't hurt to have another chat with him.'

'Are you not making a certain assumption, sir?'

Bragg looked up sharply. 'And what is that?' he asked.

'Pease may not, in fact, have been murdered.'

'He was, lad,' Bragg said firmly. 'I feel it in my bones . . . Come on!'

This time they went to the King Street offices, only to be sent to Alexander's chambers in Serjeants' Inn. Even when they arrived there, they had to wait in the clerk's office till he returned from lunch. Finally, he came hurrying up the stairs and, glancing in, saw them. A look of mild irritation crossed his face as he passed on. Bragg sprang up and, disregarding the clerk's outraged protests, followed Alexander to his room, with Morton bringing up the rear.

'What is it, now?' Alexander asked coldly.

'I just wanted to clear up one or two things, sir,' Bragg said in an amiable tone.

'Very well, but please be expeditious. I have a conference in ten minutes.'

'I want to go back to the voyage home, on the ss *Rome*. If you remember, you said you were all gentlemen, so there was no wrangling.'

'Yes.'

'Well, we have talked to other people, and they said that there was quite a bit of quarrelling, mostly involving you. Everybody agreed that you had quarrelled with Jardine.'

Alexander frowned. 'We clashed, certainly, but that was hardly surprising, considering our divergent interests.'

'They said you had a disagreement with Mr Hewitt, too.'

'He was part of a blatant conspiracy to thwart the will of the people of this country!'

'I see. They agree with you, do they?'

'Most certainly.'

'And would you say it's just a coincidence that both men are dead?'

Alexander bit back his reply, and took a deep breath. 'I am not an authority on coincidence, sergeant,' he said in a level voice.

'But you are on opium?'

'On its effects, yes.'

'You feel very strongly about them?'

'I would hardly be secretary of the society, if I were not.'

'We have also heard that you had an altercation with Arthur Pease.'

Alexander smiled grimly. 'You are well informed,' he said.

'What was all that about?'

'I must ask you to regard what I am about to tell you as confidential, since the matter is not yet public knowledge.'

'We will certainly take note of your request, sir,' Bragg said cautiously.

'You are probably unaware of the fact, but Arthur Pease and I were both on a short-list of possible Liberal Party candidates, to contest the next election in a radical constituency in the Midlands.'

'I see,' said Bragg thoughtfully. 'They feel strongly about opium up there, do they?'

'Any right-thinking person must abhor it! . . When the ship docked at Marseilles there was a telegraph waiting for me, to say that I had, in fact, been selected as the candidate. I was, of course, delighted – and, equally, I felt for Pease in his disappointment . . . It seemed to me that he would prefer to arrive in England already knowing the worst, rather than face the news immediately on his return. I therefore imparted to him the contents of the telegram.'

'And you found he wasn't grateful at all?'

'I expected him to be disconcerted, even mortified, but there was no call for such an extreme reaction.'

'So the rest of the voyage was unpleasant, then?'

'I do not know, sergeant. I left the ship at Marseilles and came home by train and the Channel packet.'

'But you have seen him since?'

'Only at a committee meeting of the society – a purely business meeting, I may add.'

'I see . . . And would you say it was just another coincidence that you were there when he died, also?'

'Dead? Pease?' Alexander asked in consternation.

'At the Guildhall reception, this lunchtime. Don't say you were unaware of it; you were there.'

'Indeed I was not!'

'I can show you your name on the guest-list.'

'That is hardly proof that I was there, sergeant! Pease and I were invited to represent the society. In the event, I was busy, and did not attend.'

Bragg looked sceptically at him. 'It's not copper-bottomed proof, no . . .' he said slowly.

Alexander suddenly exploded. 'I am tired of your snooping and innuendos, sergeant,' he shouted. 'If you are going to arrest me, please do so. If not, go away and stop harassing me!'

*

'This is an unlooked-for pleasure,' Catherine said, as she settled herself into her chair.

Morton smiled. 'I would not have you think that I have become insensible to your charms, Miss Marsden,' he said in a rallying tone.

'My parents will become concerned, lest I might reciprocate! I only had time to send a hurried note, saying that I would not be in for dinner.'

'But, surely you told them that you would be with me?'

'Is that supposed to reassure them? – a footloose, unattached bachelor, who has a demonstrably eccentric way of life!'

'Then we are well matched . . . I suggested a chop-house, because I have something in mind for later.'

'Perhaps I ought to turn tail and run, while I can!'

'Nonsense! You know that I am your guardian angel.'

'Entirely self-appointed!'

'You are certainly in need of one. I gather from the Commissioner that you were with Arthur Pease practically the moment before he died. Did he say anything in particular?'

'He parried my professional advances with the shield of his immaculate integrity! Why do you ask?'

'Sergeant Bragg is convinced that he was murdered.'

'Murdered?' she exclaimed.

'Keep your voice down. There have been two earlier deaths, each caused by a rare poison, both probably murder. Red wine was associated with both, hence the Commissioner's panic at lunchtime.'

'I wondered what that was all about. The wine is mediocre on such occasions, granted, but I had not thought that it was so dangerous! Who were the others?'

'Sir Fergus Jardine, and a colonial servant called Hewitt.'

'But Jardine was taken ill in the City! I do think you could have told me, James! You are all too ready to seek my help, but you are loth to reciprocate.'

'I am concerned for your safety. Whoever is behind these deaths seems to be a madman. The only link between the people murdered is that they were all involved in the current controversy over the Indian opium trade – though not on the same sides.'

159

Catherine shivered. 'We know all too well the degeneration that opium can bring.'

'Fowler, you mean? Oddly enough, at one time I seriously regarded him as a possible candidate for our murderer. He is certainly strange enough! Then we found a better one, in the person of J.G. Alexander, an up-and-coming barrister.'

'The Secretary of the Society for the Suppression of the Opium Trade?'

'Why, yes. We were on the verge of arresting him, until today; but he was unsporting enough not to have been present when Pease died.'

'Oh, but he was!' Catherine exclaimed. 'I saw him myself.'

'Are you sure?'

'Of course,' she said scornfully. 'No woman would mistake such a handsome man!' She burrowed into her handbag and extracted her notebook; then, flipping over the pages, pointed triumphantly to a series of names. Alexander's was indubitably among them.

'Well, this is most interesting,' Morton said musingly. 'At least the wretched Fowler should be grateful to you. We shall be able to go with a light heart.'

Catherine's face changed. 'So that is it! After dinner you propose to bear me off to pay your guilt-money to Louisa,' she said coldly.

'Yes,' Morton admitted with a hang-dog expression on his face. 'I do not even wish to reject your epithet. I do feel guilty, on behalf of all boorish and self-indulgent mankind.'

'You are being maudlin,' Catherine said brusquely. 'Louisa had no need to get herself into this mess. Women are not defenceless toys, at the mercy of the whims of men. She went to live with Fowler, because that was what she wanted above all else – what she still wants, or she would leave him. Your sympathy is misplaced, James.'

'I am sure that you are right, but I cannot help regretting the waste . . .'

'There are many ways of wasting one's life . . . Louisa always did incline to the extravagant gesture.'

The waiter came for their order, and the interruption became a truce. Throughout the meal they chatted inconsequentially and, by the end of it, they had re-established something approaching their normal relationship. As they rose to go, Catherine made no comment, but walked to the cab-rank with him, her hand in the crook of his elbow. He looked at her quizzically as he handed her into the cab, but she refused to acknowledge the implication that she could decline to accompany him. She had as much claim to him, as Louisa . . . More. She was not about to let him waste his life on her!

They kept silence until the cab pulled up in Plough Court. James handed her solicitously down the narrow steps to the area door and knocked. After some time the door opened and Louisa appeared.

'Come in,' she said softly. 'I am sitting with Ben.'

The living-room was illuminated only by a single candle, but an oil lamp was burning in the bedroom. They followed her and saw that Fowler was in bed, asleep. Louisa resumed her seat, her eyes fixed on Fowler, muffled in the bedclothes. Morton set a chair for Catherine, standing himself in the little remaining space by the door. Fowler was lying still, breathing very slowly. The expression on his countenance was one of deep repose. Catherine studied Louisa. She was sitting erect and still. There was a hard excitement in her, held in balance by a kind of hypnotic serenity.

'Is he ill?' Catherine asked.

Louisa turned her face full towards her. 'Yes, very ill.'

'When did it start?'

A look of irritation crossed Louisa's face. 'He took laudanum this morning,' she said, 'then went out. He came back at two o'clock . . . I do not know where he had been, but he was talking wildly . . . He came back to me so that I could look after him,' she added softly.

'He had been to the Guildhall,' Catherine said. 'He seemed to be indulging in some kind of mockery of the City's ethics.'

Louisa looked up. 'He said he had struck a blow for the oppressed,' she murmured. 'He would like that for an epitaph.'

Catherine looked sharply at Morton.

'Louisa,' he said, 'why do you not put him in one of the homes for addiction? There is the Dalrymple Home at Rickmansworth; they would take him.'

Louisa turned, her eyes bright. 'No, that would not be right.'

'I will gladly pay the fees,' Morton said.

'No, I know him too well, you see. It would not last. He has been taking opium, in addition to the laudanum I gave him. He admitted it. He had become like a wayward child . . . He was not always like this,' she went on dreamily. 'When we first met, he was amusing and full of self-confidence. He used to delight us with his biting criticisms of the academicians – of Frith's frenetic panoramas or the absurdity of Wells's painting *Victoria being Informed of Her Accession*, forty years after the event. When he chose me, I was intoxicated with happiness. We would take trips on the river together, picnic at Hampton Court and walk back to my lodgings throught the warm evening air . . . You may not believe it, but we were blissfully happy – until he began to strive, to feel that he must prove himself. It was not important to me, but he had to succeed as a painter – and to do so, he sought the aid of opium . . . The people who stay at the Royal ought to be sitting here, with us.'

She seemed to drift into a trance, her eyes fixed on her comatose lover.

'So these are De Quincey's "portable ecstacies",' Morton murmured in disgust. He felt Catherine's hand seeking his. They were like bemused children, needing solace, far removed from the elevated emotion in which Louisa was cocooned.

As time passed, Fowler's breathing became shallower, until it was barely perceptible. Morton leaned over the bed. The painter's features were ghastly in the lamplight. He took his wrist, but could barely feel a pulse.

'This is absurd!' he cried. 'We must get a doctor.'

'No, he would not want that,' Louisa said serenely.

'We cannot let him die!' Morton rushed out of the room, and the outer door banged.

The silence enfolded the little tableau, became oppressive. Catherine felt superfluous and afraid. She wished she had not come, but now she was trapped.

'Why, Louisa? Why?' she cried.

Her friend turned her blue eyes full upon her, then smiled. 'I love him,' she said and turned back to the bed.

After an age, there came the clatter of boots on the area

steps, and Morton flung the door open.

'Where is the patient?' asked another voice curtly.

'In the bedroom, there.'

The doctor brushed Louisa aside and bent over the bed. 'Opium, you say?'

'Yes,' said Morton.

The doctor felt Fowler's pulse and grunted; then held back his eyelid and shone the lamp on his face. 'Pupil contracted,' he murmured. He took a stethoscope from his pocket and, opening Fowler's nightshirt, sounded his chest. Then he stood up abruptly.

'There is nothing I, or anyone, can do – a typical overdose case.'

'How long will it be?' Morton asked quietly.

'Not long, now . . . Get those women out of the way, they will only become hysterical. I will sign the death certificate in the morning.' He thrust the stethoscope back into his pocket, and marched out.

'You see,' Louisa said with a triumphant smile. 'I told you!'

'Miss Marsden,' Morton murmured, 'I do feel that you should go home. I am sorry for having involved you in this.'

'If you are involved, James, then so am I. I shall stay.'

He took her hand, and they remained immobile for what seemed an eternity. After a time, there was a loose rattling in Fowler's throat. It seemed to go on interminably . . . Then, at last, it ceased. There was total silence for a moment, then Louisa gave a sigh. She got up calmly, pulled the coverlet up over Fowler's head, then smoothed her dress.

'It is all over now,' she said softly.

'Will you come home with me, Louisa?' Catherine asked.

Louisa looked up, suddenly drained. 'Thank you,' she said. 'I would like that. I will pack my things.'

'Had he any relatives?' Morton asked.

'There is a brother in Clapham Common.'

'I will find him so that he can make the arrangements. Don't worry, Louisa. Leave everything to me.'

'I will take her back to her parents' house tomorrow,' Catherine whispered.

Louisa knelt on the bed and, pulling the sheet from off the

hooks, selected a few of her clothes. She bundled them up and put them in a bag, then turned to Morton.

'Thank you,' she said. 'Give my regards to your family.' With a nod to Catherine, she walked steadily out of the house.

10

Morton glanced out of the railway-carriage window. The flat Essex countryside was muffled in a layer of thick mist, through which an occasional row of bare trees projected. It was eerie, he thought. They seemed, at a distance, to be floating erect on a spume-flecked sea. What a treacherous month March was! Only two days ago, this same terrain had been soaking up the spring sunshine; there had been a zest in the air, summer just around the corner. Now they might as well be in depressing November. He glanced across to where Bragg was sitting in the opposite corner, his pipe going well, a frown of concentration on his face.

'May I ask, sir, why you have decided to come back to Chelmsford today?'

Bragg took his pipe from his mouth. 'I don't know, lad. Instinct, if you like. This third death bothers me.'

'You still feel it is murder?'

'We shall know for sure this afternoon. I spoke to Professor Burney last night. He has promised to get his lab boys on the case first thing this morning.'

'By the way,' Morton said, 'I was with Miss Marsden last night. I do not know what weight can be placed on the remark, as she was chaffing me at the time, but she said that she saw Alexander at the Guildhall reception yesterday.'

Bragg looked up with a fierce grin. 'Did she by God! Well, she's not likely to be mistaken over a good-looking fellow like him.'

'That was precisely her assertion,' Morton said ruefully.

'You are going to lose that young woman, if you bugger

about much longer,' Bragg said reprovingly. 'She won't wait for ever.'

'Even were I convinced that she would be the right wife for me, I would be little further forward. She shows not the slightest inclination to exchange her career for humdrum domesticity – and one can hardly blame her.'

'Have you asked her?'

'Of course not! One can scarcely embarrass a young lady by an unwanted proposal. I have touched lightly on the topic, on several occasions, and she has invariably seen me off.'

'What do you expect?' Bragg said contemptuously. 'You rich folk are just bloody stupid. You are more concerned with pedigree than human worth. It's like a sodding stud-farm.'

Morton smiled. 'I assure you that my family is totally untainted by that kind of calculation. Through my mother, we have had a transfusion of red American blood. It has given us a healthy immunity from considerations like that.'

'Then, why don't you get on with it?'

Morton shrugged. 'The lady's feelings in the matter must be of some importance.'

'You will never get anywhere, lad, if you take notice of what she says. Where I come from, if you fancied a lass you would ask her to come for a walk across the fields. You would talk a bit and hold hands. Then, if you were really struck with her, you would suggest a sit-down by the hayrick. If she agreed, you were well in. It wasn't what she said that mattered, it was what she would let you do!' ·

'One could hardly apply such rustic tactics to an elegant, young society lady!'

'Why not? She's only human. At bottom, they're all longing for a cuddle – with the right man.'

Morton stared moodily through the window again. His own parents had proved to be admirably matched. Perhaps it had been because his father had been some years older than his mother. Did that mean that he was lacking in maturity? Or was it that he had no need of a wife? With Mr and Mrs Chambers to look after him, he was relieved of the necessity that must drive most men to marriage. It might be that he was destined to be coupled with some maiden still in the schoolroom. He shied away from the idea . . . Perhaps his mother had been more forthright than Catherine, more prepared to reveal her feelings. But she had not had a career . . . Clearly his mother felt that Catherine might not be the most suitable of daughters-in-law. But she was concerned with the perpetuation of the line. To her, his marriage to someone who might decline to have children, would be a family disaster. He sighed. It would be easy if they all lived in Bragg's bucolic bliss, if the slightest indiscretion did not compromise a woman's whole life . . . On the other hand, Catherine would still have her career to fall back on . . .

'I have been thinking about our friend Alexander,' Bragg remarked, knocking out his pipe. 'He tried to sound surprised, when we told him Pease was dead, but it didn't really ring true. And he showed us the door pretty smartly, once we started to probe. But it doesn't take us all the way. After all, if you knew you were suspected in connection with a similar death, you would make yourself scarce too, I reckon.'

Morton roused himself. 'I wonder if he really did have the parliamentary candidacy in the bag. His remark about the matter's being still confidential could be a ploy to keep us from enquiring further.'

'You mean that, having knocked off Pease, he was certain he would be nominated?'

'It is possible. Another thing has struck me. By leaving the ss *Rome* at Marseilles, he could have got back to London in time to send the anonymous letter to the *Echo*.'

'You still think the tea business is connected with the deaths?' Bragg asked indulgently.

'Even constables can conjecture!'

'We will have to get you a job as master of ceremonies at a music hall!'

'If you are convinced that Pease's death was similar to those of Jardine and Hewitt, sir, why are you continuing to hold Volkes? He could hardly have murdered Pease from his prison cell.'

'You should never get so set on one theory, that you ignore other possibilities, lad. It is tidy to think that one person must be behind them all, but it is not the only answer.'

'A conspiracy? That must be the alternative, if so unusual a poison is the common factor.'

'Maybe. Anyway, Volkes is much too footloose to release, until we have nailed our man.'

'Are you ruling out a woman?' Morton asked with a grin. 'What about the luscious Jane Morell? Can we afford to disregard her? You did suggest that Pease might have been yet another of her supporters!'

'Stranger things have happened! But she was not on the guest-list for the Guildhall do.'

'I know of at least one other person, not invited, who was nevertheless there.'

'Who might that be?'

'A man called Fowler.'

'Fowler?' Bragg repeated.

'At one time, I thought he might be a suspect. Do you remember the entry in Hewitt's diary, regarding an appointment with "Painter"? Well, it was for Fowler – he paints murals.'

Bragg looked up quizzically. 'Mrs Hewitt certainly said they were going to have one at their new house.'

'There was a letter among Hewitt's papers, from Fowler's mistress, confirming the appointment. I happen to know her.'

'There was no letter in the papers I saw,' Bragg said brusquely, 'and I have been through them enough times.'

'There would not be. I took it to the young lady in question and . . .'

'Who is she?' Bragg interrupted curtly.

'Miss Louisa Sommers . . . She confirmed the appointment, though she did not know if he had, in fact, attended. However, I could not see Fowler as our man.'

'You couldn't see . . .?' Bragg said harshly. 'Have you gone soft in the head? . . . When you knew bloody well that Fowler was at the Guildhall! That makes him connected with two of the deaths, even in your book! Christ Almighty! Are you stupid? Or is it that one of your acquaintances could not possibly be connected with anything as vulgar as murder?'

'That is totally unfair!' Morton said hotly. 'You are acting on the so far unwarranted assumption that Pease was another murder in the chain. Furthermore, it is very likely that Fowler did not go to see Hewitt – there were no jottings of the meeting, as there were in Volkes's case.'

'That doesn't matter a toss,' Bragg said angrily. 'You are working with me. And while you do, I have to know everything you discover, every thought in your head. A good policeman will suspect his own grandmother if there is a trace of evidence! The trouble with you, lad, is that you've got too much education and very little experience. When you have got twenty years in, you can start to make decisions about who is a likely villain.'

Morton stared back angrily.

'It may interest you to know,' Bragg said censoriously, 'that Fowler was painting a mural at the Saddlers' Hall, when Jardine was murdered.'

'I am sorry, sir, for being so presumptuous as to draw an inference,' Morton said sarcastically. 'However, if you had told me that, I am sure I would have acted differently.'

Bragg glared at him belligerently, then: 'I accept your apology,' he said curtly.

They relapsed into a furious silence, which lasted for the rest of the journey. Even when they arrived at Chelmsford station, their exchanges were merely concerned with finding transport to Brandon House. When they were at last on its doorstep, Bragg cleared his throat.

'Don't forget, we are his old friends,' he murmured.

The maid opened the door before Morton could reply, and took them down to the morning-room, where Mrs Hewitt was waiting for them. She rose and held out her hand to Bragg.

'I got your telegraph,' she said in her bright clipped voice. 'Have you something new?'

'I am sorry to trouble you again, Mrs Hewitt,' Bragg said. His tone was low and unctuous. He sounded like an undertaker about to measure a corpse, thought Morton uncharitably. 'Have the Metropolitan police been in touch with you, ma'am?'

'No, sergeant. Why?'

'I am very much afraid that I have distressing news for you.'

'Nothing could be more distressing than to lose a husband,' she remarked with composure.

'No, ma'am. However, as you will appreciate, the coroner had to order a post-mortem to establish the cause of your husband's death. You will get the findings officially, in due course. But we heard them last night, and I thought it proper that I should tell you myself.'

She looked puzzled. 'Thank you, sergeant,' she said.

'It seems that your husband died from poison, ma'am; that, very probably, he was murdered.'

'Good heavens!' Her forehead creased in perplexity. 'Why should anyone wish to murder William?'

'That is what I wanted to ask you, Mrs Hewitt. Had he any enemies that you know of?'

She gave a strangled snort of a laugh. 'I would have thought that William was far too cautious to have incurred so deep an enmity . . . No. I can confidently say that there were none, so far as his private life is concerned.'

'And his work?'

Her face took on a defiant cast. 'No man can rise in his chosen career,' she said, 'without incurring the jealousy and hostility of disappointed rivals.'

'Have you anyone specific in mind?' Bragg asked earnestly.

'There was one man, John Ward, a senior administrator in Delhi. He was considered a serious contender for my husband's present – I mean, last post. When the succession was being considered, Ward was called home to London with his family. His wife and children went to visit relatives while he stayed in a hotel. It later emerged that, in the three weeks he was in England, he had been consorting with a prostitute from Hampstead – had actually had the creature staying with him at the Metropole, would you believe! His wife is a foolish self-righteous creature. She must have heard the rumour and, no doubt, confronted him with it. However that may be, she promptly sued him for divorce – so it must have been true. Naturally enough, he was passed over. Then his supporters began to whisper that my husband had put the story about. It was utterly absurd, but it made him quite unhappy for a time.'

'I am sure it did,' Bragg said sympathetically. 'And what happened to this John Ward?'

'He went back, alone, to his old job in India, where these

things are tolerated. So far as I know, he has remained there.'

'I see . . . Well, we'll look into it. In the meantime, I wonder if you can tell us any more about that voyage back from India. You said there was a running battle between Jardine and Alexander . . .'

'So William said.'

'And, also, that Alexander had quarrelled with Arthur Pease.'

'Yes. My husband felt that it was inevitable, considering Pease's bombshell.'

'Bombshell?'

'Since the Commission had two Indian members who were reluctant to spend more time in England, it was decided to have the final meeting in Bombay, to discuss the main thrust of the report. Henry Wilson, the radical Member of Parliament, had made it plain from the outset that he would be writing a dissenting report; and it was confidently expected that Pease would join him. However, after hearing a lengthy review of the evidence, and, indeed, only minutes before they were due to embark, Pease changed sides. He said that he had been impressed with the vigorous and manly bearing of many of the natives who gave evidence. Some of them were eighty years old; all of them had been taking opium since childhood. He was, therefore, no longer able to accept the basic tenets of the Society for the Suppression of the Opium Trade's case – that moral and physical degeneration followed quickly and inevitably, once the opium habit is formed. He therefore proposed to sign the majority report.'

'What happened then?'

'Immediately the meeting was closed, all the Europeans hurried to the ship to embark. It was just before dinner, apparently. When the first-class passengers were having sherry before the meal, Alexander accosted Pease. They had a violent argument and Alexander went so far as to strike Pease. He had to be physically restrained by the others . . . They seem to have avoided each other thereafter.'

'You are certain that this happened before the ship sailed?'

'Oh yes. According to William, some of the military said that Alexander ought to be put ashore and made to come on the next boat.'

'Were there any other quarrels between them?'

'I gather not.'

'Not even in Marseilles?'

'No, though there was a curious incident in that port. The ship docked in the night. It so happened that Pease and my husband were on the same table. They had just sat down to breakfast, when Alexander approached them. He placed a telegraph form before Pease, allowed him to read it, then took it away again – and all without a word. According to William, Pease was stunned. I gather that Alexander left the ship there and hurried home by train.'

'Did your husband know what was in the telegraph?' Bragg asked.

'It was something to do with Alexander's having been chosen as a parliamentary candidate in preference to Pease. William said that Alexander's face had been a picture of vindictive triumph, as he watched Pease read it.'

When Bragg and Morton arrived at Golden Lane, Burney's assistant was sluicing the floor of the mortuary with a hosepipe. Bragg checked in the doorway.

'Is the boss in?' he asked.

The man nodded. 'You've set him a right royal conundrum, over that poison business,' he said. 'I haven't seen him so happy for years!'

They picked their way across the wet flagstones and knocked on the inner door. When they entered, Burney was stooping over a microscope on the bench by the window.

'Ah, sergeant!' He straightened up with a beaming smile. 'Thank you for sending me the latest mystery poisoning. If you keep up the supply, we may actually be able to identify the agent, in time!'

'No further forward, are you, sir?' asked Bragg gloomily.

'Scientific advance is often a matter of going round in a circle and taking the problem from the rear!'

'At any rate, Pease was murdered with the same poison?'

'Indubitably.'

'Can you tell us anything more about it?'

Burney smiled. 'A little, though I doubt if it will give you any pleasure.'

'Try me.'

'It is clear that we are dealing with a very toxic substance. As I said in my preliminary report, it acts on the central nervous system, leading to muscular paralysis and rapid death. We have now established that its effectiveness varies in proportion to the quantity used.'

'You mean a big dose would kill quicker?'

'Precisely. Though we are speaking of relatively small amounts of the poison.'

'So, somebody who knew what he was doing, could kill one person with a small dose, another with a larger one; and because of the time difference, he would not be obviously connected.'

'I presume so.'

'We have suspects, of course. But, for some of them, the poison would have to have been given hours before.'

'I see.' Burney's eyes gleamed with pleasure. 'Tell me, when death occurred, did it follow precisely the same pattern in each case?'

'How do you mean?'

'An apparently hale and hearty man, suffering a sudden physical collapse followed quickly by death.'

'We can't really say for Hewitt. But he was found sitting peacefully in his chair, if that is any indication. Certainly, that was the case for Jardine and Pease.'

'Interesting . . . interesting,' Burney murmured.

'You can see my problem, sir,' Bragg said irritably. 'Until we know how long this stuff takes to work, we can't safely eliminate any suspects.'

'Yes, I can see that, sergeant. Indeed, you could find yourself considering a whole new range of possible murderers.'

'God forbid!'

'Well, sergeant, it is dangerous to draw inferences from incomplete data, and I must therefore warn you against relying unduly upon it; but I can tell you that, in the laboratory, a relatively minute dose caused physical collapse in a rat in less

173

than half a minute.'

'Hmn . . . That's more like the Jardine and Pease pattern.'

'However, it does not necessarily follow that those results could be duplicated on a large mammal, such as a human being . . . I have often thought that condemned murderers ought to be given the opportunity of bequeathing, as it were, their living bodies for the advancement of science.' Burney's slack grin became positively gruesome. 'It would be infinitely preferable to the grisly business of hanging.'

'Would the poison be likely to have any particular physical characteristics?' Morton asked.

'Inevitably, it would have particular physical characteristics, my boy.'

'Sorry! I am not expressing myself very clearly. Let us suppose, as is possible, that this poison has been prepared by someone who is not a qualified chemist. You said that it is a vegetable alkaloid. Would it, for instance, have the colour of the plant from which it was taken, or be sticky like sap?'

Burney furrowed his brow. 'I suppose that if it were so prepared, there might be some residual coloration; but I am firmly of the view that it would be in the form of a free-flowing liquid.'

'As you realise, all of the cases you have dealt with have had a common factor. The victim had taken red wine before he died.'

'Very little, in the case of Jardine and Pease,' Burney commented.

'True, and one has to say that Hewitt drank his wine over an hour before he died. Nevertheless, we have our tentative theory that the poison, as prepared by the murderer, might have a noticeable colour, which has been concealed by adding it to red wine.'

'It is a perfectly tenable theory,' Burney said. 'All I can tell you is, that the poison would be soluble in water or alcohol. Prepared in the laboratory, it would be colourless.'

'That doesn't get us a lot further,' Bragg said gloomily.

'I am sorry, sergeant. I am afraid that we are waiting for you to catch your murderer before we can put the final pieces of the jig-saw together.'

Bragg left the mortuary in a state of exasperation. Three people murdered – two of them on his own patch – and no nearer putting together a case that would stick. Only circumstantial evidence, that a decent defence lawyer would tear into tatters.

'After our conversation this morning,' Morton said diffidently, 'there is something that I should tell you.'

'Eh? . . . What's that?' asked Bragg, roused from his reverie.

'That remark of Professor Burney's assistant stirred a chord in my mind.'

'What remark was that?'

'About your having set them a right royal conundrum . . . It is strange how selective the mind can be.'

'Come on, out with it!' Bragg said testily.

'You remember how Sir Polydor de Keyser had his hotel in building for an age, before naming it. So much so, that everyone, including me, still thinks of it as the de Keyser, rather than the Royal.'

'Well?'

'Fowler's mistress made an odd remark, last night. We were by Fowler's bed, watching him die.'

'Die?' Bragg interrupted. 'What from?'

'An opium overdose – he died last night.'

'Did he now? . . . Well, go on.'

'Miss Sommers said that the people who stay at the Royal ought to be sitting there with us. I took no notice at the time. But it suddenly strikes me that she may be the woman who went to see Jardine, the day before he died.'

'Isn't that a bit far-fetched?'

'At first glance, perhaps. But she was insistent that Fowler could be weaned from opium, until almost the end. Then she suddenly seemed to give up hope. She began to act very strangely, as if she was in a prolonged state of excitement . . . She has been making Fowler's laudanum for months. So she is not unacquainted with preparing potions. It is possible that she could have brewed the poison in some way. You remember the chambermaid saying that Jardine had tea sent up, when the young lady called?'

'Yes.'

'If it was Louisa, she could have put some poison in his tea.'

'A very small amount, that took the best part of twenty hours to work?' Bragg said sceptically.

'Let us accept the hypothesis, for the moment. If we do, there is also the connection with Hewitt that I mentioned. It is my belief that Fowler did not keep the appointment that night. But suppose that Louisa Sommers went, in his stead? If she managed to give him a large dose, he could have died almost immediately.'

'Hmn . . . and how is she tied in with Pease?'

'Pure conjecture, I must confess. But if Fowler was in the Guildhall, why not his mistress, also.'

'And what about motive? One can see that, with her fancy man bent on destroying himself with opium, she might feel murderous towards those who peddle it – so I will give you Jardine. What about the others?'

'Perhaps she went to Hewitt, not to discuss the mural, but to try to influence him over the Royal Commission report.'

'Then, when he wouldn't play, she slipped him the poison? It hardly sounds rational.'

'Whoever is committing these murders must be a lunatic.'

'And the motive for Pease?'

'I grant that this appears difficult. After all, his reputation here is firmly anti-opium. But suppose she had got wind of his change of heart? It cannot be a close secret. The members of the society's committee must have been told about it; and I am sure they will not have been able to keep it from their colleagues and friends.'

Bragg pondered awhile in silence. 'All right, lad,' he said finally. 'We could just about make out a case for a warrant. And we owe it to the opium traders still living, to err on the side of caution. Do you know where she is?'

'At her parents' home in Kent.'

'Well, since you are bent on becoming a proper policeman, you can telegraph the Kent police and ask them to pick her up . . . Now, see if you can find a cab, will you?'

When Bragg and Morton arrived at Serjeants' Inn, they found

that Alexander was in conference. They sat listening to clients conversing in hushed tones, noting the reverential way in which solicitors responded to even the clerk of the chambers. Eventually, Alexander's clients departed, and they were shown to his room.

'What on earth do you want now?' he asked, glancing up from his papers.

'I want to tidy up a few loose ends, sir,' Bragg said evenly.

Alexander laid down his pencil and swivelled his chair to face them.

'Very well,' he said, 'but I am very busy.'

'It won't take long . . . You said you are going to be a candidate for a Midlands constituency. Which is that?'

'Nottingham,' Alexander said sharply. 'What on earth has that got to do with anything?'

'And Mr Pease had set his heart on the same thing?'

'I imagine so. One does not put oneself forward for Parliament lightly.'

'So it was not surprising that he was upset, when he heard that you had been preferred to him?'

'Nevertheless, as I think I told you, I had not expected such an extreme reaction.'

'The trouble is, the people we have spoken to only remember that you struck him.'

Alexander shrugged. 'I may have pushed him. The exchange became heated on both sides.'

'What I cannot understand, sir, is why you should have become so incensed, when you had triumphed over Pease.'

'That is hardly a term I would use, sergeant.'

'No, I suppose not . . . Then again, we are told that it all happened in Bombay harbour, before the ship sailed.'

'Then your informant has a faulty recollection,' Alexander said frostily. 'What could possibly have precipitated a quarrel there?'

'I think I can answer that for you, sir. Our informants put it down to Mr Pease's change of sides, over the opium question.'

Alexander snorted derisively. 'There was nothing unexpected in that. It had been evident for weeks that he was wavering. Henry Wilson had barely spoken to him since they left for

India, for that very reason. Ask him!'

'So, it was no great matter?'

'No. It was clear, by then, that the final report would come down on the side of the opium interests.'

'I see,' said Bragg in puzzlement. 'We were told that you had a real up-and-downer when you heard – with him being on the council of the society.'

'No sergeant. It was not for me, as secretary of the society, to take action. That was left for the council itself.'

'Ah . . . Who initiated the action?'

'I did. It was my plain duty.'

'As secretary?'

'Of course.'

'And what did the society think about it?'

'At the committee meeting I told you of, it was unanimously resolved that Pease should be expelled from the society. I have no doubt that the decision would have been ratified by the whole council.'

'That would be the committee meeting Sir Joseph Pease attended. I wonder why he did not mention it.'

'I would think that he was too ashamed of his brother's conduct.'

'Hmn . . . Still, expulsion was a bit extreme, wasn't it?'

Alexander smiled superciliously. 'Is it not Shakespeare who speaks of cutting cankers from the flesh?' he asked.

'It seems that you had a brisk exchange of views with Mr Hewitt, too,' Bragg said mildly.

'On more than one occasion!'

'Yes . . . the last one at the Orleans Club.'

Alexander's head jerked up, startled.

'May I ask what that was about?' said Bragg.

'I was trying to persuade him to forgo his personal advancement and be, at the very least, objective in his preliminary draft of the report.'

'And what was his reaction to that?'

'He pretended to be outraged that I should even consider him capable of partiality.'

'I see. So you had this quarrel over the dinner table and, a little more than an hour later, he was dead.'

Alexander was silent, tense.

'He didn't die as quickly as Jardine, though, did he?'

'What are you suggesting?' Alexander asked menacingly.

'Well now, sir, we are informed by the offices of both coroners involved, that Jardine and Hewitt were murdered – killed by the same poison. Somebody must have given it to them. At the very least, we could say it was interesting that you had been drinking with each of them, shortly before his death.'

'I had nothing to do with their deaths!' cried Alexander, suddenly shrill.

'On top of that, we now know that Mr Pease was murdered in the same way . . . and that you lied about being at the Guildhall, yesterday lunchtime.'

'I swear that I was not there!'

'No doubt you do, sir. But we have people who saw you there, and are prepared to swear to that, as well. John George Alexander, I have here a warrant for your arrest for wilful murder . . . I am sure that the other tenants of these chambers would prefere you to come quietly.'

11

'Ah, there you are, Bragg!' Inspector Cotton came striding across the Guildhall courtyard.

'Good morning, sir,' Bragg said dutifully.

'When is Alexander up?'

'His name is not on the list, sir.'

'Then they will be slipping him in first – they often do that, when the defendant is someone important.'

'I see, sir.'

Cotton was bursting with exhilaration. He was like a schoolboy going on his first train trip, Bragg thought; scarcely able to keep still, for the excitement bubbling inside him.

'Come on, Bragg. Let us see if we can hurry them up. I have a meeting at eleven.'

They pushed their way into the justice room. The place was stuffed, as usual, with drunks and vagrants, petty thieves, carriers accused of obstructing the highway. Cotton wrinkled up his nose.

'Let's hope we are not kept long with this stinking lot,' he said. 'You know, Bragg, this is going to be something of a *cause célèbre*. The newspapers will make a meal of it, I shouldn't wonder. And quite right too. It will show ordinary people that the police are not under the thumb of the well-off; that even influential people get nicked, if they step out of line.'

'Yes, sir.'

'I don't mind telling you, I am looking forward to this hearing. I knew all the time it had to be Alexander. I told you so, right from the business in the Saddlers' Hall. Opportunity, motive and means, Bragg, and he had them all. I can't think why you buggered about so much; you might have saved a life, if you had been more decisive.'

'I thought you were against linking Alexander with Hewitt's death,' Bragg said mildly.

'Nonsense! I was concerned with the administrative problems arising from our investigating in the Met area. We had a bit of trouble, as you know, but I was able to fight them off . . . Anyway, cheer up! Mistakes are made all the time. You have to shrug them off and get on with the job.'

'Yes, sir.'

'It's a good thing I have had plenty of experience of court proceedings, Bragg. It isn't often you get a barrister in the dock. He is likely to be a tricky customer – that is, if he has any fight left, after a night in the cells at St Bride's! . . . No, I have done my homework, this case is going to be real copy-book stuff . . . What's going on? They are calling the first case! Are you sure we are not on the list?'

'Quite sure, sir.'

Cotton plunged into the mêlée and grabbed an usher by the sleeve of his gown.

'When is the Alexander case coming up?' he asked.

'It's been transferred to the Mansion House, sir.'

'But it can't have been! I was told last night that it was down for the Guildhall.'

'It was, but it isn't any more. The defendant's side asked for a transfer.'

'When will it be heard there?'

'Dunno – first thing, I expect.'

'Christ!' Cotton battled his way to the door and sprinted down the street. When Bragg came up with him, he was red-faced and panting.

'Good thing you organised these early-morning runs, sir,' Bragg said cheerfully. 'We might be out of breath otherwise, by the time we got to the Mansion House.'

'To hell with running!' Cotton gasped. 'Stop that cab.'

'But it's no more than a quarter of a mile.'

'Stop the cab!'

Cotton had barely recovered his breath by the time they arrived at their destination. In the wide passage leading to the Lord Mayor's court there was a throng similar to the one they had left at the Guildhall. Bragg noticed, however, a group of three sober-suited men by a window. They stood aloof from the general hubbub, conversing quietly.

Cotton went over to an usher. 'When is the Alexander case down for?' he asked.

'Ah, Inspector Cotton! We were waiting for you to arrive. I will tell the clerk you are here.'

He disappeared, then shortly afterwards returned and bawled: 'The case of John George Alexander'.

Cotton strode purposefully through the door, and took up his position on the right of the dais. Following him, Bragg saw the group by the window turn and begin to drift after them. There was a murmured exchange with the usher, then they went to sit on the benches in the well of the court.

Cotton smiled confidently. 'As I thought, he has his pals here – but I can deal with them, you see if I can't!'

The court rose as the Lord Mayor came in with full ceremony. He peered at the list before him, then had a whispered conversation with his clerk. A look of surprise and perturbation crossed his face. Then he nodded his head and, moments after, Alexander was brought in. He was unshaven and dishevelled, his eyes were red-rimmed from lack of sleep and he stumbled as he went up the steps of the dock.

Cotton grinned fiercely. 'Every inch a guilty man,' he whispered. 'I wish it was the proper hearing today, instead of just bail.'

One of the well-dressed men had risen. He was stocky and clean-shaven, with grizzled hair. He spoke in deep, measured tones.

'My Lord Mayor, may I have your permission to address the court?'

The Lord Mayor looked startled, and held another consultation with his clerk. Then he turned to the man.

'You may,' he said. 'But please be brief, we have a very full list, this morning.'

The man inclined his head in acknowledgement. 'I am Judge Hodgson, of the Queen's Bench division of the High Court. Mr Alexander is a member of my chambers. This gentleman is Sir Walter Pennington QC and, behind us, is Mr John Stephens, of counsel. They will be conducting his defence if the matter proceeds. However, my Lord Mayor, I would submit to you that this prosecution is totally misconceived; that to allow it to continue would be to besmirch the high juridical distinction that the City of London has preserved through the centuries.'

The Lord Mayor shifted uneasily, and licked his lips.

'This is a purely formal hearing, judge,' he said nervously. 'I am not at all sure that it is proper for me to consider your remarks, at this stage.'

'My Lord Mayor,' Hodgson went on emphatically, 'there are cases which are out of the general run, in which judicial discretion can, and should be exercised. This is such a one. Mr Alexander is a man of the highest reputation and integrity. His whole future could be irreparably damaged by a slavish adherence to procedures evolved to cope with a very different class of situation.'

Bragg could feel Cotton moving restlessly beside him, as the Lord Mayor once again turned to the clerk. Then he looked up.

'I have to point out, judge,' he said diffidently, 'that Mr Alexander has been charged with three counts of murder.'

'I do so believe. But the question is, should he have been so charged? You would no doubt agree that it would be a gross misuse of the judicial system, for a man to be accused of a crime, and subjected to the full processes of the law, without there being any evidence to support the charge . . . any evidence at all. Has an information been prepared?'

'I . . . I would not expect it to have been done at this stage,' the Lord Mayor said hesitantly.

Cotton sprang to his feet, eager for battle. 'I have a draft of it here, sir,' he said, pulling a fold of papers from his inside pocket.

Hodgson crossed over and took them. He looked rapidly through the sheets.

'As I suspected,' he said caustically. 'It is a mere assemblage of circumstantial evidence, and none of it is directed to the actual commission of the felonies charged against Mr Alexander. There are assertions that witnesses saw him in particular places and references to testimony in description of his actions at particular times. There is no direct evidence that he

committed the crimes charged.' He waved the papers scornfully. 'All this is pure inference by the police. It is clear to me, that
they have selected Mr Alexander as a convenient scapegoat, so
that they can clear their files. As a brother judge, I would
advise you that it would be most unsafe to proceed.'

The Lord Mayor glanced unhappily towards his clerk, but he
was busy looking up a point in a legal tome.

'Before considering your remarks, judge,' he said, 'I feel that
I ought to hear what the police have to say.'

Cotton bounced up again. 'Your honour', he said querulous-
ly, 'evidence will be given that three men – three distinguished
men – all died of poison. A poison hitherto unknown in this
country. It seems possible that the poison was administered to
them in red wine. The crown's witnesses will show that Mr
Alexander actually handed a cup of wine to the first, drank
wine with the second, and was at a reception where the third
drank red wine. We will also be putting forward evidence to
show that he had motive for carrying out each murder.'

Cotton resumed his seat.

The clerk had evidently found the paragraph he sought, and
whispered urgently to the Lord Mayor. Then the latter cleared
his throat.

'In view of what Inspector Cotton has said,' he began timidly,
'I feel that I have no alternative but to allow the matter to
proceed. After all,' he added lamely, 'it is only a bail hearing.'

Hodgson sat down gravely, then Pennington rose beside him.

'You honour,' he began quietly, 'I would not wish to add to
the appraisal of the character of my client just given by his
honour Judge Hodgson; except to point out that he is a
distinguished member of the bar, and has an enviable reputation as a humanitarian. I am sure that he will not be unknown to
you, as the Secretary of the Society for the Suppression of the
Opium Trade. It would be unthinkable for such a man of
standing, not to present himself for trial at the time appointed.
Further, let me say that if he were incarcerated without good
cause, then his charitable work would be hindered. In a very
real sense, the poor and destitute would be made to suffer for
the vagaries of our legal system. His position has inevitably
been damaged already by his arrest and appearance here. It

would be tragic if he were to be utterly ruined by being held in custody pending an unsustainable prosecution. Your honour, my client intends to plead not guilty to these charges, and will vigorously defend himself against any allegations. In all the circumstances, I ask that he be given bail.'

Judge Hodgson jumped up. 'My Lord Mayor,' he said, 'I will personally vouch for his appearance at the further hearings of these charges.'

The Lord Mayor turned towards Cotton.

'When will you be ready to proceed to the committal stage?' he asked.

'In a fortnight, sir,' Cotton said crisply.

'Very well. The accused is granted bail, in his own recognisance of two hundred pounds. Next case . . .'

When Bragg got back to Old Jewry, he found Morton sorting through the contents of Jardine's trunks, which were now piled in the corner of the room.

'Were you successful?' Morton asked.

Bragg laughed. 'It was a bit of a caper, really. Old Cotton was out to pinch all the credit, as usual; but this time things didn't go smoothly for him. The other side turned up with a high court judge and a couple of barristers, to try and get Alexander off the hook. Asked that the whole case should be dismissed, would you believe it? Before it had even got started! The Inspector had a few uncomfortable moments, I can tell you. Still, he did what was needed – though they ended up giving Alexander bail . . . In a murder case! I ask you!'

There was a rap on the door and the Commissioner came in.

'Ah, Bragg,' he said, 'I heard from Inspector Cotton, very much in passing, that Alexander was remanded on bail. It seems rather trusting, in the circumstances.'

'The other side brought up their big guns, sir. Half the judiciary seemed to be there, trying to get him released.'

Sir William gave his foxy smile. 'It sounded as if the Inspector routed them easily enough,' he said.

'Yes, sir,' Bragg replied stolidly.

'Bragg, I seem to have got myself into a great deal of trouble.

On top of our difficulties with the tea merchants, I now have the wine trade round my neck. I really ought to have been more circumspect at the Guildhall – though I was clearly expected to take some kind of decisive action . . .' He sighed. 'Now the vintners are demanding clarification of the position. They say that no one is buying red wine any more. They are talking of a permanent loss of trade, and demanding prompt action to head it off.'

'What kind of action do they want, sir?'

'They seem to be asking for a full statement to be published, setting out the facts which led to my advising people not to touch the red wine.'

'But you can't do that, sir!' Bragg exclaimed. 'For a start, the facts are nowhere near established. Beyond that, if the newspapers got hold of the story, they would make such a meal of it that you would not be able to put together an unbiased jury out of the whole kingdom!'

Sir William sighed. 'Then, what am I to do?'

Bragg pondered. 'If I were you, sir, I would issue a holding statement,' he said gravely.

'What would I put in it?'

'I would tell them to go away and hold their pieces!'

Morton laughed, and the Commissioner coughed in embarrassment.

'I wonder, sir,' Bragg said quickly, 'if you can give me a more considered idea of the timings involved in Pease's murder.'

'Timings? Why?'

'You will have to be accurate, when you come to give evidence, sir. Best to clarify it, while it is still fresh in your mind.'

Sir William looked startled. 'I had not thought that I would be called as a witness,' he said.

'I would think that it is inevitable.'

'What would they need to know from me?'

'The length of time between Pease's taking the wine and collapsing, principally.'

'I have been thinking about that, as you can imagine . . . I first noticed him walking away from the door, as if he had just entered the room. He made his way towards the line of notables

– he was in my sight all the time, because I was facing that way. When he had shaken the various hands, he was approached by Miss Marsden. I saw him raise both hands in mock supplication, so he had no glass at that moment. Then he took the glass from the tray, as I mentioned before.'

'A single glass on a tray, carried by a waitress you would not recognise again?'

'It sounds rather feeble, for someone in my position,' the Commissioner said sadly. 'But, dammit all, I have not been trained for police work, and I make no secret of it. If someone drove me over a stretch of countryside, my mind would unconsciously assess what it would be like to fight over. But faces . . . I have no skills in recalling them.'

'So, Pease got his glass of wine. What happened then?'

'He started to come towards my group. I presume that he had already recognised Thomas Ashley, who was standing opposite me.'

'Did he have a drink on the way?'

'I doubt it very much, in that crush . . . When he joined us, he greeted Ashley, lifted his glass in salute to him, and drank. At that point, I turned to catch something my neighbour was saying. The next moment, I heard the crash as Pease fell.'

'What then?'

'George Rylands, the padre chap, rushed up and tried to give him aid, or comfort or whatever. But I think he was already too far gone. Only moments later, the doctor examined him and pronounced him dead . . . Then I had my rush of blood and brought down the wrath of the vintners on my head!'

There was an uncomfortable pause, then Morton crossed over to his desk.

'I discovered a mildly surprising thing about Rylands last night,' he said. 'I was going through Hewitt's papers, yet again,' he shot a grin at Bragg, 'when I found this *London City Mission Magazine*. I know Rylands said that he helped out in the East End, but I did not expect to find him as its editor.'

He opened the front cover. 'Look, his name has been circled in pencil, and "eighteenth March", followed by a question mark, written beside it.'

'Is that Hewitt's writing?' Bragg asked.

'It is difficult to be certain, from such a small sample,' Morton said, 'but it could well be.'

'Hmn,' Bragg grunted. 'I think we might stroll up to the vicarage before lunch. You never know, he may know something new . . . Will that be all, sir?'

'Yes, Bragg . . . yes. Thank you for your advice about the vintners. I will try to formulate an acceptable way to follow it!' He smiled and went out.

As they walked along the sunlit street, Bragg felt the onset of a kind of contentment. It had been an untidy, dirty sort of case, and its conclusion was all of a piece with the rest. You could not take any real satisfaction from it, though Cotton seemed content enough. Perhaps it was too much, to expect a clean ending to such a tortuous affair . . . The Commissioner still hadn't managed to tie the China tea case in with it – if that was what he'd wanted! Now he had more pressing things to contend with. The vintners were well up in the hierarchy of livery companies; they carried a lot of political weight in the City. If Sir William didn't placate them, they would be howling for his blood! . . . That would be a pity. He was no great shakes as a policeman, true enough; and he would insist on by-passing his senior officers, to hob-nob with the lower ranks. But Bragg himself had cause to be grateful for that. If there were a new Commissioner, his special position would be ended smartly. He would find himself back under Cotton's operational control, instead of merely reporting through him. Cotton would grind him into the dirt . . . But there were other things in life besides chasing villains. Every day of sunshine, and Dorset beckoned more insistently.

'By the way,' he said with a smile, 'I gather from the desk-sergeant, that someone vandalised the new mural at the Saddlers' Hall, on Wednesday. Daubed paint all over it. Completely ruined, I gather.'

'Fowler?'

'I expect so. He didn't seem too happy with it!'

'I suppose we might call first at the church,' Morton remarked, 'since we are here.'

'Right.'

Bragg tried to shake himself out of his lethargy. It was

tedious work, clearing up the loose ends of a case, but someone had to do it – and that someone was him. They went through the west door, into the church. It was in opulent repose, its gilding glowing richly in the strong light. As they walked up the aisle, they could see the figure of Rylands, in his cassock, kneeling at the altar rail. Apart from them, the church was empty, quiet. Not even the clatter of horses' hooves, from the road outside, penetrated its stillness. They stood at the chancel steps, while Rylands finished his devotions. After a few moments he rose to his feet, nodded companionably to the altar, then turned towards them.

'Ah! Sergeant Bragg,' he said cheerfully. 'I was not aware that you were here. How nice to see you again!' He came down the chancel and joined them.

'We were lucky to catch you, sir. I didn't realise that you were so tied up with the East End.'

'How do you mean, sergeant?'

Bragg produced the magazine from his pocket. 'I didn't know you were editor of this, sir. It must take a lot of your time.'

'I suppose it does. But then, one's ministry cannot be confined by parish boundaries. The poverty and deprivation is in the East End; the wealth to alleviate it is here. I try to be a bridge between the two.'

'We got this copy from the office of William Hewitt, in St James's.'

'Ah, yes. Poor man.'

'You knew him, then?'

'I made it my business to know him, sergeant.'

'I would not have thought he was rich, sir.'

'Perhaps not rich . . . affluent, certainly. But he was clearly a coming man in the India Office. I cultivated him because he seemed destined to rise to a position of power and influence in the nation.' He fumbled in his cassock pocket and brought out a small silver box. 'Have a lozenge,' he said with a smile. 'Ah! I see that, like many other philanthropists, I am only giving away what I can well do without. My passion is for the yellow, and I see there is only one!' He took the lozenge and popped it into his mouth, then offered the box to Morton.

'Thank you, sir.' Morton put out his hand, then, suddenly,

the box was smashed from Rylands's grasp, its contents scattering over the floor. Rylands jumped back and Bragg flung himself on him, knocking him to the floor. There was a savage struggle, Morton looking on in stupefaction. Bragg was trying to hold Rylands's arms, twisting them behind his back. Morton felt in his pocket for his handcuffs. Then, Rylands gave a violent squirm and managed to get one of the lozenges into his mouth. He went still. Bragg turned him over, propped him up against the chancel steps and released his grip.

'Find every one of those lozenges, lad,' Bragg ordered peremptorily, 'and get them back in the box – every last one!'

He turned to Rylands. 'How long have you got?' he asked quietly.

Rylands smiled. 'Ten to fifteen minutes,' he said.

'What poison is it?'

'It is made from an eastern plant – of the *strophanthus* family.'

'Where is the rest?'

'In a phial at the back of my handkerchief drawer, where my housekeeper will never look!'

'Did you always administer it by way of these lozenges?'

'Yes. There have been only three occasions.' There was a curious note of satisfaction in his tone, almost of exultation.

'Jardine?' asked Bragg.

'Yes. I gave it to him when we talked briefly in the waiting room.'

'Hewitt?'

'He took one when I called at his office.'

'Pease?'

'In the doorway as he came in . . . That was a pity. He had been a fine man . . . but he was flawed.'

'It was the opium business, was it?' Bragg asked.

'Yes . . . I have had personal experience of it. Do you realise that there are over twelve million opium addicts in China alone.'

'But why you?'

'I have told you. In my younger days I was a missionary – until I, too, became addicted to opium. I have experienced the overwhelming longing for it, the brief excitement, the torment

190

and terrors that follow. I have endured the degradation, the sense of helplessness and hopelessness . . . I too have been an outcast.'

He paused, and the silence of the church enfolded them. Then he began again, speaking more rapidly, in a matter-of-fact tone.

'Thanks to God's good grace,' he said, 'I threw off the shackles of opium and clawed my way back to health. I obtained the chaplaincy in Hong Kong, spending much of my time trying to help addicts among the Chinese population. The plight of these people is desperate beyond belief – and our merchants grow prosperous at their expense. Their destitution made such an impression on me, that I began to realise my own agonies had been predestined; that without my personal Gethsemane, I would never have understood the depths of their despair. But my frail body was not equal to the enormity of the task, so I had to take my discharge and return to Britain. When I arrived here, I found myself in the midst of a gentlemanly debate about opium. Some people proffering the view that it was really rather bad for the natives; others countering by saying perhaps that was true, but it was not so bad that we need interfere. So they talked airily, about this diabolical instrument of hell! . . . Then I felt God calling me to act – to make it apparent that His wrath would fall on the heads of the ruthless and greedy.' He smiled. 'I seem to have been guided aright in my selection.'

'Would you have gone on?' Bragg asked.

'Oh yes. Mowbray, Fanshawe, the Sassoons . . .'

'Did you send the anonymous letter to the *Echo*? About the tea being poisoned?'

Rylands smiled. 'Yes. It seemed a good idea, until I realised that sterner measures were required of me . . . Now, sergeant, if you would indulge me, I would like to spend some moments in prayer . . . I am about to go to my glory.'

He got up painfully, and walked to the altar rail. He stood looking at the crucifix for a time, then knelt down and bowed his head over his hands. Moments later, they saw his body slump sideways to the floor.

12

'So it was a case of an upright, honourable man, who decided that his convictions put him above the law?' Catherine remarked.

She was sitting with Morton in the drawing-room of her parents' house, the door left open by Mrs Marsden, as a gesture to propriety.

'I do think you are the limit, James!' Catherine exclaimed. 'You knew all this yesterday afternoon. If you had given me the story then, I could have written something for our Saturday edition . . . Though I cannot see Mr Tranter wanting to print a story about a homicidal City clergyman!'

'You could still get copy to the *Star*,' Morton said with a smile.

'Only for the Monday edition. It will be old news then.'

'Perhaps you could pursue the Alexander side of it. He would welcome every opportunity to publicise his innocence and his outrage. When we told him, last night, that we were dropping the charges, he was fuming. Sergeant Bragg was quite aggrieved. After all, he had spent only one night in the cells – and we had proved his innocence!'

'Poor Alexander!'

'Even poorer Volkes! It was only this morning that we remembered he was still locked up. He is being set free at this very moment.'

'I suppose we should be pleased that justice has been done,' Catherine said meditatively, 'even if it has not been seen to be done. Nevertheless, I would be sorry if anyone felt that the grossly improper pressure on the Lord Mayor's court had anything to do with it.'

'Now, there is a subject for one of your crusading articles!'

'No. That is a phase of my life that somehow seems to have run its course . . . How did you discover that it was Rylands?'

'I can only say that it was a blinding flash of intuition on Bragg's part – and very grateful I am. He saved my life . . . I had developed a most astonishing obsession. Because of the coloration of the stomach contents, I was convinced that the poison must have been in the red wine. True, all of the victims had recently drunk red wine – though, in Hewitt's case, it had been a considerable time before his death. Instead of rejecting the wine hypothesis, because of this inconsistency, I even tried to invent people who might have called on Hewitt, just before he died.'

'Something must have triggered the sergeant's intuition,' Catherine said.

'According to him, it was the fact that we were offered a different box, coupled with Rylands's unexpected lack of politeness in taking his lozenge first. When he glimpsed that all the others in the box were red, it all clicked into place.'

Catherine put her hand on his arm. 'Thank goodness for that,' she said softly.

'This opium business seems to de-humanise everyone it touches,' Morton went on gloomily, 'whether they are pro or anti. At one stage, Sergeant Bragg seemed to be hell-bent on brutalising me because of it.'

'Surely not?'

'In my futile efforts to reason away the snag with Hewitt, I had proposed that Louisa might have called on him, in Fowler's place, and somehow given him the poison. Bragg listened to my ramblings, then, so that I could prove I am a proper policeman, ordered me to arrange for her arrest myself. It is hard to believe that, isn't it? Particularly as he knew that she is a friend of mine . . . Have you heard any news from Kent? I have not.'

Catherine looked at him mistrustfully. 'Louisa stayed with me, here, on Wednesday night,' she said in a low voice. 'I took her back to her parents' home on Thursday. Mrs Sommers is a rather silly woman, and she took it into her head to become distraught at Louisa's condition. She required from me an explanation as to why she looked so ill – after she had reduced her daughter to hysterical tears with the same demand. All this, after being content with seeing virtually nothing of her for three years!'

'It was what Louisa wanted,' Morton said gently.

'That is no excuse whatever!' Catherine retorted angrily. 'Would you abandon your daughter?'

Morton smiled. 'How you have deceived me!' he said. 'I thought you were a committed feminist, wanting nothing so much as to strike off the shackles from the shapely limbs of the modern woman.'

To his surprise, Catherine did not riposte. She looked probingly into his face, then dropped her eyes.

'Mrs Sommers finally decided that Louisa was seriously ill,' she went on, 'so she sent for the local doctor. As you would expect, he found nothing physically wrong, so he gave her a sedative for her nerves.' She paused.

'And?'

'He gave her ten ampoules of morphine, and a hypodermic syringe to inject them with.'

'Oh, no!' Morton exclaimed.

'On Friday morning, the maid found her sitting up in bed, clutching her portrait to her bosom.'

'Dead?'

'Yes . . . She had used all the morphine she had been given. Your policemen arrived, pat on cue, to create the most distressing scene I am ever likely to witness.'

'Dead! I cannot believe it,' Morton said dully. 'She was so vital! . . . Vulnerable too, I suppose. The stress must have been more than she could bear.'

'Don't talk rubbish!' Catherine flashed out angrily. 'Keep your patronising platitudes for some less fraught occasion. Louisa loved Fowler. She wanted him to die, because he had destroyed himself. But when he was gone, there was nothing left for her.'

'I do not mean to be patronising,' Morton said meekly. 'it is just that one normally takes life as an interesting, joyous . . . adventure, I suppose. Then something like this happens, and one does not seem to know where one is going, or why.'

'Are you asking me to hold your hand, like a lost child?'

Catherine said acidly.

'No . . . but I would like you to consent to be my wife.'

Catherine started. 'Oh, no James! You have no need to feel pity for me. I do not want to be enfolded in your all-pervading gloom. When I marry, it must be a relationship of continual excitement and wonder!'

Morton screwed his mouth up ruefully. 'I can at least take comfort from your "when",' he said. 'I know that this is not an auspicious moment for a proposal. You are upset, and so am I. But you will not forbid my raising it again?'

'You sound as if you are promising sweets to a half-witted child!'

'I am sorry.' Morton got to his feet. 'My compliments to your mother . . . And I shall ask you again.'

Catherine rose, her hands tightly clasped. 'That is your privilege, James,' she said.

Historical Note

On the 16 April 1895 the Royal Commission published its report. With the exception of Henry Wilson, the Commissioners concluded that the arguments for the prohibition of the opium trade had not been sustained by the evidence they had received. However, Indian exports of opium had already begun to decline and that trend continued.